The White Star Continuity
Book 4

INTO TEMPTATION

by

Jeanie London

The legend continues... MI6 agent Lindy Gardner
is determined to capture bad-guy fixer
Joshua Benedict—and the stolen amulet in his
possession. The man is leading her on a sensual
cat-and-mouse game across two continents that will
only make his surrender oh, so satisfying.

Dear Reader,

THE WHITE STAR legend continues.... The amulet is now leaving the United States to follow its destiny into several sexy European locales. While it journeys to places both familiar and new, it weaves the power of true love over two new lovers.

True love is about the last thing MI6 agent Lindy Gardner expects when she crosses the big pond to pursue the man who can lead her to the amulet. Joshua Benedict isn't expecting true love, either. He doesn't believe in legends or curses—only in the luck he makes for himself.

But the White Star possesses a power that finds the pure of heart even in the unlikeliest places.

The instant I heard about this continuity series, I knew *Into Temptation* was the story for me. I hope you enjoy! Let me know in care of Harlequin Books, 225 Duncan Mill Road, Don Mills, Ontario, M3B 3K9 Canada, or visit my Web site at www.jeanielondon.com.

Very truly yours,

Jeanie London

Books by Jeanie London

HARLEQUIN BLAZE
128—WITH THIS FLING
153—HOT SHEETS*
157—RUN FOR COVERS*
161—PILLOW CHASE*
181—UNDER HIS SKIN
213—RED LETTER NIGHTS
     "Signed, Sealed, Seduced"
231—GOING ALL OUT**

HARLEQUIN SIGNATURE
SELECT SPOTLIGHT
IN THE COLD

*Falling Inn Bed...
**Red Letter Nights

INTO TEMPTATION
Jeanie London

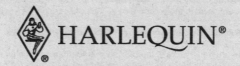

HARLEQUIN®

TORONTO • NEW YORK • LONDON
AMSTERDAM • PARIS • SYDNEY • HAMBURG
STOCKHOLM • ATHENS • TOKYO • MILAN • MADRID
PRAGUE • WARSAW • BUDAPEST • AUCKLAND

To all the folks who had a hand in creating this wonderful world…my continuity buds: Lori Wilde, Carrie Alexander, Kristin Hardy and Shannon Hollis; our project manager extraordinaire, Kathryn Lye; and my own always-brilliant editor, Wanda Ottewell.
It has been a pleasure, ladies!

ISBN 0-373-79252-2

INTO TEMPTATION

www.eHarlequin.com

Printed in U.S.A.

The Legend Continues

A warm breeze stirred branches, filling the air with the incense of eucalyptus. Yet Egmath glared into the sultry night, a mixture of defiance and despair making this magical place seem unfamiliar, though he had always found refuge here.

"How can so perfect a night herald such heartache?" he demanded of the dark that lay as sweeping velvet over the river, studded by stars and illumined by moonlight.

He would find no shelter this night. He could escape neither destiny nor duty, for on the morrow his marriage would take place in the Hall of a Thousand Pillars.

Always, Egmath had intended to speak the sacred vows with his beloved Batu, but the priests had sworn him to her sister, the heiress to the throne. And the gods would mock them all, for he and Batu would flank their future queen before the altar while he uttered vows binding him to the wrong woman, tearing the heart from his beloved's chest, from his own.

These past days of feasting and preparation had blurred together, marked only by his spiking dread as the wedding approached. He told himself a feted warrior who had faced death in battle should be more courageous of spirit and reconciled to duty, yet obligation lay as a death pall over his future. When he could finally endure the agony no longer, he had summoned Batu, knowing he would not find the strength to endure the morrow without holding her in his arms one last time.

He stared into the moonlit darkness with eyes hungry for the sight of her. She emerged from the shadows as she always had, bereft of the adornments of the royal court, a simple gown flowing around her, tempting him with sleek curves and raven hair that gleamed silver and gold beneath the night.

In her welcoming smile he found his shelter.

"You came to me," he said.

She approached with a grace that had made her fiendishly difficult to catch when they had played their youthful games as children, liquid strides that had enticed him since his arrival in manhood. Feasting on the sight of her, he extended his hands. She slid her own within.

"I would look upon you one last time as we have always been." Her heart glowed in her eyes. "I would look upon you as you always will be—my love."

Their bodies swayed close, drawn together as naturally as the pull of the tide, barely touching, yet her nearness soothed away the ache in his soul and righted the universe.

Then he brought his mouth down upon hers. For the spate of one shared breath, the promise of a future that should have been theirs lay between them—the prelude to their kiss, so agonizingly sweet, before need crashed in, and passion reigned.

Batu yielded beneath the press of his lips. He thrilled to her giving response, his own yearning that defied destiny and circumstance, made him ache to toss obligation to the four winds and follow the call of desire. This woman was his lifeblood…his friend, his strength, his fantasy.

With his mouth upon hers and his tongue tasting the demand of her kiss, Egmath would have laid down his life to avoid the morrow. But self-indulgence was not to be his. Only in his strength would Batu find her courage to face their future. He loved her too much to deny her any chance to find peace.

When finally they broke apart, their passion lingering in their ragged breaths, in the whispers of the palms on the breeze, she pressed something into his palm.

"What is this?" He gazed down upon a mother-of-pearl amulet fashioned in the shape of a star.

"I would give you my heart." Her voice trembled through lips reddened by his kiss. "To keep with you forever."

"I will cherish your gift always. Your heart shall be my strength and my beacon through this darkness."

When she held her hand over his, he knew she understood all his feelings so poorly conveyed.

"I would beg such a prize of you as well, Egmath."

"It is yours, my beloved, as is my heart."

"Then grant me tonight, where I will be yours alone. Gift me with a memory I shall cherish forever."

The amulet blazed in their clasped hands, a fire that captured the power of their love, the force of their shared passion, a heat that would bind them in spirit forever.

Egmath brought their hands to his mouth, breathed a promise in the kiss he pressed to her smooth skin.

She trembled.

"Tonight shall be ours," he vowed.

Loosing the clasp at her shoulder, he swept away the gown to expose her golden loveliness. The double-edged blade of desire pierced his heart as she came into his arms, unfolding in a sweep of lush curves and warm flesh that aligned perfectly against him.

"A memory to cherish always, my beloved Batu, a reminder that neither duty nor fate nor death can separate us, for true love will endure."

TO BE CONTINUED...

1

New York City, where the chic and commonplace clash along busy streets that make the perfect place to pursue a man.

"OH MY, MY, but the man is even more dishy in the skin," Lindy Gardner said to no one in particular as she focused the digital-cam binoculars.

The device had been designed to look like a pair of stylish sunglasses, so she didn't concern herself with the passersby on the street, but zoomed in on the tall blonde leaving the ritzy Piazza Hotel.

Joshua Benedict aka Stuart Temple. Approximately thirty-eight years old.

Origins: unknown.

Current residence: Nice, France.

Occupation: Fixer.

She produced the man's stats by rote, but peering through those lenses, Lindy didn't see a familiar image from the surveillance photos the Secret Intelligence Service, MI6, had collected during recent months.

Life sparked the lifeless images she'd studied during mission briefing into a wholly 3-D man. He stepped onto the pavement, his smile dazzling as he inclined his head to the doorman and moved past with smooth strides.

Definitely a man her old school chums would have called a cut above bog standard.

With the depression of a button, zoom lenses magnified her vantage again. Startling black eyes and brows contrasted with his pale hair and tanned skin. His hair glinted in the late-afternoon sun.

Joshua Benedict looked as if he spent much of his time sailing, fishing and windsurfing on the deep-blue waters of the French Riviera.

According to her intel, he did.

But Lindy also knew he spent the rest of his time jet-setting around the globe conducting business.

Legitimate society believed this man to be nothing more than a businessman with many areas of interest. But the world of the Secret Intelligence suspected Joshua Benedict of conducting *illegal* business, which was precisely why he was in New York City on this bright spring afternoon.

And why she'd followed him here.

Tracing her finger along the binoculars in what would appear to the casual observer as an adjustment to her sunglasses, Lindy depressed another button and captured the man's image as he moved beneath the Piazza Hotel's marquee.

Target acquired.

Joshua Benedict appeared to be a tourist, looking for all the world as if he belonged in the crush of people that ebbed and flowed along the street.

Lindy knew there was nothing casual about this man's visit, however. An informant had relayed reliable intel that connected Joshua Benedict to a recent auction-house theft.

Not as the thief, though.

This man maneuvered easily through the layers of

society, from the wealthy glitterati to the shadowy underworld of international organized crime. He rubbed elbows with power brokers, from global financiers to old-money families who made up high society on three continents.

He had established his reputation as a man who could mastermind brilliant business deals, "fix" any sort of unexpected situation and leave behind no prosecutable evidence. Most importantly, he could keep secrets.

A regular Johnny of all trades.

The thought made Lindy smile. Ironically, his job description didn't sound so far off from hers.

Except that Joshua Benedict worked for the bad guys, and one bad guy in particular.

Henri Renouf.

The man SIS wanted to apprehend in a big way.

In much the same fashion as Joshua Benedict, Henri Renouf was known to the general public as a businessman with a cutthroat reputation—a reputation built through rumor, innuendo and suspicion. Since Renouf had been around for over four decades, he'd established himself as a private and very powerful man whom most people didn't dare to cross.

According to Secret Intelligence, the rumor, innuendo and suspicion surrounding Renouf was well-founded. The man was known to be an obsessive antiquities collector, but Renouf didn't let the availability of artifacts deter his acquisitions. In Britain alone, he was suspected of "acquiring" numerous priceless relics from museums and private residences through thefts spanning several decades.

Since Renouf had the resources to conduct his shady actions through intermediaries, he protected himself with distance. But with each passing year, he got bolder. While no international agency had enough evidence to prosecute, after a recent rash of heists all over the globe, her agency, in conjunction with Interpol, had deemed the time ripe to make contact with one of Renouf's associates.

Joshua Benedict was a means to an end.

With that thought, Lindy watched him cross the street then found herself suddenly on the move.

In her chic two-piece ensemble, she could have been any resident of this big city, where people favored practical walking shoes and relegated more stylish footwear into carryalls until reaching their destinations.

Her own carryall contained shoes, plus a few items that would mark her as a visitor to the Big Apple. Mostly cover essentials. Passport. Notebook computer. Cellular phone.

Hiking the bag higher on her shoulder, Lindy marked their path along Fifth Avenue, keeping her gaze on her target, admiring the way he affected the perfect blend of casual disinterest and purposeful concentration as he passed upscale stores.

Admiring the man himself.

Benedict moved with a boldness she knew would make him a native of any city on any continent. Confidence. He wore it as easily as the lightweight blue shirt and tan slacks—clothes that had clearly never seen a rack, judging by the way they molded the athletic lines of his body. If she could see his feet, Lindy knew she'd find him wearing something butter-soft and expensive.

So far, the man fit his profile to a T.

Except that she hadn't expected him to be quite so handsome.

When he stopped to await a signal to navigate another cross-street, Lindy slipped the digital-cam binoculars back up her nose and snapped a second image, just to see if she could capture his expression as he glanced up at a building, surveying his environs as skillfully and inconspicuously as she might.

But there was no question in Lindy's mind that he was taking stock of his surroundings. Something about the stone cut of his jaw, perhaps. Or maybe the furrow between those dark eyebrows that suggested a deliberation she recognized.

It took one to know one—someone who was up to a lot more than he appeared to be.

Hanging back a step, Lindy moved behind an older woman wearing a wide hat, who had just enjoyed a spree at Amali's, according to her sacks. And when the traffic signal changed, she made her way around the woman with a quick smile and a cordial, "Lovely bonnet."

While she wasn't sure precisely what to expect from Benedict, she'd come prepared for any number of scenarios. She knew why he'd come to town, but had no way of knowing how he would take care of his business.

She'd come up with a few likely guesses, of course, but not one of them had led her to the sweeping spires of St. Patrick's Cathedral. Yet that was exactly where he was heading—right up the bloody front steps.

Well, well, well. What business did her handsome target have with God today?

Now there was a question she wouldn't spend too much time mulling. Lindy wasn't particularly religious, but she had been reared in the English countryside, where Sunday trips to the village church had been a way of life.

As a result, she had a healthy respect for passing judgment and throwing stones in places where she herself wouldn't want others passing judgment or throwing stones.

With her work as an intelligence agent over the past decade, she'd found herself in enough situations that some might label morally questionable. Unless Joshua Benedict's business with God had something to do with Henri Renouf, Lindy wasn't interested.

But she couldn't help thinking a cathedral would be an ace place to hand off a stolen artifact, so she strode lightly up the steps and made her way inside.

Given that her work covered every European city in what was once known as Christendom, Lindy thought old Gothic cathedrals pretty standard fare. While she didn't know much about this one—and honestly hadn't thought to research more—she did know the place was the seat of New York's archbishop.

Stepping inside the cool interior, she found the cathedral no less majestic than any other she'd ever been in—a tribute to the architects, as America was regarded as distinctly substandard in architectural grandeur.

The bustle of a busy city vanished behind the heavy doors, and the silence—a tangible serenity that seemed a unique and integral part of churches everywhere—settled over her like the mist after a London rain.

Sliding her digital-cam binoculars on top of her head, Lindy sighted her target. She attached herself to a small group of women, all hastily affixing lace chaplets onto their teased curls, and bowed her head reverently.

Through her periphery, she watched Benedict stroll down the main aisle, taking in his surroundings almost absently, as though he made a habit of visiting churches. Sun spilled through stained glass, throwing light that splintered his handsome features with color.

Had he come to this place to make a pickup?

During mission briefing, Lindy had decided her target's usual MO consisted of using busy public places to cover his shady business dealings. She'd watched video footage of the man strolling into Queen's Cross as boldly as he pleased to take possession of Princess Charlotte's tiara and scepter from a man believed to have conducted the museum theft.

Unfortunately, even with the video footage, her agency didn't have enough evidence to prosecute the thief or the man who allegedly had delivered the goods to Renouf.

Joshua Benedict was bold, to be sure, but a *cathedral?* Maybe her prosaic upbringing made conducting shady business in a church seem to be tempting fate too closely for comfort.

As long as it wasn't *her* eternity at stake…Lindy followed her little holy ladies to a bas-relief statue of a saint.

She watched him head to an altar flanked by two stone saints and several-dozen-odd tourists as if he owned the place, and her heart raced to think he'd take delivery of the stolen auction-house artifact in plain sight.

Shades of Queen's Cross?

Disengaging from the holy ladies, she slid into a pew, knelt and lowered her head as if in prayer. She slid the digital-cam binoculars down her nose to watch her target move toward a station filled with tiers of votive candles.

Lindy could see no one else approach, detected nothing about the man to suggest he might be searching for anything that had been left concealed for him.

He made a donation and lit a candle.

Lindy observed him, the moments stretching almost painfully as he stared at the flame, his expression thoughtful, an almost-smile playing around his lips.

He did *not* meet with anyone to make a handoff.

He did *not* reach underneath the station and come up with any small package.

He just genuflected before the altar, made the sign of the cross then headed down the aisle the way he came, leaving Lindy staring after him with a narrowed gaze.

Joshua Benedict had come to church to light a candle.

Had she been made?

Lindy had no choice but to consider whether this seemingly purposeless side trip was for her benefit. Instinctively, she stood and moved down the aisle before he reached the doors. Wouldn't do to lose him now. Not until she could decide whether or not he was on to her.

Timing her paces as he paused to hold the door for a couple, she veered sharply right and headed out of a side exit. She sprinted around the corner of the building, swung around a gate and onto Fifth Avenue just as he stepped onto the pavement.

And headed straight toward her.

Turning toward the curb, she raised her arm as if flagging a cab, clearing the path and covering her face from view as he swept past. So close that she caught a whiff of his aftershave—subtle, expensive, but all spice and warm male. That scent stuck with her as she spun on her heels to follow.

No eye contact. No visible sign of any awareness. If Benedict had made her, he was exceptionally good at hiding it. But that didn't really come as any surprise to Lindy. No man could elude capture for so many years without being good.

Damn good.

This time her target led her to a traditional co-op

building overlooking Central Park, the sort of place Lindy knew consisted of upscale apartments with large rooms, high ceilings and thick walls that cost more than her accumulated salary since the day she'd signed on with Secret Intelligence.

She recognized this particular building as the prewar variety, showplace of the wealthiest New York society families, modernized with a thrust of tall windows that revealed the lobby chandelier and the stairwell rising to several upper stories.

Joshua Benedict handed a card to the white-gloved doorman then swept inside as if he were the crown prince expected for tea, leaving her to bimble about on the street while he conducted business where she couldn't see him.

Sometimes she *hated* surveillance.

Today was one of those times. She needed to find a less conspicuous place to ride out her watch. She couldn't be sure whether he'd led her here intentionally. He would know that any interested parties could easily find out the names of the building residents.

In fact, the job would only take about two minutes of uninterrupted satellite uplink on her notebook. But Lindy stuck to her spot. If her target reappeared on the stairwell, he just might cut that time in half by showing her what floor he went to…

Luck was hers.

He took the stairs two at a time, not at a bound but with the fluid strides of a strong, long-legged man. Since he didn't use the lift, she knew he only headed up a few flights, so, slipping the binoculars up her nose, she enjoyed the show.

Those lead-paned glass windows showcased the man as if he'd posed for a bloody portrait—and quite the dishy one at that. Zooming in closer, she admired the way his thighs played against his slacks with his movements, how the fabric pulled enough to give her a clear shot of his backside.

Mmm-mmm. Joshua Benedict's profile had missed the part about him having the nicest bum she'd seen in forever, the kind that made a gal think about smoothing her hands over it. Lindy might have laughed at her own unexpected reaction to a target, but her instincts chose that exact moment to go live.

She spun around just as a no-nonsense voice barked, "Excuse me, miss."

Not at all used to being taken by surprise, Lindy schooled her expression and stared at the uniformed security guard who frowned down at her from his superior vantage.

"Hullo, Constable," she said cheerily, letting a bit of her British accent leak out.

She slipped off the sunglasses—the magnification made the man look like the worst sort of Picasso—and maintained eye contact. "Lovely spring afty, don't you think?"

The man's gaze didn't waver, which suggested he wasn't going to fall easy victim to her charm. Good for him.

"Not interested in the weather this afternoon. I'm interested in why you're loitering."

"Loitering?" She gave a sparkly laugh and toyed with the idea of admitting she'd been staring at a man's bum.

A definite first in her experience.

But as the security guard looked all tetchy and by the book—relatively new to his job, she guessed—Lindy opted for a more conservative approach.

"Actually, I'm here on business." She patted her carryall. "I'm with Hampstead, Heath and Associates. We're based out of London with offices all over Europe and Asia. We're scouting a North American site. Of course, the CEO will need housing if we open a location here. That's where I come in—I'm checking out the neighborhood." She tossed a glance back at the building, and the guard followed her gaze, clearly wavering.

"Do you have identification?"

"Of course. If you'll let me go into my bag, Constable, I'll give you my card. And my passport if you need it."

The man inclined his head then stepped back to give her space. She produced a passport and business card that supported her claim and stood quietly while he inspected her credentials.

Americans were hyper-security conscious nowadays and rightly so, but that this guard would catch her with her binoculars snagged on a pretty sight and her usually sharp senses blinded to her surroundings was just plain unlucky.

Lindy was a stellar field agent, which was precisely why she'd been assigned this case. But she hadn't done much more than surveillance yet, and for things to go pear-shaped so early on…she hoped this didn't foreshadow what lay ahead.

"All right." The guard gave a curt nod. "What else do you need before you can move on?"

"Nothing really. I've already researched the demographics on this and the other buildings we're considering. The big boys will let me know which leasing agencies to make contact with, but I'll be sure to tell them this co-op has the best security of the bunch."

That earned a smile. "Well then, good day, miss."

It was an obvious effort to move her along, so Lindy returned his smile, hiked her carryall higher on her shoulder and shoved off with a bright, "You have a good one, too."

She could feel the guard's gaze follow her down the street, where she rounded the first corner and ducked inside a conveniently located subway station to regroup.

Lindy had to act fast because she had no intention of losing sight of her target now. She had to return to that co-op without drawing the security guard's attention again. No problem. Lindy liked challenges.

She hoped Joshua Benedict proved to be one.

JOSHUA NOTICED the woman as soon as she entered the gallery. Amid the attendees of the Classical Greek Antiquities exhibit opening, she somehow managed to look...*fresh*—no easy job in this human sea of designer labels, artful grooming and cosmetically-enhanced perfection.

Curious, he studied her from his position near a marble diorama of the Graces, where he sipped Moët and chatted with the exhibit's benefactress, Lily Covington.

Perhaps Lily chatting *with him* better described what took place, as the society matron hadn't stopped to draw air in a while. But Joshua didn't mind participating in any conversation that left him free to observe this beauty who paused to admire an oil painting of Artemus with a quiver of arrows.

Maybe it was her flawless skin, touched with only the barest color to enhance a mouth designed to kiss. She wore a chiffon gown to distinguish her from the crowd of the flashy sequins and beads that defined American haute couture, the filmy off-white gown clinging to her body with classic lines hinting at all the long curves below.

She was subtle seduction as opposed to bold temptation, a woman who made him imagine two bodies close in the darkness and the sound of breathless sighs. Soft brown hair fringed around her face and neck, sexy for the way it framed her features. His gaze followed the graceful lines of her throat, and the pulse beating there, another place ripe for kissing.

He would have noticed this woman even if the gala kicking off this new exhibit hadn't been a bore. But he couldn't fault his hostess. As a member of the Covington family—one of the mainstays on the New York society scene since somewhere around the mid-nineteenth century—Lily had perfected hosting philanthropic events into an art form.

Select members of the Westbrook Philharmonic filled the gallery with music. Le Kevin, hailed as Manhattan's latest culinary genius, catered the event with a menu of shellfish flown in from Maine and delicate hand-pressed pasta that melted on the tongue. Champagne flowed.

But not even Moët could wash away the taste of the business that had brought him to New York.

No, he assumed all responsibility for his current mood.

Forcing a smile, Joshua mouthed all the polite responses to Lily's comments about the Graces under discussion while covertly checking out the lady in white, as he christened her.

The sight of her, at least, improved his mood.

He watched her accept a champagne flute from a passing waiter, the gesture graceful, her smile fast and real. There it was again…that *impression.*

This woman struck him as having much beneath her surface that she didn't bother to hide. It was only a sense he got from watching her, but he didn't question his perception. He was an exceptional judge of character.

A skill that always served him well.

Putting that skill to work now, he sliced his gaze across the crowd, passing over several potential prospects to mark the wife of a state senator who'd captured his party's interest.

"I see Carolyn Vandeveer came in from Washington to attend tonight," he said.

"She and the senator are wooing support for their upcoming presidential bid." Lily's tone remained unimpressed.

But Joshua knew his hostess would credit the senator's wife with the appropriate attention. Lily respected the status of her social standing, and presidential hopefuls were only a small percentage among those who sought favor from the Covington family.

So Joshua maneuvered Lily away from the Graces with questions about another artifact and steered her in Mrs. Vandeveer's direction. He needed to get about the business that had brought him to this museum. Only then would he be free to enjoy the night ahead.

To make the lady in white's acquaintance.

Hooking up Lily and the senator's wife over an urn, he participated in their conversation for a respectable few beats then begged his excuses and headed across the gallery.

Resisting the urge to glance at the lady in white, who'd been drawn into conversation with Jeffrey Baldwin of the Boston metals conglomerate—a slick bastard who never missed a trick—Joshua nodded to an usher and stepped into the hall.

While turning, he pitched a nickel behind him with a surreptitious motion, and the tinkle of the coin hitting the floor resounded exactly where he'd meant it to—inside the gallery. When the usher turned around, Joshua vanished down the hall that led to the restrooms.

Chattering voices over the smooth strains of classical music soon faded, yielding to the muted silence of an after-hours museum. Glancing at his watch, he pushed open the restroom door and entered a foyer decorated in the fashion of a gentleman's drawing room. Joshua peered around the corner to confirm he was alone then retrieved his cell phone from a jacket pocket. He depressed a series of numbers.

The ring tone sounded only once before a gravel-voiced man picked up and asked, "You're on schedule?"

"Yes. What about you?"

"No problems."

"Good. Three minutes."

Joshua severed the connection, depressed another button to activate the vibrating ringer and swapped the phone for a pair of black gloves. After donning them, he withdrew a small electronic device from his pocket and cracked the restroom door again. He glanced into the hallway to find it empty, although voices carried from the nearby ladies' room.

Moving quickly past, Joshua raised the digital imaging device above his head and paused long enough to capture a shot of the dim hall leading to a stairwell exit.

The security monitor was positioned in the upper south corner of the ceiling, and he stopped directly beneath the camera to remain out of range.

It was a trick to balance with a foot on the narrow baseboard and the other bracing the wall, but even at six foot two, he couldn't easily make the stretch to the ceiling. Slipping the captured image in front of the camera lens with a practiced move, he pressed down to activate the adhesive and secure the device to the crown molding.

And shut down the live feed. Until he removed the device, the security monitors on the basement level would show only the captured image of the empty hall, leaving him free to move to the stairway without detection.

He hoped this device was an unnecessary precaution. He'd arranged for tonight's contact to bypass this security zone. But Joshua didn't trust his fate to any man, and the idea of a camera documenting his travels into places that would raise questions wasn't a risk he would take.

He trusted his fate to no one.

Not that tonight's business associate presented a significant risk. This career police officer had more to lose than Joshua. In fact, *until* their business, this officer had been an upstanding citizen with an exemplary career record.

Unfortunately, no man was perfect, and Joshua had built a career out of uncovering other men's imperfections.

Shaking off the thought, he moved quietly toward the exit at the end of the hall and slid through the doorway as he heard the ladies'-room door hiss open.

The third-floor stairwell was empty, but he waited until footsteps echoed below before beginning his descent. Joshua couldn't remember exactly when he'd gotten so cautious, but cautious he'd become. Pausing in the shadows, he waited for his contact to appear for a visual verification.

There he was.

Dressed for tonight's stint as a rent-a-cop, the man's neatly pressed NYPD uniform fit snugly on his thick shoulders and barrel chest.

"Any problems?" Joshua descended the last few steps.

The officer shook his head. "We're covered. I disarmed the sector. You brought the reports?"

Joshua ignored the question. "Let's see the amulet."

The man reached inside his pocket and withdrew a box.

Joshua had seen an auction-house photo of the White Star while researching this job. He'd thought the ivory amulet plain for Henri, who usually had an eye for more spectacular pieces. But the allure was the amulet's legend, which prophesied love for the pure of heart and a cursed future for all else.

Joshua didn't believe in curses, or in any luck except what he made for himself, but as he weighed the amulet in his palm, the ivory felt warm, somehow alive. He wondered if he imagined the sensation or if the police officer had noticed, too.

This NYPD veteran had bought his way out of an indiscretion on the vice squad about three years back. Joshua had uncovered this indiscretion and blackmailed the man into removing the amulet from the precinct property room. Then he'd arranged for immediate delivery. So far everything had gone according to plan. Not that he thought the officer would have had second thoughts about keeping the amulet.

The officer's one indiscretion in an otherwise exemplary career hadn't been hard to figure out—a substantial drug bust had gone down around the time the officer had been sending his twin daughters off to college: one at Yale, the other at Vassar.

Joshua suspected that facing Ivy League financial commitments on a policeman's salary would have the noblest of men thinking twice about taking the high road when a windfall of drugs had fallen into his path.

That's what had made this officer invaluable. He wasn't a criminal, but a good guy who'd made a mistake. That distinction meant he could be manipulated.

But the officer's luck wasn't all bad. Joshua played fair. One unsupervised visit to a precinct property room, a stolen amulet and a meet on a museum stairwell, and the officer could go back to his wife and second mortgage with no one the wiser.

As Joshua turned the amulet over, he knew he'd chosen his target well—the officer was more interested in covering up a mistake than profiting by it.

Setting the White Star back inside the box, Joshua extracted a sheaf of papers from his inside jacket pocket. He waited while the officer skimmed the documents before asking, "You're satisfied?"

"If I could trust I won't see copies of these again."

"I'm not interested in you, and the people I represent don't know who you are. Those documents are payment for services rendered. No more or less."

The man inclined his head in grudging acceptance. Joshua knew the officer didn't believe him and wondered if it mattered.

Guilt only plagued men capable of feeling it.

Without a backward glance, Joshua took the stairs two at a time and paused with his ear to the door, listening for sounds from the restrooms, hearing nothing. He cracked the door and peered down the hallway in both directions to find it empty.

Edging the door wider, he slipped through then eased the door shut behind him. It wasn't until he'd taken a step into the hall that he heard a soft laugh.

Spinning toward the sound, he watched the lady in white emerge from another doorway.

She was smiling.

2

"WELL HELLO, beautiful," Joshua said coolly, no trace of surprise in his voice. "Lose your way?"

She shook her head, a sultry move that drew his gaze to her pouty mouth, the impudent tilt of her chin. Though the dim light cast her in shadow, he could see humor flash in her gaze. "I wanted to catch you coming out of the loo."

British, Joshua thought, which could explain why he'd picked her out of an American crowd. But nationality didn't explain why she was waiting *behind* the exit door when the restrooms were down the hall. His instincts went wild. He wasn't used to being caught by surprise.

"To what do I owe this pleasure?" he asked.

Whatever else this encounter might prove to be, it *was* a pleasure. Just seeing this woman up close meant admiring the way she leaned back against the wall, that dress hugging her curves with delectable precision. A long slit left her leg exposed from the knee, and he glanced down the length of shapely calf and ankle to a sandal that showcased a delicate foot.

"It seemed a crime to admire a sculpture of Eros when I was starved for good company." She exhaled a sigh that managed to shoot his already-rushing adrenaline into the red zone.

"Old Jeff wasn't filling the bill?"

"So you noticed me? I'd hoped you did, but to answer your question…*no*. Mr. Corporate Yank didn't impress me nearly as much as he seemed to impress himself with his assets and company's ranking on the stock exchange."

Joshua laughed, deciding right then and there he wanted to continue this conversation. Unfortunately, he wasn't free just yet. He would have to extricate himself from this lovely lady to remove the digital imaging device.

Leaving the device behind wasn't an option. Once the night generator shifted on, security would notice when this hallway's lighting didn't change. They'd investigate. While the device couldn't be traced, museum security procedure would demand that every guest involved in tonight's gala be questioned.

Joshua preferred not to appear on anyone's suspect list. A man with his reputation could never be too careful. His most valuable skill was moving through social circles around the world. If red flags popped up whenever he crossed an international border, his autonomy would be affected. He'd worked too many years to get where he was today—connected with a man of Henri Renouf's stature.

He did not want this particular alias tarnished now.

"Joshua Benedict." Reaching for her hand, he brought it to his lips, found that she tasted as feminine as she looked. "And you are…."

"Lindy Gardner."

"Lindy." He let the name roll off his tongue, liking the sound, sensuous and feminine like the woman herself.

He also liked the way she trembled when his breath burst over her skin. It was only a slight reaction, but Joshua had made a career out of noticing details.

This lovely lady's shoulders quivered oh-so-gently. Her chest rose and fell on a quick breath.

"A beautiful name for a beautiful woman." He released her hand, but to his surprise, she held on.

Her gaze slid from his. "Gloves, Joshua?"

"I was handling a sculpture."

She stared down at their clasped hands with a smile playing at the edges of her mouth, a mouth that looked even more perfect for kissing up close.

She ran her thumb along the back of his glove. Just the sight of her fair skin against the fabric was so much more intimate than a touch should allow.

"They have some very beautiful pieces on display tonight," she said.

"They do. But you couldn't have toured the entire exhibit yet. Let me show you around."

"I'd like that."

Her acceptance was all he needed to make his move. Looping their arms together, he turned to lead her down the hall. Once inside the gallery, he would ply her with champagne then excuse himself to take care of business so he could return to the pleasure of making this lady's acquaintance.

But as they reached the restrooms, Lindy came to a sudden stop. "Aren't you forgetting something?"

With his adrenaline still pumping, he couldn't pinpoint what it was about Lindy that had his instincts on edge.

"What?" he asked.

Raising a slim finger, she pointed above their heads, directly at his digital imaging device.

One small gesture and Joshua had his explanation. As

usual, his instincts were on target—this woman was a lot more than a pretty lady in a white dress.

Following her gaze to the security camera, he said, "Well, that doesn't look like it belongs there, does it?"

"Sure doesn't."

"What makes you think that device belongs to me?"

"Simple arithmetic."

"As in two plus two equals four?"

She inclined her head so the exit light threw fiery highlights onto her hair. "The usher couldn't confirm where you'd gone, so I guessed you'd given him the slip. And you weren't wearing gloves when you left the gallery, so that would mean you were handling a sculpture *where*…? On the stairs? Another gallery on another floor? I don't believe the loo factored at all, and I'm not generally wrong."

No, there was nothing *wrong* with Lindy Gardner except that she was toying with him.

"Are you trying to pin something on me?"

"Do I hear an emphasis on *trying?*"

He laughed. "How do I know *you* didn't plant that device to frame *me?*"

"You don't." She glanced at her watch then back up at him, the smile twitching around her mouth again. "I will say I'm very impressed, though. Given my calculations, which began when you left the gallery, you placed that device on the security camera at least nine minutes ago. I've just chewed up another two chatting, which puts you at eleven minutes give or take. You won't want to leave that device behind because you know as well as I do when security discovers it, they're going to run the guest list. You won't want to be called in for questioning whether or not they can pin the goods on you."

"So, what impresses you?"

"That you haven't broken a sweat yet."

Joshua didn't get a chance to respond because as he registered that tonight wasn't the first time Lindy Gardner had heard his name, feminine laughter rang out in the hall behind them—women headed to the restroom.

"Think they'll wonder what we're doing down here?" Lindy asked.

"They'll know what we're doing."

Her mouth pursed. "Really?"

"Really."

In one move, he pinned her against the wall and brought his mouth down on hers.

Now it was Joshua's turn to be impressed. Lindy didn't react with surprise. She only exhaled a laugh that burst against his lips in a champagne-laced breath before her mouth yielded to his—soft, warm, arousing.

Definitely a kissing mouth.

Lips parted. Breaths collided. Tongues tangled, leaving Joshua the one feeling impressed and surprised. By the way Lindy threw herself into the moment, sliding her arms around his neck and pressing all those lush curves against him.

And by the way his body reacted. His pulse rushed. His blood crashed south so fast the sensation made him deepen their kiss just to share her air.

If Lindy's mouth had been made for kissing, the woman herself was all about making love.

Their bodies aligned perfectly. With her face tipped upward, her mouth fitted his just right for this soul-dragging kiss. She toyed with his neck, fingers sliding into his hair and caressing places he hadn't realized could feel intimate.

Feel intimate they did.

She was an enticing armful. Long, lithe, much more toned than her slim curves appeared at a glance, she possessed a strength that suggested an active lifestyle. Her smooth stomach caught what wanted to become an erection—this woman aroused him faster than he'd ever been aroused.

And he wasn't the only one feeling the effects of their closeness. Something about Lindy's swaying hips felt *real*. He didn't think this was a performance. Another question to add to his growing list about this woman.

Was she a bold thief sent to trap him?

British…MI6?

Joshua only had one answer—he was in trouble here.

He'd stepped out of a stairwell, and life had taken an unexpected turn. He might not know who Lindy Gardner was yet…he might not know why they were fire together… but he damn sure recognized trouble.

It was kissing him full on the mouth right now.

By the time they finally broke apart, the intruding women had long since entered the restroom. In fact, for all Joshua knew, they might have come and gone. The only thing he was sure of was that his blood was pumping so hard he wanted to brace himself against the wall for support.

He would never let on that one kiss had leveled him.

"Excellent cover," Lindy said breathlessly, drawing his gaze to her lips and that just-kissed look. "I'm impressed again, Joshua. You think fast on your feet."

He was lucky to be standing on them.

"Thank you."

She pointed up at the ceiling. "So we're back to leaving that device there."

"Does sound like a problem. I'm not sure for whom, though."

She chuckled, a silky sound that filtered through the quiet hallway and drove another bolt of need home so he had to control an urge to pull her back into his arms.

"Your problem, Joshua, whether or not you admit it."

"Guess we'll never know. So what are we going to do? Will you let me tour you through the exhibit, so you can keep your eyes on me?"

"Actually, I'm going to rescue your cute bum."

"Really?"

That had promise. A rescue wouldn't be unwelcome, whether he admitted it or not. Joshua found himself both curious and pleased she thought his bum cute enough to save.

Now to find out who she was and what she wanted….

LINDY STARED into Joshua's face, into an expression that revealed nothing. He was even more attractive up close, *impossibly* attractive with that dashing smile and those broad shoulders. She wondered if his appearance accounted for the way she felt right now, all fluttery and so off-kilter she might have been crossing the deck of a boat in dodgy weather.

All from a kiss?

Apparently. Everything about her still felt keenly aware of this man. Adrenaline made her blood hum, threw her senses into overdrive, a feeling she knew well—a familiar sense of danger.

But Lindy stood inside a quiet hallway of a museum, a highly trained agent of the Crown, perfectly capable of defending herself should this man attempt anything funny. Not to mention that there was an usher and a gallery filled with philanthropists all within yelling distance.

So where exactly was the danger?

Another glance into Joshua's gaze, and Lindy decided her attraction to this man was the only thing dangerous around here.

She wasn't the only one feeling the attraction, either. Joshua's oh-so-affable expression might not let her see what he was thinking, but she knew a real reaction when she felt one. There'd been no missing the bulge of his crotch while they'd kissed.

Chemistry—it changed *everything.*

Dragging her gaze from his, she helped herself to one of his hands and peeled away his glove.

"Quite handy." Slipping her fingers inside, she gauged the roomy fit. The man's hands were as large and attractive as the rest of him. "Will you lift me?"

He arched an inky-black eyebrow. "Lift you?"

Lindy knew he understood, but played along. Joshua obviously wanted to cover himself to give her nothing to implicate him since he didn't know who she was.

She couldn't blame him. Caution was a prized commodity even on her side of the law. Caution often meant the difference between anonymity and exposure, sometimes the difference between life and death.

Grabbing a fold of her gown, she aimed a foot his way, letting the fabric part to reveal a long stretch of hose-clad leg and a sandal.

"It's these strappy shoes." She displayed the shoe as his gaze followed appreciatively. "I won't be able to brace myself, but if you give me a boost, I can reach."

He didn't reply, but suddenly his hands were around her waist, a move that told her so much about the man. Aggressively agile. Ruthlessly honed physical condition. Strong enough to haul her against him effortlessly.

For a breathtaking instant she could feel the hard outline of his body against hers again, and heat flooded her senses, a purely physical response that made every cell in her body yearn for another go at kissing him.

Almost before the thought registered, Lindy found herself spun around and hoisted off her feet. It took a conscious effort to remind herself she had a job to do—one that needed to be done with an ample level of skill.

Presumably, Joshua wouldn't have needed to deceive the security camera if he'd had a connection inside the museum, someone who could have disabled this security zone.

This information prompted more questions about what he'd been up to tonight.

Operating alone?

Picking up a delivery or meeting with someone?

How was tonight's event linked to his New York City visit?

Secret Intelligence hadn't uncovered any evidence that Joshua Benedict was a thief and, as a result, Lindy believed he'd come to town exclusively to *fix* some trouble that had arisen with a recent auction-house theft.

She intended to find out, and to do that, she couldn't let anything come between them. Especially not an imaging device that could place him in jeopardy with museum security and, subsequently, the local authorities.

This man was all hers.

So tracing the edge of the device, she tested the connection to the ceiling. Okay, she needed a fast and clean break to avoid creating a distortion on the live feed in the security monitoring station downstairs.

Gathering her focus, Lindy blocked out the feel of his hands on her waist, the way he easily lifted her off the floor.

She ignored the feel of her bottom brushing against all

his hard tummy muscles and how her panty hose and dress didn't protect her from his body heat.

This man was one big distraction.

With brutal precision, Lindy trapped the device between her fingers and pulled it away in a hard, clean stroke.

"Got it."

"Impressive," he said, but she couldn't be sure whether he meant her work or her*self* as he lowered her to the floor, treating her to a tour of his every body part along the way.

Sliding against him in a prolonged and very tantalizing move, Lindy tried to sound casual when she said, "Thanks."

"Pleased to be of service. So tell me, Lindy. What are you going to do with that device now you've got it?"

Good question. Unfortunately, she didn't have a good answer—yet. So she leaned close to stay out of camera range and forced him back another step before turning to meet his gaze.

A very approving gaze.

An interested gaze.

A gaze that made her rethink her point of entry.

This man was Henri Renouf's fixer, a man who used his talents to manipulate situations to the bad guys' advantage. They had too much chemistry to ignore, chemistry she might use to gain his cooperation.

"I've got a plan." A *bold* plan. One that involved smoothing her way to his cooperation with seduction.

"Do you, Lindy?"

"Always." Dropping the device into her evening bag, Lindy peeled off the glove and returned it. "Thanks."

He hid the gloves away in a jacket pocket. Then he extended his hand. "The gallery. Shall we?"

Securing her evening bag on her shoulder, she let him

lead her down the hall. She had some quick decisions to make. First she must decide how best to dispose of her new electronic acquisition. She couldn't be certain what Joshua had been up to and didn't want to be caught with the goods.

She knew there would be nothing to incriminate him on the small device. He was far too skilled to be careless—far too cool when he had to be burning up with questions about who she was and why she was covering him.

Then she had to decide how to play this man. Physical awareness had changed things between them, given her a new weapon in her arsenal, and she had to decide whether or not to use it.

The man lived up to his profile as a charming host. They'd barely set foot inside the gallery before he plied her with champagne and grilled her about what exhibits she'd like to see. He was oh-so-cool, and she was determined to be as impressive.

She motioned across the gallery. "I overheard that woman wearing the ostrich feathers mention a vase with depictions of Eros and Gaea."

"You mentioned Eros earlier. Are you interested in early mythology?"

"No. Just Eros." She gazed up at him from under her lashes, a flirtatious glance she hoped would pique his curiosity and get them to the end of the buffet table.

Her gracious host led her toward the display asking, "What specifically about Eros interests you?"

"Lust and passion, of course. What do you think of them, Joshua?"

"I'm interested in attraction, too. It can happen when and where you least expect it." He reached out and dragged his thumb along her cheek, a bold touch that she felt straight to her toes. "Did you know in early mythology, Eros was about the force attracting two people to each other? It wasn't until later myths that he was Aphrodite's son and represented lust and passion."

"Did you research for tonight's event or is Greek mythology a hobby of yours?"

"Let's say I take a great deal of pleasure in learning and use every opportunity to do so."

No doubt research was an important part of his work. "Very diplomatic."

He raised his champagne flute in salute then brought the glass to his lips. Their gazes locked over the rim, and Lindy raked hers from the top of his expensive haircut over the terrain of his handsome face.

But she didn't stop there. Oh, no. When she considered how he'd finagled an invitation to tonight's gala from one of the Ladies Who Lunch—a woman well known for her philanthropy—Lindy decided *subtle* wasn't in this man's vocabulary.

So she perused the tailored collar of his Egyptian cotton shirt then the sleek lines of his tux. The jacket draped those broad shoulders to perfection before descending to the trim V of his waist. She'd felt all those hard muscles up close, so the fact he was yummy shouldn't keep surprising her.

Somehow it did. Or maybe that was the strength of her attraction to him.

"Tell me, Lindy, whose guest are you tonight? I don't recall seeing you with any of our hosts and you haven't said."

"No, I haven't said."

"Top-secret information?"

"Not really."

"Would you like me to guess?" he asked.

"Are you fishing?"

"I like to fish. That's no mystery."

"No, it isn't."

He appeared to consider that. "I'm also not very patient."

"Is that a warning?"

His dark gaze twinkled, but Lindy didn't answer when the opportunity she'd been looking for appeared. She needed to seize chance before it got away.

Setting her flute on the buffet table, she helped herself to several wedges of foie gras. Bypassing the plates, she grabbed napkins and popped the wedges into her mouth whole.

Joshua watched her curiously. "Hungry?"

Since her mouth bulged with a delicacy she truly despised, she couldn't do more than shake her head and try not to dwell on the creamy, meaty texture coating her teeth and tongue.

Joshua waited as if sensing something was coming then glanced absently at the server serendipitously making his way from behind the buffet table with a full trash bag.

Lindy made a gagging sound, loud enough to draw the server's attention. Dragging the napkin over her mouth, she spat out her nasty mouthful.

"Foie gras. Looked like some sort of hummus." She pulled a face then pointed to the trash bag. "May I, please?"

"Vegan, don't you know?" Joshua added, and she could see he fought back a smile.

The server eyed them grimly and held out the bag. Stuffing the napkins deep in the debris, she hoped the regurgitated goose liver would deter anyone from inspecting the mess.

"Thanks ever so much."

The server took off, and once he was out of earshot, Joshua laughed, a deep lustrous sound that sent prickles through her.

"I assume that device you took from the hall just made an exit."

She only smiled, which he clearly took to mean yes.

"Nicely done, Lindy. Inventive, clever and clean. I believe the owner of that device is in your debt."

"I certainly hope so."

"Do you?"

She retrieved her flute and fought the urge to gargle away the nasty taste. "I do."

"Why?"

Lindy considered her answer while considering the man. Cool, yet curious. Displaying the exact right mix of persistent and pushy. She appreciated how fine a line that was.

"I want something from you."

"What?"

Deciding that nothing short of a toothbrush would clean away the aftertaste, Lindy relinquished her champagne flute. "Let's find some place private."

He didn't hesitate but led her away from the buffet. They made their way through the crowds, forced to stop several times as he greeted acquaintances. He was as charming as his profile suggested, and as he introduced her to people he'd obviously socialized with before, she observed how this man had become so successful at running his game.

He was likable and knew exactly how to place people at ease. Some he let lead the conversation. With others he directed. He was a veritable social chameleon, and that was a skill Lindy knew came in handy.

They ultimately wound up inside the bisected glass walls of a timeline display of classical Grecian antiquities, and she glanced around as Joshua led her forward.

"Perfect." They would be able to hear approaching guests before being happened upon.

"So you're finally going to end my suspense?" Folding his arms across his chest, Joshua eyed her expectantly.

"From what I've heard, you like suspense."

"Heard from whom?"

"My agency."

"MI6?"

Lindy feigned a pout. "You guessed?"

"Simple arithmetic."

A man with Joshua's specialized skills would recognize hers. From there her accent would make an equation of two plus two equaling an answer that wouldn't be difficult to guess.

"What does your agency want with me, Lindy?"

Rising up on tiptoe to whisper in his ear, she pressed so close that her breasts brushed his arm.

"We don't actually want you."

He inhaled, a sound that was the second honest reaction she'd gotten from him tonight.

Their kiss had been *very* honest.

"What do you want then?"

"We want Renouf. We want you to give us everything you have on him."

"If I had anything on him, why would I give it to you?"

"Because…" She let her words trail off for dramatic effect. "My agency can provide you with a new identity and a well-heeled life outside the organized crime world."

3

RIGHT UP FRONT Joshua saw problems with Lindy's offer. All of them *his*. Staring into her eyes—into green and gold lights sparkling in the glow of the Classical Antiquities display—he tried to guess the thoughts behind her mysterious gaze.

Lindy had to be playing him. MI6 couldn't easily extricate him from his world. Men like Henri were not only meticulous at choosing their associates, but also at eliminating them when they no longer served a purpose. Joshua had made himself invaluable so elimination never became an issue.

Lindy made her deal sound like a one-off, but a new identity meant paying for the privilege. MI6 might start with wanting everything Joshua had on Renouf, but there would always be someone else they wanted information on. And they would know he had the resources to get them what they wanted.

Joshua had no illusions about how government agencies operated, and they weren't squeamish about breaking the rules. Especially intelligence agencies. They conducted as many illegal operations as the bad guys, but frankly, Renouf and his associates paid better.

Which was Joshua's next problem with the deal.

Until he discovered exactly what MI6 had on him, he wouldn't know how to handle Lindy.

The fact that she'd shown up at this function proved she knew more than she should. How *much* more remained the question.

"What makes you think I know Renouf?" he asked.

She gave a sultry smile. "I'm having déjà vu. Didn't we have this conversation in the hall?"

"Where you failed to prove complicity on my part."

"I wasn't trying to prove complicity. I was proving a point. Several actually."

"I got the obvious. You're following me, and you're clearly not just a pretty lady in a fancy dress. What did I miss?"

"The olive branch. I solved your little problem to prove I was acting in good faith."

"What does your agency want with Renouf?"

"We believe he has been funding the thefts of various relics from British museums and Royal residences. We've found connections that go back decades. The man's a menace. An extremely dangerous one."

"I'll have to take your word."

Lindy only smiled.

Great. This was a no-win situation if ever he'd seen one. Renouf was obsessed with expanding his private art collection, and Britain had every right to be pissed about its lost relics. Joshua was caught squarely between them—he even had the White Star burning a hole in his pocket to prove it. While not originally a British relic, the amulet had spent a good century in England.

"Answer a question," he said. "If you think I can connect you to Renouf, why did you choose tonight to make contact?"

"I received a tip you were coming to town to conduct *business* here in Manhattan."

He'd have loved to know where that tip had come from. "Business at the museum? Were you thinking entrapment?"

She shook her head, sending wisps of light-brown hair around her cheeks and neck. He could see the pulse beat low in her throat, the tempo steady. Whatever else might be happening, he wasn't rattling Lindy, which meant she thought she had the upper hand.

"Why tonight?"

"All right." She exhaled a tiny sigh that closed the distance between them. "I've been briefed on you, Joshua, and I have to admit I'm impressed. You've led me on a merry chase since I started following you."

He couldn't tell if she thought he'd known he was being tailed. He hadn't, unfortunately.

"So what did I do to lead you on a merry chase?"

"Well, tracking you to the Piazza Hotel wasn't any trouble, of course. But you spent your first day in town inside the hotel. I couldn't get close to you while you were inside your room, but there was that lunch in the bar. You took a call on your cell phone. A secured line."

She must have seen something in his expression because she waved a dismissive hand. "Don't look so surprised. I happen to be very thorough."

Damn straight. "How did you know I'd be here tonight?"

"You came out of your room today."

He swallowed back a relieved breath. His first day in town had been spent arranging to have the White Star stolen from a police precinct property room, so Lindy had missed all the good stuff. Today he'd only arranged social events with acquaintances in an effort to legitimize his visit and provide cover for the White Star's delivery.

"You followed me today." Not a question. Let her think

he was playing the game so she couldn't confirm whether or not he'd known about his tail.

"Right to Lily Covington's co-op. From there it was two plus two and all that. Since I know why you're in town, I figured you were likeliest to take delivery during some busy social function. It seems to be your MO. I'm prepared to follow you wherever you go for however long it takes."

Two things struck Joshua in that instant—that she claimed to know his business and that she thought he had an MO—something he'd worked hard *not* to establish.

"Take delivery? What do you think I've come to collect?"

"The White Star."

He was too skilled to reveal his surprise, but with the amulet in discussion suddenly weighing heavily inside his pocket, Joshua felt the confines of this display—and this museum—as if the walls were closing in.

No matter how attracted he was to this woman, Joshua had zero reason to trust her.

Forcing a manner of calm he wasn't close to feeling, he said, "Okay, Lindy. Obviously you think you have something, and you do—my attention. But I'm a businessman with connections to most of the people attending this event. Would you mind continuing this conversation elsewhere?"

"Not at all."

He didn't say another word while leading her from the gallery, without even bothering to pay his respects to Lily Covington. He'd send a gift tomorrow to make up for the slight, but right now he needed to clear his head and collect his thoughts to deal with the problem at hand.

The lovely lady strolling along by his side.

She was obviously very confident in her ability to

defend herself because she left the museum and took to the streets with that pulse still keeping even time in her throat.

Of course, if MI6 had a file on him then she had backup—if anything happened to her, he would be the likeliest suspect.

Amazing how he could feel so hemmed in on all sides in such a huge city. Ironically, tonight was one of those classic New York nights from the movies. Lights from a million windows sparkled beneath a low-hung moon that cast the city in a star-drenched sheen.

Joshua remembered his first visit to New York—the clichéd kid from the sticks who'd been overwhelmed and impressed by everything. He could still recollect that first trip down Fifth Avenue…and the definitive moment when he'd decided to turn his life around. Ironic that he'd be back in the same city where he'd made that life-altering decision.

So how much of his career had MI6 documented?

Joshua had worked with many powerful men, but he'd allied himself exclusively to Renouf over the past few years for one simple reason—Henri had proven himself the most disciplined.

Joshua admired the man's skill as a strategist and appreciated his caution. Those qualities had earned his respect, and in a career where risk was the name of the game, Henri's qualities had lessened those risks dramatically.

Until now, at least.

Joshua had honestly never expected to hear Henri's name pop out of Lindy Gardner's pretty mouth. Not that he would let her see his surprise. She already had enough of an advantage without him helping her out.

"Tell me about the White Star," he asked as they passed under a street lamp.

"I was hoping you'd tell me."

"To do that I'd have to know something about it."

"Back to complicity again?"

"So it would seem."

"Do you deny knowing Henri Renouf?"

"I'm a businessman, Lindy. So is Henri. We've done business from time to time. No mystery there. Don't tell me you didn't know that already."

She shrugged, keeping her secrets as close as he kept his. The light of a streetlamp bathed her in a golden glow, another glimpse of this woman he suspected wore many guises, the woman who had changed his life.

No matter how this situation played out, Lindy had changed everything with her investigation. An international tail, even a gorgeous one, was the kiss of death to a man in his position.

Checking his pace, Joshua switched direction. The Starbucks on the corner was still serving coffee at this hour, but he found himself lured by the night quiet and the sight of the stars glimmering overhead.

Leading Lindy to a nearby bus stop, he motioned to a bench and waited until she sat before settling beside her. He hooked his hands on his knees and stared into the street.

"Why did they assign you this case?" he asked.

"Because I'm good."

That much he knew already. Lindy sure as hell shouldn't have known where to find him tonight. Not when he hadn't even known where he'd take delivery until after visiting Lily Covington this afternoon.

Lindy shouldn't have known he'd be in New York.

As frequently happened in his business with Henri, the situation with the White Star had arisen unexpectedly. A call on a secure line had signaled Joshua that an acquisition had gone bad in the States, which had come as a surprise.

Henri had worked with Jean Allard before, and the thief had always proven efficient and reliable. Perhaps there was something to the White Star's curse after all.

Allard had been cursed—by old-fashioned greed.

He'd held on to the amulet and upped his price. Henri had promptly sent in a hit man to deal with the thief. Then he'd sent Joshua to retrieve the amulet.

"What exactly do you want to know about the White Star?" Lindy asked.

"Anything you can tell me."

"It's an interesting piece. I'd never heard of it before. Seemed a little tame for Renouf, so when we got word he was connected to its theft from a high-end auction house, I wasn't convinced my intel was accurate."

"What convinced you?"

"You did."

Joshua responded with a noncommittal nod. "You're not accusing me of stealing, are you?"

"Of course not. The local authorities found the thief floating in the East River. They're calling his death a random murder. You and I know better, don't we?"

"Do we?"

She nodded patiently. "We do. The White Star's theft went pear-shaped, and you're here to pretty things up so the trail doesn't lead from the thief to the man who hired him—Renouf."

"Are you accusing me of murder?"

"Your arrival doesn't coincide with the time of death, so you're out of the running for that crime."

"How convenient for me."

"Very." Her sultry eyes narrowed and she grew tense around the edges. "What I don't know is where the White Star is now. The local authorities obtained the amulet from the bank's security guard, but it seems to have disappeared from the precinct property room, where it was being held as evidence. I've questioned the officer associated with the case. He doesn't have a clue. But you're here, Joshua, so I did the math. Your appearance summed up the situation nicely."

Unfortunately, it did, which meant this woman wasn't bluffing. "Why do you think Henri Renouf wants the White Star if it's not his typical fare?"

"You tell me. You know the guy."

Joshua didn't expect the question, didn't expect her to admit she didn't know. Lindy wasn't playing this game the way he would expect an agent to play, and that kept throwing him. Her deal threw him—whether it was real or a double play. And then there was the disappointment he felt because she was turning his life upside down to get to Henri.

Would he rather she had chased him down that hallway because she'd been interested in him?

The thought almost made him laugh. He wasn't normally sentimental. But this woman seated beside him provided a very beautiful reminder that tonight wasn't normal by any stretch.

"I don't know why Henri Renouf would want the White Star," he said. "I don't really care. I'm more interested in knowing why you think I'm involved in all this."

She turned to face him. The light spilled onto her features, detailing her mouth and reminding him of the way she'd felt against him when they'd kissed.

"Took me *days* to brief on you," she admitted wryly.

"Is that a long time?"

She nodded. "Had to wade through a boatload of circumstantial evidence from MI6, Interpol and a few other international agencies you've probably heard of."

"When did they start looking at me?"

"About six months ago."

They'd been an active six months. Joshua had masterminded the heist of a classical manuscript in Vienna and *fixed* situations on three continents. In between, he'd helped design and approved the blueprints on one jewel of a boat.

"What if you've got the wrong man, Lindy? I told you I've done occasional business with Renouf. What's to stop me from picking up the telephone and making a courtesy call?"

She didn't flinch, and her confidence impressed him. "I don't have the wrong man."

"What if I refuse to cooperate?"

"I'm authorized to threaten you. I can bring you in and use our evidence to build a case against you."

"Think you have enough to prosecute?"

"No. Just enough to trash your reputation and drive you underground. My agency is hoping you'd rather deal than live as an international fugitive."

A slave to MI6 or a life on the run.

"Mmm. That's a tough one. I thought you said the whole point was not letting Renouf know you're interested in him."

She laughed. "Ideally. In my business, we don't always achieve the ideal. You're our best-case scenario. We've devoted a lot of man hours to tracking your movements over the past six months. If you won't deal then we move on to plan B—eliminating you from the game. You're valuable to Renouf. It'll take him time to replace you. That will shake things up, slow down operations and make him more vulnerable. We'll flush out someone else who's willing to talk."

"Sounds like you've got all the angles covered."

"So what's the problem then? Why aren't you negotiating terms yet?"

He debated telling her that he didn't believe her, but he'd rather wait and see what she'd do to try and convince him.

The bottom line was that she'd compromised him. The instant Henri discovered MI6 had Joshua on their radar, he would become a liability. Henri would send a hit man to eliminate the problem, the way he'd eliminated Allard.

Which meant Joshua was on a time limit to figure out what to do about Lindy and her alleged deal.

Henri was expecting delivery of the White Star immediately, which didn't leave Joshua much room to maneuver. But he couldn't hand over the amulet with Lindy on his tail, and given this turn of events, he wasn't even sure he wanted to.

Rubbing his temples to soothe the ache starting there, he stared at a car that sped past, tires chewing up the street and echoing off the buildings. There had to be some way to work this situation to his benefit. But he couldn't figure out how until he knew what he wanted the outcome to be.

Lindy's investigation meant someone would be served up to MI6. Did he want to risk his life and freedom to protect Henri's interests? Of all the questions he'd been faced with tonight, he actually had an answer for this one.

No.

While Joshua had learned much under Henri's tutelage, they were business associates. Friendly ones, true, but Joshua felt no loyalty to Henri, expected none in return.

Fortunately, problem-solving and cleaning up messy situations happened to be Joshua's specialty.

This situation was a mess. The timing was bad, and he was more vulnerable than Henri at the moment. But there would be a way to turn things around to his advantage.

Joshua just had to find it.

LINDY COULDN'T REMEMBER the last time she'd hung on to a man's every word—had she *ever* hung on to a man's every word?

She didn't think so, but she was hanging now.

Perhaps it was being in such close proximity to an extremely attractive man. Every time one of them moved, they touched—their shoulders, their hips, their thighs. Slight touches with electrifying effects. She found it hard to stay focused.

Perhaps she was challenged because she had no idea what question would pop out of Joshua's mouth next, or how she would reply. She'd come to New York City to conduct surveillance and figure out how to get close to this man, but she hadn't expected chemistry. She was flying by the seat of her pants, as the Americans would say.

Or maybe she could credit her unprofessional reaction to the fact that so much hinged on gaining Joshua's cooperation. Her entire career had gotten tangled up with getting close enough to Renouf to bring him in.

But whatever the reason for her hyperawareness of this man, Lindy found the experience invigorating.

Challenges always invigorated her.

"What's it going to take to convince you to cooperate?" she asked. "Another show of faith? Or do you want more proof—shall I ring one of my superiors so you can chat?"

She could just imagine what Malcolm Trent, her direct superior, would have to say to this fellow.

"I don't want to talk with your superiors."

With his chin braced on clasped hands, Joshua inclined his head enough to face her. A fluorescent bulb behind pitted plastic cast his features in a glow that did nothing to diminish his startling good looks. His gaze captured hers, and that hum she'd felt since their kiss, an awareness that had ebbed and flowed on her internal tide, surged yet again.

"Joshua, I understand I've placed you in an awkward position—"

"Only if I'm the man you're looking for."

Inclining her head, she conceded the point even though she knew MI6 only had an infinitesimal percentage of this man's career on paper. No one got to be as accomplished in the field as Joshua Benedict without years of experience.

She knew that firsthand.

"Talk to me. What's it going to take to get you to deal?"

"I still need…*convincing.*"

Convincing. Well, she hadn't expected this man to roll over, had she? To tell the truth, she'd have been disappointed if he'd proven an easy mark. But she hadn't expected him to look quite so yummy when he was wheedling, either.

"Convincing, hmm?" She willed her thoughts to behave. "About my integrity? About my agency's intentions?"

"That my future's in good hands."

There were several places Lindy could take that statement, but with his deep voice resounding in the late-night quiet and his gaze steady, the only place she wanted to take it would place their attraction square on the table.

Lindy had always been a risk taker, so she sidled around and leaned toward him until they were face to face, so close she could make out the stubble on his cheeks, a shadow that contrasted with his hair.

The move threw sex between them as surely as if she'd flashed a neon sign. And the arrogant man only held her gaze, searching for something. The truth, perhaps, because he didn't strike her as needing reassurances.

"I told you what we're offering. Don't you believe me?" The least she could do was shoot for earnest here, or as earnest as she could for someone who was lying through her teeth.

"It's not that I don't believe you...of course, I'm not saying I do believe you."

"Of course."

A smile appeared, twitching as if he was trying to hold it back. A good sign. He had such an attractive mouth, one that made it difficult not to remember his kiss.

She suspected his thoughts must be traveling a similar path because he closed the distance between them. Suddenly she could catch the scent of his aftershave on the night air—that hint of spicy fragrance and masculine ambrosia.

"To accept your deal, I'd have to trust your abilities, Lindy. And your agency's." His voice was low and sexy, drawing attention to their proximity.

"We've been watching you for six months, and I followed you to New York. Doesn't that count for something?"

"It's the reason I'm sitting here."

Absurdly, she wanted him to admit he was sitting here because he was as tempted by her as she was by him. It was a ridiculous thought that had no place in her head while she was working. Yet with his confident statement ringing in her ears and the brush of his warm breath on her lips, her reactions were physical, distracting, *real.*

"You'll have plenty of chances to take my measure, Joshua. I plan to stick to you like glue."

"You can try."

There was emphasis on *try* again, but she deemed it time to move past *try*. His mouth hovered against hers, a prelude to a kiss.

She was through *trying* to tempt him.

He seemed to be waiting, taking her measure, perhaps, or seeing what she'd do next. Sliding her hands into his lapels, she dragged him into their kiss, rewarded when his breath caught audibly.

It was odd at first. She'd kissed all sorts of men before, but lovers, never strangers, and never one of the bad guys.

But now *she* kissed *him*.

Lindy had always found control a liberating thing, and that feeling apparently ran to kissing bad guys, too. Slanting her mouth across his, she coaxed his lips wide with her tongue, savored the erotic taste of moist warm breath, felt challenged to make him respond.

He'd kissed her in the museum hallway as cover, but she kissed him now because she couldn't resist. All this awareness happening between them was simply too delicious to ignore, too intense. She liked that she had this unexpected attraction to add weight to her cause. *Almost* as much as she liked kissing Joshua Benedict.

Almost as much as she liked him kissing her back.

Remembering the cathedral, Lindy wondered if she shouldn't light her own candle.

Attraction this strong could only mean trouble.

And he proved the notion by raising a hand to touch her. She wanted him to go for the kill, to reach for her breasts, which were within easy range. Could he tell her nipples had gone all peaky or did her dress hide the evidence?

He dragged his fingers up her throat, a touch that felt

more intimate than a bolder touch might have. Especially when he arched her neck so he could deepen their kiss.

Thrusting his tongue inside her mouth for a warm stroke, he took the lead with an assurance that rolled her insides as if they were as gooey as that first melting bite of a fresh-from-the-oven brownie.

She sank against him, caught up in the feel of his hands on her, the power of their clashing breaths and tangling tongues. Who knew they'd be so hot together? The thought had certainly never occurred to her, not even when she'd been caught staring at him.

But all questions about reactions vanished beneath the thrill of the moment, the fire of their kiss. Lindy sensed the instant he was about to lose his control, felt the gathering of his muscles before his arms came around her with whipcord strength. Suddenly, she came up hard against him, feeling the difference between close and *closer.*

He surrounded her with his broad chest and strong arms. Her breasts crushed against his chest so she could feel the steady thumping of his heart. Sliding her arms around him, she hung on, unable to resist the warm, solid feel of him, the way his body seemed to tuck around her in all the right places.

It was a moment that chased away all thoughts, all distractions. Indeed, how could work claim even a shred of her reason when excitement pulsed through her like a tide, when that soft place between her thighs grew warm?

Lindy arched against him and was rewarded when Joshua ground out a sound from low in his throat, a sound that assured her he was as caught up as she.

The night fell away, the city along with it, and not until a bus screeched to a halt directly in front of them did Lindy become aware of anything but the way her body sparked to life in contact with this man's.

The bus doors hissed open with a whoosh, and Joshua and Lindy broke apart. She blinked stupidly as he disentangled himself and stood. He stared down at her, his dark gaze a caress, then he flashed a grin that was all satisfied male.

"I want to see what you're made of, Lindy Gardner. If you can keep up with me, I might actually consider your deal."

With that he turned and hopped onto the bus, leaving her staring at that cute bum as he strode up the stairs.

The doors shut with a whoosh. Joshua paid the fare and headed down the aisle as the bus lurched into motion again. Lindy watched it roll down the street in a gleam of red taillights, and she laughed, a sound that resounded through the late-night street.

"I've MADE CONTACT with our target," Lindy said when the familiar image of her boss appeared on the high-definition notebook display.

Malcolm gave a curt nod, a gesture she knew translated into approval. "Care to share the details?"

"Not just yet."

"Brief me."

"We're playing cat and mouse."

"Care to define *that*? Just enough to assure me you're the cat."

"Meow."

As her direct superior, Malcolm Trent ran Lindy's life, and had since she'd completed her SIS training nearly a decade ago. On approach to his fiftieth birthday, he was a stoic man with black hair, who somehow managed to look younger than his age.

How he'd avoided graying while maneuvering the often-treacherous shoals between the Joint Intelligence Committee, the Ministry of Defence, the Government Communications Headquarters and outside agencies like Interpol was a mystery of incredible genetics as far as Lindy was concerned. Then again, Malcolm was good at his job with a knack for diplomacy. That knack had shot him up the ranks of SIS with impressive speed.

They shared a solid relationship, not always pleasant, but based on mutual respect, with a bit of indulgence on Malcolm's part, as he'd been responsible for recruiting her from the police force in her home town.

Lindy shamelessly admitted to taking advantage of that indulgence sometimes. Like *now* when she didn't admit to hedging her bets with Joshua Benedict. The boundaries could be liquid in her line of work—one of the reasons she liked her job. Malcolm set the parameters. She did what she felt necessary to accomplish her mission objective.

Bottom line: Malcolm wanted Renouf.

"He acquired the White Star," she said.

"You got a confirm on that?"

She shook her head. "But I'd bet my Man U tickets. Everything adds up. The thief whom we believe stole the White Star from the auction house rented a security box in a local bank. He winds up a floater in the East River and the bank's security guard is arrested for drunken and disorderly conduct, where the NYPD find an amulet in his possession. Suddenly our target shows up and the amulet disappears from the precinct property room. What would you surmise?"

"Sounds like you've been tailing him closely."

"Closely, but not too closely. Didn't want to scare him off. You said it yourself—he's our only lead to the target."

"Think he'll take the bait?"

"I'm letting him put me through my paces. He wants to see what I'm made of."

"Sure that's the best way to handle him?"

Here was a place she could have admitted Joshua had thrown her a curve, too, but Lindy didn't want to be directly responsible for Malcolm's first gray hair. "Trust me. I'm playing him exactly the way he needs to be played. Let me do my job, so you're free to do yours. Speaking of, you look tired. MOD giving you grief?"

"Afghanistan."

That was all he had to say. The Ministry of Defence relied upon the intel from SIS to protect and serve, and with the rumor of ties between the United Kingdom and a new, potentially well-funded terrorist cell harbored in Afghanistan, the MOD had been applying pressure to produce the information needed to assess the threat.

"Anything I can do?"

"Bring me enough to build a case against Renouf. That'll make folks around here smile again. For a while at least." He forced his own smile.

Lindy nodded. Malcolm was right—catching Henri Renouf would soothe frazzled tempers. When British relics disappeared, more than art enthusiasts noticed. People took the thefts personally. The recovery of any artifacts, or bringing the man who'd funded the thefts to justice, would throw good light on their agency at a time when the public needed reassurance.

With political events shifting and terrorism breeding in some of the most unexpected global cubbies, a climate of uncertainty existed everywhere. There would be media attention on bringing in a man who'd eluded international capture for as long as Renouf had. He was exactly the sort of example the intelligence community needed right now to reassure the public that justice did indeed prevail.

Which was precisely why ending Renouf's reign had become Lindy's personal crusade.

He was also *her* example, a way to force a move up SIS ranks. For ten years, she'd been confined to the field. A series of lateral moves with more responsibility and freedom had kept her from running her own ops. Lindy had a theory about why.

Her field expertise was a double-edged blade.

Malcolm and his cronies relied on using her extensive connections to hunt down the bad guys. They relied on her to train new agents to become effective team players.

They relied on her to make them look good.

Lindy *was* good. Too good. And she loved working in the field. But field work consumed her life. She had no time for relationships. No time to spend with the friends who'd hung in there with her unpredictable schedule all these years. So few knew she was an agent of the Crown—with the covert nature of her work it was safer that way.

But as the years passed, *safe* was proving a damn isolated existence. She couldn't have a relationship with a man that involved more than a few dates. Hell, with the amount of time she spent away, she couldn't even own a cat. She'd bought a corn plant, and frequently came home to find it looking droopy and sad from lack of attention.

Lindy believed her work worth the sacrifice, a reasonable trade-off for the life she led. But the work needed to keep being worth it. She wanted the challenge of running her own ops.

With the capture of Renouf, the spotlight would spin

toward the agency and politicians who supported their funding, whose gazes would then swing to the woman who'd made the case.

Lindy didn't want glory; she wanted leverage.

Henri Renouf was the best-case scenario to get it.

"Our target wants to play hide-and-seek," she told Malcolm. "I expect he's checking out of the Piazza as we speak. He'll be on his way to parts unknown before the sun rises on this Yankee jungle. Trust me."

"He wants you to chase him?"

She nodded.

Malcolm frowned. "This one's awfully slippery, Lindy. You want me to assign you someone?"

She considered that. Malcolm was more right about Joshua than he knew. "No. As long as I have access to our resources, I'll be fine. His game is all about earning respect. I've got to impress the man—on my own."

"Can you?"

"Meow."

Malcolm rolled his eyes, and the screen went blank.

Logging off their secure channel, she ran protocol to erase all traces of the transmission. She reached for her phone and keyed in a number from the open telephone book on the desk.

"Good morning," a cheery voice said. "Piazza Hotel."

"Joshua Benedict's room, please." She buried all traces of Britain beneath her most practiced American accent.

There was a hesitation on the other end, and Lindy glanced at her notebook display.

Two o'clock in the morning.

Definitely outside the realm of polite behavior. "He asked me to make sure he was up to catch his flight," she explained. "But he's not picking up his cell phone. I'm afraid he's still asleep. Could you call him for me? He either won't pick up, which means he's on his way to the airport. Or he will pick up and be quite grateful."

Lindy knew the switchboard operator wouldn't ring a guest's room at this wee hour, but with any luck she would check on the guest's status.

"It looks as if your party has already checked out."

"Perfect. Thanks so much for your help."

Ending the call, Lindy set the phone on the desk and leaned back in the chair with a sigh. The lights from a nearby building shone through the sheers covering the windows in her suite, and she stared at the steady glow while focusing her thoughts on the puzzle at hand.

Joshua had flown into New York City on a commercial carrier via Newark Airport, which was an easy traveling distance to Manhattan. Would he fly out the same way he'd come, now that he knew she was on to him?

There were two schools of thought here. Joshua would either dodge her or trick her. If he went the dodging route, he'd likely leave the country in a wholly different manner than he'd arrived. Private airline, perhaps. Or maybe he'd scoot north to Canada and head out from there. If he tried to trick her, he might cover his tracks and head out from one of the three nearby airports.

Lindy considered all she knew about Joshua, bad-guy fixer and yummy kisser extraordinaire. She reconciled the profile with the man she'd met tonight, calculated how he might reason.

Dodge her or trick her?

"I still need...convincing," he'd told her earlier, which brought Lindy back to the fact that she hadn't had enough of a chance to prove herself to the man.

Joshua wasn't convinced he had anything to dodge yet, which meant he would trick her.

Or *try.*

Reaching for her notebook, she logged on to the agency mainframe, split the display and made contact with Blythe.

An image appeared on half the screen, and as Lindy smiled at the woman who stared back with a deadpan expression, she wondered again what had prompted this agent's alias. Blythe looked nothing like her traditional name might suggest, with cropped hair dyed to a shoe-polish black and silver piercings all over her pale face. She always struck Lindy as someone on the piss in one of London's many underground clubs rather than the brilliant computer analyst who ran the systems for SIS.

"Hello, Blythe. You're looking lovely as always," Lindy said cheerily.

Blythe scowled but didn't glance up from her keyboard. "Bugger off, Gardner, or jump to the punchline. I'm busy."

"I need inside the reservation systems of all the carriers flying out of the three airports that service New York City."

"Hope you're not on a time crunch."

"I am, in fact."

That brought up Blythe's gaze. "Need someone?"

What was it with everyone thinking she needed help tonight? "I'm good, thanks. I've got a lead on the target. Should be able to weed through the chaff with our subroutines."

Blythe shrugged, banged out a series of keystrokes, and scrolling data suddenly appeared on the other half of Lindy's display monitor. "Yell if you go balls-up."

"Thanks."

The image faded, and Lindy implemented a program to

process the reservation information of males traveling with companions and families. Setting a six-hour departure parameter, she would create a list of possibilities by process of elimination.

She set no parameters for destination because she had no idea where Joshua would go. The man wanted to play hide-and-seek, and the world was a bloody big playground.

But it happened to be a playground Lindy knew well.

4

London, where wet weather turns the city into a misty maze of intimate squares and narrow streets where sexy surprises lurk around every corner.

INSIDE THE GALLERY of Stanforth Hall, Joshua toured the small room in the north turret to view the displayed brooch. The spray of diamonds and rubies in an intricate platinum setting had been designed sometime in the mid-eighteenth century for the lady of Stanforth Hall.

While Joshua didn't much care for the piece's design, he did appreciate the British sense of drama and style. Lady Kenwick, the current lady of Stanforth Hall and hostess of tonight's soiree, made it a habit to display some trinket from the family coffers whenever opening her home to guests. The brooch sat on a satin-draped stand without the security of tempered glass to detract from the gems' brilliance.

Trust—a gift to her guests.

Not that security wasn't close at hand. Joshua couldn't miss the plainclothes personnel posted at both gallery entrances. Trust was all well and good, he knew, and while Lady Kenwick might be a generous old dame undeniably proud of her heritage, she was no one's fool.

But she was a gracious hostess. Her guest list included an impressive array of British aristocracy and elected members of the House of Commons. Her get-together to celebrate a favorable vote of a bill her nephew had championed through the House would surely garner interest in her nephew from both parties.

Dinner had been an elegant affair, and upon retiring to the gallery for entertainment, the conversation proved an oratorical battleground in the dignified fashion that only the Brits had ever managed to pull off, in Joshua's opinion.

Now the night was wearing away. After paying his respects to the brooch, he continued from the turret alcove, venerating the long gallery along the way. The room was decorated in the original creams, pale greens and golds of the last architect to refurbish the interior back when the gallery had been a place for ladies to retire after dinner, leaving their men to conversation and port.

Painted ceiling medallions. Requisite family portraits. China, books, urns and statues. Wealth and heritage abounded, but instead of appreciation for period refinement, everything reminded Joshua of Her Majesty's Secret Intelligence Service.

And one of their agents.

He'd chosen to start the chase in London for several reasons. First and foremost, he had business. While he'd been inside Stanforth Hall before, he needed tonight's soiree to reconnoiter. Henri had his eye on a bronze sculpture of a Roman gladiator that Lady Kenwick permanently displayed behind museum-quality glass in a dining-room alcove.

The only privately owned San Gabriel left in existence. A piece worthy of Henri's notice and, hence, Joshua's.

He'd conducted a fairly thorough inspection of the premises before the meal. While dining, he'd inspected the protection around the sculpture. And as guests mingled, he'd located the surveillance cameras.

After some research on the private security company and routine of the house staff, Joshua would have the information he needed to make recommendations to Henri. Of course, after meeting Lindy, whether or not he'd get the chance to make recommendations became a question. Which led to the second reason he'd chosen London.

A perverse sense of pride.

He'd had a good twenty hours since leaving her looking delectable on a Manhattan street. Much of that time had been spent covering his tracks out of the U.S.

The rest had been spent researching Lindy.

It had taken far more time than expected to confirm she was even affiliated with MI6. Given Joshua's resources, that lack of information had come as a surprise, which confirmed two things.

The first was that Lindy was as good at her job as she claimed. So good that MI6 had buried her identity completely.

The second was that his instinct about her had been dead on—this woman was Trouble with a capital T.

Since she'd been so forthcoming, she obviously knew her identity was well protected. Clearly she didn't fear much from him. And from what he'd been able to unearth so far, she had no reason to.

After confirming her affiliation with MI6, his information flow had dried up. He didn't know much about the woman except she spoke with an accent he'd pegged as Northern England. He also had a photo he'd taken with his cell phone while she'd been perpetrating her foie gras maneuver over the buffet table. Not much to work with.

Normally, digging up information on an invisible woman would have been a welcome challenge. But Lindy had compromised him, which had closed off his normal connections. Now he could only gather information from places Henri wouldn't think to look—at least until Joshua came up with a credible explanation about why he was researching an MI6 agent.

He hadn't had time to come up with that explanation yet. Not with covering his tracks and keeping a step ahead of Lindy.

Joshua accepted a snifter of cognac from a passing waiter, sidestepped Larry Northrup who made a move to catch him in conversation, and wondered where Lindy was now.

What would she do when she couldn't catch up with him?

He figured that after a few days of this game, he'd make contact, proving an important point to his lovely tail—that she'd seriously underestimated him.

Of course, what he'd do about her bogus deal and MI6's interest afterward still remained a question, but he was buying himself time to come up with the answer.

To uncover her true identity.

Once he knew who Lindy really was, he'd have something to work with. She'd pursued him competently and had ruthlessly attempted to use their attraction to her benefit. The woman was a player, and without a doubt, there'd be something in her life he could twist into leverage.

Maybe he'd have her erase his MI6 file. Maybe not. Their chase would give him time to look at where he wanted to go next. Lindy's arrival and his reaction to her had proven one thing loud and clear—his life hadn't been serving up much of interest lately. But after nearly fifteen years spent earning the reputation and connections he now enjoyed, Joshua supposed he shouldn't be surprised. He'd been a kid when he'd first starting playing this game.

He wasn't a kid anymore, and though he couldn't pinpoint when, somewhere along the line, jobs such as acquiring the White Star had become nothing more than interference when he'd rather have been at home taking delivery of his new boat.

Maybe he was just getting old.

There were damn sure enough younger men entering the game nowadays to remind him of how long he'd been around. And this new generation was looking to distinguish itself at any cost.

Joshua had crossed paths with enough of them to know how anyone would put a bullet in his brain without so much as blinking for a chance to step into his place in Henri's empire.

Had he ever been so ruthless?

He didn't dwell on the answer. The passage of time had anesthetized whatever morals he might have once possessed, which meant the only question he needed to answer now was about his future.

But before he could sink any further into his analysis, he heard Lady Kenwick's voice from a distance.

"Lindy, dear," she said. "It's such a pleasure."

Disbelieving, Joshua glanced around and saw *her.*

She stood just inside the gallery, hands clasped in Lady Kenwick's. Her smile widened, a clearly satisfied smile as she peered over her hostess's shoulder and winked.

The gut punch she delivered might have made him laugh—if there was anything funny about her showing up.

Somehow Lindy had managed to track him despite his evasive maneuvers, which meant the point Joshua had hoped to prove was moot. *He'd* been the one to underestimate his opponent.

And his reaction to her.

If Lindy Gardner had been subtle seduction last night, she was all about cool allure now.

Her look was distinctly British, the cream-and-gold gown fitting her slim curves to perfection. The pencil-thin skirt showcased long, long legs.

She'd swept her hair into an elegant twist, and he found himself admiring her classic bone structure—high cheekbones, angled chin, gracefully bared throat.

Bringing the snifter to his lips, he took an absent swallow, the smoky liquor going down hard as he tried to control the effects of a sudden adrenaline rush.

His pulse throbbed so hard in his ears that he didn't hear Larry Northrup approach until the guy stood right beside him.

"Now there's one I could fall arse over elbows for," Larry said, waxing poetic. "Haven't seen her about town, have you, Benedict? Any idea who she is?"

"Out of your league, Northrup. That much I know."

Northrup sniffed, but Joshua didn't give him a chance to reply before taking off toward Lindy and their hostess.

Before he got out of earshot, he heard Larry say, "You're going to cop off with her? That's poor sport. I saw her first."

"You looked, Larry. I moved."

Another disgruntled sniff, and Joshua was out of range, zeroing in on his target.

The lovely lady who shouldn't be here.

Sucking down a last fortifying swallow, he deposited the snifter on a marble-topped credenza and moved in for the kill.

Lady Kenwick caught sight of him first and offered a welcoming smile. "Oh, Joshua. You must meet Lindy Gardner. She's a friend of the prime minister, in town from Berwick-on-Tweed."

Northumberland. He'd nailed the accent. It was something.

Joshua had always been fond of Lady Kenwick, a woman who by her own declaration didn't mince words or stand for minced words from others but, fondness notwithstanding, the lady looked distinctly pug-like with her jowly features and thick stature when standing beside the exquisite Lindy.

He reached for Lindy's hand, amazed by the awareness that practically crackled as they touched.

Joshua had almost convinced himself last night had been a fluke and their steamy kisses a product of his imagination, but apparently he and this lovely lady really were attracted to each other on a molecular level.

Bringing Lindy's hand to his mouth, he couldn't resist tasting her skin, inhaling the light scent of her perfume, reminiscent of gardenia. Her fingers were warm and smooth against his lips, and he found his heart racing, that adrenaline working a number on him that had nothing to do with MI6.

Meeting her gaze above their clasped hands, he found the color riding high in her cheeks. He suspected that this oh-so-cool agent wasn't used to reacting against her will, and he was pleased by how she reacted to him.

He needed an edge.

"So what brings you to London, Lindy?" he asked.

"Business. I'm a freelance journalist working with the *Historic Post Herald* on a long-term assignment. I'm investigating a story that's been unfolding into a modern-day treasure hunt."

"Really?" Lady Kenwick exhaled the word. "Treasure here in London?"

Lindy nodded.

"Who's hunting this treasure?" Joshua asked.

"It's a bit of a race, actually," Lindy said. "I can't reveal the particulars, of course, but I can tell you an archeologist who's funded by a collector of historically significant artifacts has been staying in London. There's speculation that he wouldn't be here unless he'd made a discovery of some importance, and if he finds the treasure, he'll smuggle it out of the country and deliver it to the man who funds his work."

Lady Kenwick gasped. "Aren't there laws to prevent that from happening?"

"Laws only protect us if the authorities can enforce them. Without proper evidence…" She let her words trail off and gave a shrug that did amazing things to her cleavage.

Joshua forced his gaze up from the skin swelling over her fitted bodice and reminded himself that this woman was nothing more than a siren luring him to the rocks. "So that's why you're here, Lindy?"

Before Lindy had a chance to reply, Lady Kenwick said, "No wonder the prime minister is concerned. Why, our historic artifacts belong to the public. Having them snatched from beneath our noses would be…*theft*."

"Agreed," Lindy said. "That's why the *Historic Post Herald* has sent me. We're hoping to raise public awareness to deter others from believing they can just stroll into the U.K. and help themselves to our treasures."

"Sending a message to the thieves?" he asked.

"Precisely."

Her eyes sparkled, and Joshua knew exactly what Lindy was trying to do—provoke him. Entice him. And prove that while he might run, he couldn't hide.

He wasn't willing to concede that point yet, but he did caution himself not to underestimate this woman again. And as Lady Kenwick paid Lindy the honor of touring her around the gallery, he attached himself to them, enjoying the view of Lindy from behind while he considered how she might have followed him to Stanforth Hall.

Unless Henri himself was her informant, Lindy couldn't have possibly known about his interest in the Roman Gladiator, which meant she'd followed *his* trail, when he'd made every effort to bury his movements.

"Joshua dear," Lady Kenwick said. "You haven't yet told me what you think of Alexandra's portrait."

Joshua glanced up perfunctorily at the full-sized portrait of a young girl decked out for her sixteenth birthday. "Your granddaughter is growing up to be as lovely as her mother."

Lady Kenwick beamed as she reached out to pat his hand fondly. "I'll tell Erica you said that."

"Please let her know I was asking about her."

"I shall, dear. I shall. But you should ring Erica sometime yourself. I know my daughter would love to hear from you."

Joshua inclined his head, knowing Lindy listened with interest and feeling her gaze as a visceral connection that sliced the distance between them.

He wanted to excuse himself from Lady Kenwick's solicitous attention and drag Lindy off for a private question-and-answer session, one that would most likely involve kissing the glossy sheen off her mouth just to knock the lady down a notch.

But he knew privacy wouldn't be forthcoming any time soon. Lindy's alleged connection to the prime minister warranted the special treatment. Lady Kenwick obviously wanted to impress as well as show off her new connection, so she regaled them with an abridged version of Stanforth Hall's history.

The family home had a respectable background as far as British residences went, mainly for the central location in a park surrounded by the Thames and London's suburbs.

Lady Kenwick began with the origins of the site. The Britons had dug stakes into the riverbed to stop Caesar and his legions from crossing. She continued through the Reformation, when old Henry chased away the inhabitants of the monastery that had been built several centuries before, and titled both building and land to the Earl of Kenwick.

Joshua had heard it all before and almost sighed in relief when they approached the north end of the gallery, where the brooch sat on display, and was—hopefully—the end of the tour.

When Lady Kenwick got sidetracked by a waiter, Joshua seized the opportunity to whisper in Lindy's ear, "The prime minister?"

"I wanted to impress you." She flashed one of those smiles that dragged his gaze to those shiny lips again.

And she had.

Not only by her resourcefulness, but by her cool skill when she directed her attention to Lady Kenwick again and delighted the old woman by saying, "I haven't seen any brooch this lovely since I last visited Topkapi Palace."

"Surely you don't mean the Eye of the Tiger."

Lindy nodded. "I do indeed."

"Oh, dear, you are delightful to notice the similarities."

"Actually, Lady Kenwick's ruby is two carats larger," Joshua said.

Lady Kenwick laughed, but Lindy leaned close to peruse the brooch.

"So I see," she said.

While Lady Kenwick chatted with them, Joshua debated ways to get Lindy all to himself, and as they—*finally*—moved out of the turret, he cast a parting glance at the sparkling brooch and found his answer.

HAD LINDY been paying less attention to the handsome man accompanying her on the gallery tour with their hostess, she'd have immediately noticed how security personnel had closed off the exits before a guard arrived to escort Lady Kenwick away.

Unfortunately, she'd been so aware of Joshua moving along in her shadow that details were slipping her notice.

Well, the important details, anyway.

The scent of his aftershave shouldn't have been occupying a top slot in her awareness just now. Or the way his broad shoulders blocked out the light whenever he moved in to stand close behind her. Yet worthy or not, these were the details currently distracting her... And how could she really expect *not* to notice the man when he kept stepping so close she could feel the warmth of his crotch against her back.

He was needling her, Lindy knew, his pride probably pricked because she'd followed him to London. Oh, he'd led her a good chase, and had he been trying to outwit an agent without the benefit of her resources—both official and unofficial—he might have given her the slip.

"I'm afraid you'll have to excuse me, Lindy." Lady Kenwick shot a worried glance at the security guard who'd whispered a discreet message into her ear.

"I'll entertain your guest until you're free again," Joshua offered.

Their hostess gave an absent nod. "Thank you. You'll be in good hands, Lindy. I promise."

Lindy smiled at that turn of phrase. The memory of Joshua's hands on her was still so fresh that she tingled... *tingled,* for heaven's sake.

Lady Kenwick hurried off to convene with the guards at the opposite end of the room, and none of their fellow guests seemed much interested in how the gallery's only two exits had been sealed up as tightly as a canister of nuclear waste. But Lindy watched the proceedings curiously, resisting the urge to speculate as Joshua passed off a glass of what turned out to be very tasty burgundy. "London, Joshua. Should I be insulted?"

"Insulted?"

"You obviously didn't think I'd be much of a challenge. You flew out of New York City on the same commercial carrier out of the same hub you flew into. True, Joshua Benedict dropped off the grid after you disembarked in Canada, leaving me to assume you'd stayed in Montreal. I suppose I could have searched the city, but that would have been a waste of time."

"Why's that?"

She raised her glass in salute. "Because when Joshua Benedict dropped off the grid, Stuart Temple appeared."

To his credit, he didn't flinch. His dark eyes held hers. His smile remained steady, an expression that didn't tell her a bloody thing.

"Stuart Temple?"

"The man who flew from Montreal to Heathrow."

Stuart Temple was a little-used alias from Joshua's past that went back a good decade, an alias that, to her knowledge, he'd never used in his dealings with Renouf.

Admitting she had this information revealed a few of the cards she held, but since he seemed to have such a low opinion of her abilities… "Now you're in *my* town, visiting *my* countrymen, right under the very nose of *my* agency. How can I be anything but insulted?"

"No insult intended. Testing you is the only way I can get the information I need."

"So you're admitting that you're Stuart Temple?"

"Of course not."

She chuckled. "Did you get the information you need?"

He inclined his head and the light from the cut-crystal chandelier overhead winked off his fair hair, drawing her gaze, and grudging attention, to the contrast against his tan skin.

He might blow off the fact that she'd known his alias, but Lindy suspected this was a detail of great interest—it would have been to her if their situations were reversed.

"Information gathering?" she said. "That happens to be exactly what I'm doing."

"Have you gathered any?"

"Absolutely. You acquired the White Star."

"What makes you think so?"

She nodded. "You wouldn't have picked up and left New York so fast. I have it on good authority Renouf really wants that piece, and I don't believe for a second you'd let a British agent interfere with a job."

"Even when that British agent is dogging my heels?"

"I thought you wanted me on your heels. Wasn't that the point of playing your game? You hide so I can find you?"

"Or *try* to."

She waved a dismissive hand. "What *try?*"

With a laugh, Joshua took a step toward her, crowding her against a bookcase and blocking her view of the security guards breaking away from Lady Kenwick.

She wanted to see what was happening across the room, but there was simply no ignoring this man. Even if he hadn't towered above her, his sheer maleness demanded her notice. Even clutching her wineglass between them, she felt surrounded. Heat flushed her, made her feel overdressed at an affair where she fitted in perfectly. She couldn't help but imagine their bodies pressed as close, naked.

Tipping her gaze to meet his, she recognized the heat in his expression, and wondered if he entertained similar thoughts.

She suspected he did.

"As far as my work in New York goes," he said, drawing her thoughts away from naked and back to kissing. "You threw me a curve when you arrived. I wouldn't insult your intelligence by pretending you didn't."

"So you do have some opinion of me."

"I do." Since he stared at her mouth, she suspected his opinion had less to do with Her Majesty's Secret Intelligence than how she kissed.

"Speaking of your work, Joshua, were you able to send the White Star off to its new owner? Or did you decide to deliver it personally after you shake off your tail?"

"Fishing?"

"It's a pastime of mine as well."

"An interest we share then." Plucking the wineglass

from her, he set it on a shelf then trailed a finger along her cheek where hairs had strayed from her stylish twist. His touch was subtly bold, warm, his fingertip faintly rough, and she added another piece to the Joshua Benedict puzzle that hadn't been in his profile.

He *used* his hands.

She'd read that he liked to fish, and his boats factored heavily into the life he lived for the public's viewing. Lindy couldn't be sure what else he might like to do with his hands, but from the easy, thorough way he touched her, she knew he would be skilled at whatever he did. She could feel it in the almost gentle way he brushed the hair from her cheek.

She was struck again by the same impression she'd had while first gazing through her digital-cam binoculars at this man—there was so much more beneath the surface, so much that no profile or image could capture.

Maybe it was their proximity or how he stared into her face as if he could see straight inside places she didn't dare look, but Lindy suddenly felt exposed.

"You have a smudge on your nose." He backed up a step, freeing her up to deal with her appearance.

Lindy was ridiculously relieved for an opportunity to break away from his overwhelming nearness. Just one step and she could breathe easier. It was absurd, really. She couldn't remember ever being so affected by a man, let alone a target. Yes, she'd decided to play the attraction card, but she hadn't expected to be all tied up in knots every time the man came near.

Automatically reaching into her purse for her compact, she mentally warned herself to get a grip. True, she hadn't dated in a while, but that had been by choice. The little free time she'd had out of the field had been better spent with family and friends.

And nursing her ailing corn plant back to health.

Raising the mirror, she shifted around so she could break completely free of Joshua's proximity to see what security was doing in the mirror's reflection.

"Wonder what's going on?" she said. "Security's questioning the guests. Lady Kenwick looks upset."

She watched for a moment, and her instincts—now that she wasn't preoccupied with this tall, handsome male—went wild. "Considering they've locked us inside like criminals, I can only assume they don't want us leaving. Do you suppose there's been a theft?" Tilting her compact, she caught Joshua's gaze. "This is your area of expertise, after all."

"Alleged expertise."

"Humph." Looking for the smudge on her nose, she couldn't find a thing wrong with her appearance. Wondering what the man's game was, she returned the compact to her bag, where her hand bumped into something unfamiliar....

Lady Kenwick's brooch.

5

JOSHUA WATCHED the play of emotions across Lindy's face when she discovered the surprise he'd planted in her purse and guessed she didn't often reveal so much in a glance.

Her thickly fringed eyes widened and her whole body went still. From her expression, he pinpointed the exact instant she identified the brooch and connected the locked gallery to the piece she now had.

She swung her gaze his way and laughed, a silvery sound that wasn't the response he'd expected, but when hearing it, Joshua knew he should have.

And again he was impressed.

"Well, I knew being a thief factored in somewhere." She snapped her purse shut and cast an amused gaze around the room. "Well done, Joshua."

"What have I done well?" He couldn't argue the thief part tonight.

"You've played me. Now I'm curious to see what your next move will be. I don't guess you would have directed me to my bag if you were planning to take off and leave me to be caught with this?"

"That wouldn't be gentlemanly."

"You're a gentleman?"

"I promised Lady Kenwick I'd see to you in her absence."

"Hmm. That doesn't quite answer my question. I suppose I'll have to formulate my own opinion."

She scanned the room, no doubt looking for a way to unload the brooch, which was exactly what he wanted—to watch her in action. He needed to know everything he could about this woman.

When security split into groups to work the gallery from both directions, she frowned, but instead of showing signs of panic, she reached for her wineglass and sipped.

He'd been hoping to catch her off guard, but found her cool under pressure. "Not worried, Lindy?"

"We're in the middle of the room. The guards are still working the perimeter. I've got a few minutes until they show up and ask me to upend my bag."

"Would you like me to rescue you?"

"Do I look like a damsel in distress?"

Despite the distinctly castle-like qualities of Stanforth Hall, there was nothing distressed about Lindy. "Not after watching you dispose of that electronic device last night," he admitted. "I'll take my time before stepping in."

"Oh, arrogant. Why do you think you'll need to?"

"Because I want to prove I'm a gentleman. Fair is only fair."

"Sounds like you think you owe me. Are you admitting that imaging device was yours?"

"No."

She gave a snort of unladylike laughter, and he couldn't help but smile.

"Y'know, I might actually buy a gentleman bad guy, Joshua. If you carry a hanky."

He obliged, watching as she went for her purse. By the way she fished around inside, he knew she was wiping the brooch clean of prints. The consummate professional. And one of the worthiest opponents he'd ever met.

Glancing around the room, he watched Lady Kenwick motion a security guard away before pairing off with a woman he recognized as a close family friend. Both ladies looked upset, and he had a momentary pang that he'd marred Lady Kenwick's otherwise enjoyable affair to put Lindy on the spot.

The new security guard lent effort to the cause, speeding up the investigation. Joshua knew Lindy noticed those proceedings, too, but she still looked cool, unaffected, even as his own pulse sped up while precious seconds ticked by.

The opportunity for escape was fast slipping away as two security guards wrapped up business with one group of guests and moved on to a couple standing on the opposite side of the fireplace—not far from him and Lindy.

"Ready for that rescue yet?" he asked.

"You'll have to find another way to prove yourself tonight."

She openly challenged him. No coyness or subtlety. She wanted to use him, didn't care how she'd trash his life in the process. All she cared about was catching her man.

And he wasn't even the man she was after.

"Come on." Suddenly she was on her way, heading across the room in a silken glide of swaying hips and smooth strides. He followed, both appreciating the scenery she made and curious to see her next move.

"Oh, Joshua, look at those Stargazer lilies." She beelined straight for a fresh-flower arrangement that adorned a credenza. "Aren't they the most beautiful you've ever seen?"

The arrangement showcased an array of colors and shapes, but Joshua didn't recognize the flowers. "They're pretty."

"Pretty?" She sounded incredulous. "Just smell them."

Passing him the wineglass, she leaned into the arrangement, inhaling deeply. He passed off the glasses to a nearby waiter, who was obviously doing his bit to accommodate the guests under unusual circumstances, just as Lindy came up from the arrangement in a fit of sneezes.

"Bless you," he said.

She pulled the handkerchief from her purse and buried her face inside it, still sneezing. He wondered if he was being treated to a repeat of last night's performance. But Lindy wouldn't dispose of this piece in the trash. No one would be leaving Stanforth Hall until the brooch turned up. Security would search the gallery then the rest of the house. If they didn't recover the piece, guests would be held for questioning until the local police arrived.

And Joshua would be back to hoping his name didn't turn up on a suspect list.

"I need water, please." Lindy motioned to the waiter, who immediately did an about-face and headed toward the service bar.

She followed the waiter, and Joshua followed her. When she brushed close to another flower display, this one designed from silk blooms that matched the gallery's color scheme, he braced himself to catch it.

But the arrangement didn't topple over, and he did a double take when he saw the jeweled brooch suddenly peeking out from the greenery, noticeable without being too obvious.

A respectable hiding place.

"Well done," he whispered to her as they arrived at the bar. "Now what?"

After accepting water from the waiter, she offered

thanks and moved out of earshot before saying, "We entertain ourselves until someone notices it. Come on. Let's go chat with Lady Kenwick. The poor dear looks nearly hysterical."

He felt another pang of guilt as they approached their hostess to find her indeed distraught. But as she and the Duchess of Bradborough explained the brooch's disappearance while he and Lindy took turns reassuring them that security would locate the piece, Joshua knew Lindy had set him up. This was a test. She gauged him now, watched how well he held up under pressure. And except for the guilt…

Fortunately, it didn't take long for security to stumble across the brooch. Joshua felt an unfamiliar relief when Lady Kenwick bustled across the gallery. "Oh, thank goodness."

The guests cheered.

"We've already paid our respects to the hostess," he said. "Now seems like a good time for that rescue. Shall we?"

Lindy looped her arm through his. "We'll look suspicious if we leave."

"We've already spoken to Lady Kenwick, so I think we might slip away in all this commotion without drawing any notice if we don't leave the way we came in."

"Are you suggesting we jump out a window?"

"Trust me—unless you'd rather spend the next few hours debating theories about who moved the brooch from its display. They'll think we've slipped away for a tryst."

Lindy's gaze sparkled. "Then rescue me. Fair's fair."

Inclining his head, he led her on a tour, remarking on various features around the gallery. When they reached the turret room at the south end, Joshua stepped close while pointing to a portrait high on the wall.

While relating the history of that particular Kenwick ancestor, he slipped a hand under the authentic Spitalfields silk wall hanging. The fabric had worn through the centuries, faded to a dull red that managed to accent the room's décor.

And create a respectable place for a getaway.

Lindy didn't hesitate when he motioned her behind the drapery, but slipped quietly inside, pressing close to the wall until he joined her. He made his move, and suddenly they were ensconced in the narrow black space.

He could hear her shallow breaths in the darkness, the sounds of conversations muted through the silk hangings, and he groped along the wall....

A mechanism hissed. Crowding Lindy inside an open space that smelled of stale air and age, Joshua blinked to adjust his gaze to the complete blackness and entered behind her. He could feel her come up against him, all warm and sexy woman, and a sudden rush of awareness quickened his own breaths.

Another brush of his hand and the panel slid shut to sequester them together.

Reaching for her hand, he twined their fingers and cautiously led her from the secret entrance until they stood just inside a narrow tunnel that wound down three stories along the building's exterior.

"I had no idea Stanforth Hall had a secret passage," Lindy whispered.

"A family secret."

"Which begs the question about how you know...ah, Erica."

"Erica," he confirmed, pulling out a pocket flashlight.

The beam illuminated the narrow tunnel that had been erected with the castle's original structure. Stone walls glistened almost cave-like beneath seeping moisture. Although Joshua couldn't see beyond the beam at the moment, he knew iron sconces perched high on the walls at intervals and panels led to other rooms as the passage wound down toward the first floor.

"Did you date Erica?" Lindy asked. "I didn't read a thing about her in my profile, which surprises mc since she's part of a prominent British family."

"We dated for a while."

"I'll have to look more closely at your ex-lovers. Thanks for the tip."

"Not even Lady Kenwick knows I'm in on her family secret."

"Then I'll red-flag Stanforth Hall in our systems to see if any artifacts come up missing."

He laughed. And made a mental note to tell Henri that his plans for the San Gabriel would need to be shelved for a while.

"This tunnel leads outside?" she asked.

"We'll have to time our exit, though. Security sweeps the grounds. We won't want to be seen leaving."

She didn't ask why he knew details of Lady Kenwick's security, but he didn't think she'd dismiss his knowledge as another by-product of dating the lady's divorced daughter.

Something about that challenged him. In fact, everything about Lindy challenged him—from the opinion of him she might be piecing together to the way she'd managed to track down an old alias and follow him to London.

Depressing the power button, he dropped the light into his pocket and cast them into total darkness. Lindy came up full against him with no protest, no feigned surprise, just the simple melting of their bodies together.

Here was that feeling again. Joshua wasn't sure what it was. Given that Lindy threatened his future with her MI6 profile and cutthroat manipulations, they were adversaries. Attraction shouldn't explain the effortless way she felt in his arms.

Dragging his fingers along her jaw, he urged her head back so he could make out her expression. Her features were shrouded in the gloom, so Joshua sensed rather than saw her sudden uncertainty. He felt it twining through the stale air, inhaled it with every breath. He wasn't the only one surprised by the awareness between them, and he wondered how sassy Lindy, accomplished agent of Her Majesty's Secret Intelligence Service, felt about being attracted to her target.

"Are you thinking of ways to thank me for the rescue?" he asked.

"You said fair's fair. We're even."

"We never established that you rescued me last night, which means you're in my debt."

"You planted the brooch on me."

He thumbed the curve of her jaw, depressed the smooth skin of her throat until he could feel her pulse quickening. "We've never established that as fact either."

His statement lingered in the darkness between them, words that held tangible power and so many possibilities with their bodies pressed close, their hearts throbbing in rhythm. Their breaths threaded through the muted quiet, edgy, as though each of them struggled not to cue the other on how their awareness had filled the moment with thoughts of sex.

Joshua tightened his arm around her waist, anchored her against him until he shared her body's warmth. She'd been designed to fit against him, and in any other scenario he'd have pursued this woman without a thought, considered himself fortunate to have made her acquaintance.

He'd met many lovely women in his travels and enjoyed his share of satisfying relationships. But this was an impossible scenario if ever he'd seen one. Ironic, really. He was the prey of a woman who aroused him more than he'd been aroused in so long, involved in a high-stakes game with his future resting on each move and countermove.

"You know, Joshua." Her voice throbbed with a want he recognized. "You didn't only rescue me, you rescued yourself."

"How is that any different than your rescue last night? *If* that electronic device belonged to me—and I'm not admitting it did—you rescued me from dealing with museum security so you could interrogate me yourself."

"Are you saying I was self-serving?"

He dragged his thumb along her chin, traced the defiant tilt, worked his way toward her full lower lip that made him remember what their mouths felt like when they kissed. "I am."

"No less self-serving than you were tonight. You didn't want to answer questions about the brooch either."

"I didn't," he admitted.

"Then, I repeat, we're even."

He couldn't resist anchoring her a little closer, until his groin pressed against her. "You owe me."

"What do you want as payment?"

"Another kiss."

He wasn't sure who made the first move, but suddenly their mouths came together on an exchange of breath, their lips yielding on a rush of need that was physical, undeniable. His heartbeat spiked, a sudden ache in his chest, a languid thud in his ears.

Any questions Joshua had about their attraction vanished the second their tongues met in a clash of excitement that had nothing to do with circumstances and everything to do with passion. This was *hunger,* elemental, consuming, the sort of soul-deep wanting he'd never felt quite this intensely.

He'd enjoyed an active love life for enough years to become discriminating in his tastes, yet when he held Lindy…there was something so unexpected about the way he felt, so *real.* When she slipped her arms around his neck, snuggled closer, he guessed her reaction was as unexpected as his own.

Joshua had never felt this sort of excitement, a need to get under her oh-so-accomplished facade. He wanted to win more of these reactions from her. He wanted to convince her that she needed more than his kisses.

Without conscious thought, he found himself caressing her throat, feeling the silken skin yield beneath his fingertips, so supple, so alive with the steady throb of her pulse. He embraced her tightly, wanting to explore the heat that simmered when he held her in her arms.

Molding a palm over her shoulder, he skimmed a hand down her bare arm, skin against skin, such a simple touch that felt intimate and erotic in the extreme.

Time stopped inside this ageless passage, the stale air lending to their breathlessness, the stony chill contrasting sharply with the heat burning between them.

Joshua didn't understand the effect Lindy had on him, but he knew he'd never enjoyed kissing more. He should be using their attraction to take the advantage. But he didn't think this savvy woman would fall for any obvious maneuver. And he couldn't think beyond obvious when he held her. With Lindy in his arms, he could only think about the sexy way she melted against him.

When she began rocking against him, her sinuous moves turned an ache into a full-fledged erection. Blood plummeted to his crotch in blinding surges that echoed his pulse, made his legs leaden.

Sucking in a hard breath, Joshua broke their kiss and trailed his mouth along her jaw, her cheek, her temple. She shivered in reply, a tremor that rocked her from head to toe. He breathed against her ear and made her tremble again.

Lindy laughed, a low sound that echoed through the passage and sparked his need even hotter. Tipping her head, she exhaled another throaty sound, only this one burst against his ear, rocketing heat to all his sensitive places.

Fighting fire with fire.

He was ready.

Nibbling his way down her throat, Joshua distracted himself from the way she mirrored his actions with moist kisses and tantalizing nips, the way she rode his crotch with a sultry motion that mimed two bodies making love.

Her hands slipped down his back, nothing coy or shy about her desire to explore him, and when she slipped her arms free to reposition them so she could reach even lower, Joshua knew he was in trouble.

Sliding her hands beneath his jacket, Lindy molded his hips, dug her fingers into his ass until she could put thrust behind her strokes. And she almost had him. His hips had started moving of their own accord.

He couldn't resist the mounting pleasure, the sweet little

moans that slipped from between her parted lips when he nibbled at the base of her throat.

Joshua intended to fight back. She'd given him an erection that demanded satisfaction, so he prodded the neckline of her gown aside, molded a breast with a hand.

She gathered and tightened against him, a long "Oh" of pleasure tumbling from her lips, gusting against his neck in a warm exhalation.

He smiled, taking the opportunity to crowd her against the opposite wall of the narrow passage, a short two steps that changed the entire dichotomy of their embrace.

With the wall to support Lindy, Joshua had both hands free.

He went straight for the kill before she could protest, a search-and-rescue operation for the fastenings that held her gown wrapped around her luscious body.

God, he loved these Brits. The style was elegant and conservative, but deceptively so, because the tailored fit was actually nothing more than a simple wrap. He found a fastening at her bodice, another at her waist, and with one tug of an inner tie, her gown fell open, exposing a wealth of pale skin.

She was lovely. Firm breasts swelled over a silky bra with each rise and fall of her chest. Sheer panty hose clung to the smooth expanse of her stomach and perfectly-rounded hips before descending legs that would haunt his dreams. He wanted to lift her into his arms, feel her wrap those legs around him, knew a need that suddenly felt bigger than his restraint.

Words came to mind as he raked his gaze over her, her skin pale in the darkness, her body arched on the edge of desire, simple words that humbled him. He swallowed them back, still rational enough not to add to Lindy's advantage.

She didn't need to hear that he thought she was beautiful. She would have heard those words from other men, men she'd probably invited into her life, men whose kisses she'd pursued.

But wasn't she pursuing him? Responding to him?

Yes.

A spray of goose bumps pebbled her skin, and he might have blamed the chill had it not been for the way her eyes had fluttered half-shut in a dreamy expression.

He reached out to touch her, unable to resist.

"Joshua—"

Kissing his name from her lips, he revealed his own need in how hard his mouth caught hers, the way he drank in the taste of her. He wouldn't give her a chance to protest, or to think about who he was and all the reasons why she shouldn't give in to the way she felt. Not when her body responded so vitally to him. Not when his desire raged out of control.

Slipping his hands between them, he shoved her bra up. Her breasts tumbled free as he speared his tongue inside her mouth, explored the warm recesses as he molded his fingers around perfect handfuls.

Her skin was supple, her nipples tight peaks that stabbed his palms, begging to be touched. Catching them between thumbs and forefingers, he squeezed. A shudder rocked her slim body, and he tugged again, taking liberties, fondling her until he could taste her pleasure in the breathy little gasps that tumbled from her lips, feel her mounting need in the way she swayed against him.

This woman was fire, and Joshua wasn't exactly sure when he broke their kiss, wanting to test her and push her until she came apart in his arms.

Trailing his mouth down her throat, along the pulse beating there, he lifted her breasts toward his mouth, so turned on by the erotic sight of her pale skin gleaming faintly in the darkness.

The moment stretched in painful anticipation as he zeroed in and sucked in a tight peak with a slow, wet pull. Lindy writhed against him in reply. Joshua might have enjoyed a moment of triumph but his own response sabotaged any thoughts that he possessed the upper hand.

This desire felt bigger than both of them.

Just the taste of her flooded his body with need, spiked an ache inside until he wasn't sure how long he'd remain standing.

His body reacted instinctively, sensing her responses, touching her in places that made her tremble, growing bolder when she rocked against him as if trying to knead her own ache into breaking.

Coaxing a hand into the waistband of her hose, he sucked hard on a nipple to distract her so she wouldn't think about stopping him. He wanted free reign over her body, wanted to see if he could push her over the edge.

He found the core of her heat, wet with desire, and targeted the tiny bundle of nerve endings that made her hang on to him for dear life. With his thumb starting up a knowing rhythm, he slid a finger inside, felt her clench tight.

She rode him in an eager stroke, and the sight of her boldly taking her pleasure made his own breath hitch as her thighs began to quiver and he knew he'd pushed her to the brink.

Then she came apart, the sound of her moan pulsing through him like a living thing. His crotch tightened until her pleasure subsided and she finally relaxed against him.

And in that instant, Joshua wanted this woman in a way he hadn't known he could want. The urge to shove her back against the wall and convince himself that what he felt in her arms was real overwhelmed him.

Would she resist if he dragged down those hose and took advantage of her need? His every instinct urged him not to ask for permission, not to give her any chance to think rationally. There was nothing rational about what he felt right now.

"Make love with me." He knew each second allowed her to regain her equilibrium—exactly what he didn't want. Not when his own need drove him. When every instinct he possessed urged him to start kissing her again, to coerce her, to convince her to toss reason to the wind.

He recognized uncertainty in the way she gathered herself together, as if it took every ounce of her will to resist.

"You're trying to distract me, Joshua."

"Trying?"

She chuckled, a throaty, sexy sound that arrowed need through him almost painfully.

"Make love with me, Lindy." The roughness in his voice gave her every advantage.

"Are you convinced your future is in good hands already?"

Lindy raised her chin defiantly, an act of pure bravado. He could see the yearning in her beautiful eyes, knew if he pushed, he might yet win this round.

That was all the concession he needed to know he'd already won.

6

DAWN PALED the snug maze of London streets before Lindy finally accepted that process of elimination wasn't going to serve up Joshua this time.

She wasn't surprised. Having admitted to uncovering the Stuart Temple alias, she knew Joshua would assume she'd unwound his trail through connections made under the alias.

A correct assumption.

This wasn't rocket science, but covert ops. Joshua wasn't a thief but a fixer, and that made a difference in the way he maneuvered. He might work for the bad guys and utilize different resources than she did, but the process was disturbingly similar. Once she'd admitted to uncovering his alias to verify her resources and—*try*—to intimidate him, she'd complicated tonight's job immeasurably.

Correction: *today's* job.

With a sigh, Lindy flung wide the drapes of the agency safe house where she'd holed up after escaping Lady Kenwick's. Joshua had led her across Stanforth Hall's grounds before vanishing into late-night London. But not without a damned cheeky grin that had told her he'd had her at his mercy, and known it.

She tried to shake off her restlessness while staring into the morning. Dawn bleached the shop fronts on the street below in drowsy shades of gray, decidedly lifeless terrain if not for the market awakening.

Traffic had been blocked off at both ends of the street, and from her vantage of the mews bisecting the lane, she watched life happen. Vendors filled carts with vegetables, fruits and flowers, spoke with customers as the milling crowd thickened.

Crowds were great places to become anonymous, as Joshua Benedict well knew.

So where was he now?

Out of the country she assumed, by a trail she couldn't seem to unravel. Trying to prove himself—of *that* she had no doubt. While tracking him to London hadn't been exactly easy, Lindy knew he hadn't expected her to show up at all.

She'd accomplished a giant stride toward getting him to take her seriously, and as she reviewed the events of the previous night, she was pleased overall by the outcome.

But she struggled for objectivity about their interlude in the secret passage, when emotion kept clouding her vision.

Shame, or pleasure?

Lindy felt an honest measure of both. She'd made the decision to use their attraction to her advantage, so getting nearly naked didn't bother her.

Losing herself in his arms did.

Feigning passion was one thing. Surrendering to it was another entirely. Lindy had lost herself in the pleasure of Joshua's kisses, of his skilled touches. She'd abandoned her control for an orgasm the likes of which had scattered her wits.

She had several old school chums who waxed poetic about the merits of bad boys, but Lindy had always made a distinction between bad *boys* and bad *guys*. She didn't see a thing wrong with a brooding hero. Some women enjoyed chipping away at an attitude the size of the Lake District to uncover the noble man below.

Bad guys were missing the nobility beneath the attitude, and Joshua Benedict was that particular breed, which meant she should be having only one kind of orgasm with him— the el fake-O kind. Wit-scattering orgasms had no place in their relationship. Then again, Lindy supposed temptation wouldn't have any real power if it wasn't…well, *tempting*.

She needed to be on guard with Joshua.

Provided she could track him down again, of course.

Staring out at the marketplace, Lindy took a sip of rapidly cooling Earl Grey and cleared away the surplus emotion. She couldn't let the surprise and pleasure and shame of what she'd experienced in his arms last night interfere with her work. Not when she needed her analytical abilities honed to the nth degree.

After hours of playing the process-of-elimination game, she knew Joshua had switched aliases again. Unfortunately, this time he'd apparently switched to one she couldn't trace. She'd spent an hour running the list of men who'd traveled alone via various means from London during the time frame, but she could only go down so many layers in the time available.

So far, each name had come up real. That didn't mean the man behind the name was real, of course, just that she didn't have the time to keep digging until the trail ended. She should have called Blythe for backup long ago, but with the turn this mission had taken in a secret passageway last night, she'd rather not give Malcolm any reason to start asking questions.

As much as Lindy hated to admit defeat, she didn't see another choice. She needed to backtrack and trace Joshua's money trail from last night with the hope she could uncover some clue as to what he might be up to today.

Unfortunately, diving into the extensive worldwide network where crime syndicates laundered money to find out where Joshua had hidden his would take time—exactly the commodity she lacked. To stay in the game meant keeping up with the man. If he got a full day ahead, he'd move beyond her reach, and the game would be as good as over.

Lindy had no intention of falling out of the race.

She'd made a bloody study of Henri Renouf and knew his trusted associates were few and far between. Joshua Benedict was her window to the man. Period.

So, the money trail it must be, which meant…

Inhaling deeply of the wet dawn air, Lindy turned back to the room, her tired body aching in protest as she sat in front of her notebook computer where she'd spent most of the night. She was admittedly knackered—no sleep and orgasms combined to take a toll—but she willed away all physical traces of weariness and got back to work.

Her fingers flew through the keystrokes as she secured a connection and waited for a familiar face to appear on the monitor. "G'morning, Blythe."

"Morning, is it?"

"Haven't shut your eyes yet?"

"*Shiiit,*" Blythe exhaled the profanity on one long breath.

As Blythe was cranky before three o'clock in the afternoon on the best of days, Lindy just raised her teacup in a silent suggestion to try more caffeine. A cure-all.

"What do you want, Gardner? In case you hadn't noticed, I'm a little busy monitoring an active mission here. And where the hell is your report? Malcolm's curious about how you got to Number One Safe House. If you'd care to share the details, of course. I hope you are because the man is getting crabbier by the hour. You know how he hates being out of the loop."

"I'll send him my report—as soon as you help me track down a money trail."

"Bloody hell, Lindy. I'm not your damn lady's maid. I told you I'd assign you backup."

"But you're the best, Blythe. I just need two minutes."

Which was a shameless stretch of the truth, as they both knew. The network of banks, companies and countries where Joshua might have hidden his funds was as expansive as the globe, which was why Lindy needed Blythe exclusively. Otherwise, she didn't stand a chance of tracking down a money trail that might bounce around the world like a drunken ping-pong ball.

"Please." Lindy tried to sound sweet.

"Quit your whining. It's too early. Or is that late?" Blythe glanced around at the row of clocks displaying international times on the wall then narrowing a gaze so thick with liner her eyes became black slits. "Two minutes, Gardner. Clock's ticking."

Vienna, where spring storms douse the nooks and crannies of this historic city and lightning strikes—not once but twice.

JOSHUA KNEW he was playing with fire, but he didn't see too many other choices. Breaking into this lawyer's office didn't trouble him. The man had been in Henri's unofficial employ for a dozen years that Joshua knew of, trustworthy for his part, which was usually in the role of document courier.

Henri kept men of varying prominence positioned around the world—men who did as they were asked for generous favors, were competent at their various jobs, and didn't ask questions.

Joshua had used this man before, although the lawyer had no knowledge of Joshua's identity. They'd worked via secure phone connections with prearranged code words. Joshua always made deliveries directly to this law office, always after hours. The lawyer would arrive for work the following morning to find documents prepackaged for shipping on his desk, knowing he'd been paid an illegal visit during the night. To date, Joshua had never bypassed building security the same way twice.

Tonight had involved a climbing rope.

This law firm held offices in a prime location in a business section of Vienna, an address Henri had secured and one that made illegal access somewhat less than a challenge. The newer buildings in this part of town had been built alongside the historic, designed to blend in with the medieval facades rather than for security.

Tonight Joshua had decided to work off restless energy with a free solo climb to the eighth-floor office. Just to interest himself, he hadn't bothered bringing along much gear—the sheer rebelliousness of the climb suited his mood.

He didn't like being pushed into a corner, and that's exactly what Lindy had done. He'd decided to push back. Before leaving London, he'd forwarded her photo to a British private investigator. And the man had turned out to be good. He'd called back less than twelve hours later with a report.

A resident in a Northumberland hamlet known as Kirks Moor claimed to recognize Lindy's face from a high-school yearbook. Since there were only two high schools in the vicinity, pursuing the lead was simply a matter of research at a local library.

Joshua had been pleased with the break, glad for a place to start, a first step in uncovering her true identity and ascertaining how he might push her to get what he wanted.

No man was perfect. No woman, either. She would have a vulnerability, and once he uncovered it, he would know how to exploit it to his benefit.

Watching for any signs of movement in the alley, Joshua coiled his rope and pulled it inside the office so the stretch still dangling from the rooftop anchor wouldn't be easily noticeable. He wouldn't underestimate Lindy again.

Easing the window shut, he slipped the pack from his shoulders and made his way to the desk. He sat in the lawyer's plush leather chair, letting the late-night stillness soothe away the edges of his mood.

Opening the pack, he withdrew a box wrapped in plain brown paper. No bigger than a standard ream of copy paper, this box held a prize worth a vast sum more.

Mit Vergnügen!

Josip Franzparz was considered one of the great Austrian playwrights, so five months ago when his original German classicism manuscript had been stolen from a city museum in what had since become known as the Franzparz Heist, the authorities had issued an international red alert.

As Henri had anticipated Interpol's involvement while orchestrating the theft, he'd enlisted Joshua to resolve the problem of removing the stolen manuscript from the city.

Joshua's solution had been *not* to remove the manuscript. Instead, he'd arranged for a safe hiding place and a delayed removal. Now, when the commotion of the theft had abated and the investigation, although still active, had worked its way down from key status, he deemed the time right to retrieve the prize.

During the planning stages, Joshua had intended to use this particular lawyer's services. The man was an Austrian native who traveled often on business. Having him courier a package believed to contain documents to a standard drop point seemed a safe bet. Now Joshua was glad for his caution.

Henri had been eager to reclaim this manuscript, and after their telephone conversation last night, Joshua had decided to arrange the delivery as a consolation prize until he could transport the White Star.

Joshua had told Henri he'd been detained, sidestepping specifics about MI6 and the woman who prevented him from showing up on schedule. He'd claimed something personal had come up.

He knew that Henri would be wary after dealing with Allard's sudden reversal and the resulting mess. But he had no reason to distrust Joshua. *Yet.*

Eying the wrapped box containing the manuscript, Joshua questioned again whether he should risk a second-party delivery of the White Star. Sending the amulet along with this manuscript would buy him more time to deal with Lindy.

Instinct, however, urged against such a risk. Aside from the obvious danger of turning one priceless manuscript into a double treasure of incalculable worth, Joshua wasn't ready to part with the amulet. Not because of any imaginary curse, either. Unlike Allard, he hadn't succumbed to greed.

The White Star was Joshua's insurance policy.

He'd been compromised by MI6. Life as he'd known it was in jeopardy. All the years he'd spent developing connections under this alias would be traceable if he couldn't get Lindy to erase his file. He couldn't retire his alias and resurface under another, not without compromising himself.

Henri Renouf wasn't the sort to let anyone walk away. Especially not someone who knew as many secrets as Joshua. No, if he didn't find a way to resolve this situation, he could very well wind up the target of a hit man.

The White Star would provide leverage should he need it.

Henri had obsessed over the piece in a way he had no other. Joshua would stall Henri as long as he could, giving himself time to dig up something on Lindy. Then he would decide what his next step in this game would be.

He knew what he wanted it to be.

The sweet sounds of her breaking climax had been playing in his memory all day, sultry low moans that haunted him with visions of pulling her into his arms to enjoy the luxury of time spent with a beautiful and compelling woman.

Even now, his fingers tingled with the memory of touching her. She'd been tempting in her passion, uninhibited in a way that promised such pleasure. He wished he could seduce her into helping him, rather than resorting to blackmail—a fantasy if ever there was one.

Giving in to the restlessness he'd been feeling all day, he pushed away from the desk and stood, exhaling a short laugh at his absurd disappointment that Lindy hadn't shown up.

He would see her again, he reminded himself. As soon as he could force her to deal. Until then, he'd relegate the fantasy into the deep dark recesses of his mind and out of his work.

Shrugging on the backpack, Joshua eased open the window enough to search the alley below for any signs of life. A security guard patrolled the outer perimeter of the building every half hour between stints behind a desk in the main lobby, where he watched cable sports or dozed.

Joshua glanced at the lighted display of his watch, knew

he only had to descend and stow his gear before disappearing into predawn Vienna a good fifteen minutes before the guard would make his next round.

He'd make it back to his hotel ahead of schedule.

Grabbing his climbing rope, he slithered the coil through the window and lowered it. He hopped onto the ledge. Exiting the building without leaving behind proof of his visit proved even easier than entering, and with another glance to ensure the alley was still clear, Joshua began his descent.

He willed the exertion to dull his restlessness so he could think clearly, get his plans for the day in place then sleep on the flight out of Vienna. God knew he needed a few hours of decent rest. He'd been on a dead run since first crossing Lindy's path and needed clarity to turn the minute amount of information he had on her into something serviceable.

He broke a sweat somewhere between the sixth and the fifth floors, began to feel his muscles burn somewhere between the fourth and third floors. When his boots hit the asphalt, he was ready to be on the ground.

"Boo."

The word snapped at him through the darkness, and Joshua spun toward the sound, locked his gaze into a service entry doorway and the woman who stood within the shadows.

Disbelief mingled with satisfaction, a conflicting blast of emotions that reinforced how much trouble he was in. But once he could see past his own reaction and Lindy's smug smile, Joshua realized she hadn't dressed for a night of climbing. Her linen tunic ensemble looked more suitable for an afternoon tea rather than a jaunt through a dark alley.

"Anyone ever tell you that you look yummy in burglar black?" she asked.

"No."

Her smile gleamed in the dark. "You do."

He inclined his head at the compliment, more interested in knowing if she'd seen which floor he'd come from.

He couldn't be sure, but since he'd aerially mounted his climbing rope and she'd been standing on the ground, her vantage had been straight up. With the storm clouds scudding before the moon and his dark clothing to conceal him, he could have been coming from any of the upper stories. He didn't want to think he'd led her straight to the lawyer's office before *Mit Vergnügen!* began the journey to Spain.

"This was a trick, Lindy." He kept his voice to a whisper. "How did you find me here?"

"Uh-uh." She shook her head. "You got a freebie last night. If I tell you how I found you today, then you'll make my job harder the next time I try to find you."

"Glad to hear tracking me wasn't so easy."

"It's never been easy. I'm just good."

That smug smile still clung to her lips. He wondered what pleased her more—catching up with him or that he hadn't denied her skill. He hoped for both, and hoping wasn't something Joshua had done for a very long time.

"Then let me guess. If you followed me to Vienna, you knew I'd need transportation. I don't doubt MI6 can hack into any rental car company's computer system. If so, you could have tracked me through the GPS in my rental to this vicinity."

"Are you saying you have a rental car?"

"Are you saying you didn't already know?"

She chuckled. "First of all, I *did* follow you to Vienna. And your rental car is parked on the street in front of an apartment building across the park. Looks like you're a resident all tucked in for the night."

"But that doesn't explain why you're standing here if my car is across the park."

"Your climbing rope."

He darted his gaze up to the roofline then back to her incredulously. This woman had the devil's own luck. The city park was hardly Central Park, but even an acre-plus tract had a substantial perimeter. She would have had to stroll around these streets looking for a visual confirmation of where he'd gone until happening across his rope. He'd even used an anchor that was granite-colored like the stone. Nearly impossible to see in the dark. Not even the building security guard had noticed.

"I'm very impressed." Not only by her eye, but because she admitted to not having had such an easy time of it. "So you didn't dress for the occasion tonight because you didn't know where you'd find me."

"True enough. But I'm still hoping to impress—" She broke off suddenly, spinning toward a sound—footsteps.

Crouching, Joshua clutched the rope tightly in his grip, steadying it so not to draw notice and pressed Lindy back into the doorway, a position that minimized her visibility from the street. He wanted to drape his dark sweater over her as an added precaution, but knew any movement might draw notice.

So he waited silently in the darkness, heart beginning to race when a flashlight beam pierced the night and a figure appeared, rounding the corner and warily scanning the alley in the beam's sweeping motion.

The security guard appeared to be looking for intruders, but when his cursory investigation turned up nothing in the alley, he moved toward the gated entrance of a subterranean parking garage.

Joshua's chest constricted around a breath as he mentally willed Lindy not to move. He felt his vulnerability all too keenly, and she could so easily betray him.

Lindy Gardner was an MI6 agent with diplomatic immunity. Any jurisdictional bullshit she might step into would simply be a matter of government communication and string-pulling. Joshua, on the other hand, would wind up in a prison cell.

He always got uneasy when his fate rested in another's hands. Since he had no idea what Lindy intended, he wasn't about to rely on a repeat performance of her New York rescue. Sure, she wanted information, wanted it enough to sidestep security. But he wasn't willing to bet she wanted it enough to put her own future on the line. If bullets started flying, she'd no doubt sell his ass to the authorities and let MI6 bail her out.

But Lindy had frozen into position, and he hoped some of her uncanny luck would keep the guard moving.

Didn't look as if he'd get his wish, though. The rhythmic grind of rubber tread over wet asphalt signaled an approaching car. A police cruiser eased past the alley.

The security guard must have radioed in a disturbance, an assumption borne up when the guard went to meet the cruiser.

Joshua caught Lindy's gaze across the distance, a glance of silent understanding, and they waited, breathless in the shadows, as the car stopped.

Muted voices carried toward them. Joshua couldn't hear the conversation, but he breathed a sigh of relief when the cruiser began moving again, circling the block while shining a spotlight along the sidewalk.

Perhaps luck was with him, after all.

The guard didn't reappear, and they waited while the

cruiser circled again. Joshua could hear the hum of the cruiser's engine at slow speed, suspected the police would continue casing the side streets.

He and Lindy couldn't remain here until the cruiser returned. Departing via the street wasn't an option. He had no idea where the guard had gone.

Which meant the only place to go was up.

Catching Lindy's gaze, he inclined his head toward the roof and found himself holding his breath as he extended his hand. Only when she slid hers inside did he breathe again.

Apparently they were in this together.

Gauging the distance up to the roof, he regretted not bringing along a full complement of gear. One glimpse at Lindy's stylish shoes made him frown.

She didn't ask where they were headed, just slipped off her shoes and passed them to him. He placed them inside his pack. Tugging off his sweater and gloves, he leaned close enough to smell the scent of her hair, feel her body heat as he worked the dark sweater over her head. There, at least half of her didn't glow like a beacon.

"Ladies first," he whispered against her ear, and any question he'd had about Lindy's top-roping skill vanished when she slipped on the gloves and maneuvered the lines around her waist. She swung into easy motion and headed up.

Joshua followed with a smile. The night wind kicked up again, this time with a cold drizzle. He focused on Lindy's bare feet moving in a steady motion above him, leading the way. She moved agilely, silently, a professional no matter what clothes she wore.

The exertion soon made him sweat, only without his sweater, the weather cooled his skin, made him feel the keenness of the night, made the silence so much sharper.

He watched as Lindy worked her way past the eighth floor and half expected her to glance down and wink as they passed the lawyer's window. She did nothing to indicate she knew which office he'd visited.

The cruiser appeared on the street below again, shining a spotlight into the alley. Without discussion, they both paused in their ascent, waiting until the beam moved on before continuing to the roof.

Lindy obviously knew this drill, and he wondered how often she dodged the authorities while scaling a building ten stories above the street. He supposed he'd have to revise his opinion of MI6 agents, if this woman was the standard caliber.

When the first droplets of real rain fell, he was relieved that Lindy was only five feet from the roof's ledge. He fixed his gaze straight ahead to keep the rain from his face and waited while Lindy hoisted herself onto the roof before completing his ascent.

The rain fell harder as she took off to survey the rooftop while he stowed the gear, removing any evidence that could betray them. Familiar with the building's specs, he already knew the only way off this roof was down an emergency stairwell that would place them back in security's line of fire.

Lindy presented an interesting alternative. She found equipment stowed beneath a tarp. The scaffolding, ladders and poles had apparently been stored by workers and used for some building renovations.

"We can cross over the back alley to that building," she said. "Maybe we can find a way down from there. The alley's barely seven feet wide."

Peering over the side of the building, Joshua decided a tightrope walk was not only a viable alternative, but a good one. If Lindy felt comfortable, he was game, but even seven feet over a ten-story drop...

"The ladder or the scaffolding?" he asked, unsure if she intended to crawl or walk.

"Scaffolding."

She wanted to walk in the rain. Bold woman.

Joshua retrieved the rope coiled inside the backpack. "Tie this around your waist."

"Afraid I'll fall?"

"A precaution."

"Being a gentleman, Joshua?"

"Wasn't that in my file?"

"Must have skimmed over it."

With a laugh, he pulled her toward him. Mistake. She was wet and breathless from the climb, entirely too tempting, and trying not to touch her proved an effort of will.

"Has nothing to do with being a gentleman." He distracted himself by winding the rope around her waist. "If you fall and die then I'll lose any chance of getting my file away from MI6."

"There's only one way to do that." She dared him with a glance. "Accept my deal."

"There's always more than one way."

When she didn't reply, he dragged the scaffolding to the roof's edge. The beam was thick and solid, about a foot wide, adequate to support Lindy, all one hundred and twenty pounds of her. But he hoped like hell the beam would support his weight.

She helped him balance the scaffolding as he fed it to the neighboring rooftop. The beam easily covered the distance but sloped to the lower roofline, making passage slick and tricky.

"I'll go first," He tossed the backpack ahead of him, where it landed on the other roof with a solid thump.

"I'm lighter. If you break the thing, I won't have any way to get across. I don't want to get caught up here."

Her candid assessment of the situation heightened his tension, and transformed the moment into a dare.

She reached out for a boost onto the ledge. He obliged, and she eased into an upright position. After gauging the distance, she breathed deeply, raised her arms and took the first step.

Joshua's heartbeat stalled. She crossed the distance with steady strides, never hesitating, never glancing down, never seeming fazed by the wind that lifted her hair and tossed razor-sharp drizzle over them.

The crossing took less than a minute, but he didn't move until she safely reached the other roof. Only when her smile flashed in the dark, did he suck in a hard breath, a powerful relief hitting him like an iron punch.

Then it was his turn to impress her.

All thoughts of Lindy vanished when the sky opened up and the rain lashed down at him, and he focused solely on keeping his balance, on placing his steps solidly on the slippery beam.

Lindy reached toward him as he covered the final distance, and he latched onto her hand, calm washing through him as he jumped down and felt the solid roof under his feet.

"Bloody good show," she said. "Thought you were going over. File would have been useless then."

Her laughter carried on the wind, and the sound proved the catalyst that unleashed Joshua's tension along with the storm.

She looked wet and delicious with the rain plastering her hair to her cheeks, making her blink away drops from her lashes. The sweater clung to her, molding her breasts, drawing his gaze to the rapid rise and fall of her chest.

For all her boldness, she was physically jolted by their predicament. It was in her shallow breathing, in the laughter that tumbled from her lips.

Their shoulders touched and their hands brushed as they maneuvered the scaffolding toward themselves, lowering it to the floor out of sight to leave no evidence behind.

And when she peered up at him with that sparkling gaze and said, "Now we just have to escape from here," Joshua couldn't resist her. Not when they were bound by pounding hearts and racing breaths. Not when adrenaline rushed so hard he couldn't feel the needling rain. Not when he wanted Lindy more than he could ever remember wanting a woman.

He wouldn't let her escape just yet.

7

JOSHUA'S MOUTH came down on hers hard. Lindy tasted the rain on his lips, the urgency in his kiss, and her body replied with a yearning so intense it startled her.

Her control evaporated around this man. She didn't know why, but the frustration she'd felt while unsuccessfully tracking him only served to heighten the effect.

This chase had become personal. Sometime during the past twenty-four hours catching Joshua had become less about Renouf and more about checking Joshua's moves with moves of her own.

And proving herself, although Lindy had no idea what she could prove. He was the bad guy. She was the good guy. Black and white. Matching wits was only a way to win his cooperation.

It all made sense in her head. But when Joshua's arms came around her, spun her away from the outer roof wall and crowded her back against an inner wall with decorative cresting…desire slammed through her hard. Her body rose to the challenge of their escape, of *him*.

With the night roaring around them in a lashing of rain and wind, there was no denial, no reason, no shame. There was only the memory of the pleasure she'd found in his arms and an ache that was undeniably physical.

There was no resisting temptation.

She'd meant to seduce her way into gaining his cooperation. Liquid ethics, perhaps, but in this line of work, Lindy did what she must to get a job done. Not this time. Somehow her lack of control, the reality of her reaction to Joshua made this so much more than work.

She wasn't sure why, only knew that the impulse to slide her hands around his neck was too strong to deny in this moment, the fury of the weather crashing around them.

Thunder rumbled though the storm-soaked city, and the very idea they might be struck by lightning barely penetrated the haze that had her trapped. Reason could only tug at the edges of her brain, battle for attention in a body that had gone live with pleasure.

She wanted to rise up on tiptoes and press against him, feel his body against hers, all those hard places that had felt so impossibly right in a dark passageway.

So she did.

Giving herself to the moment, Lindy pulled Joshua deeper into their kiss, allowed the thrill of their colliding mouths to lead her wherever it willed.

He cupped a hand behind her head, trapped her so he could thrust his tongue deeper, press his body closer until she could feel him everywhere. He dared her to resist with each bold caress of his mouth. He challenged her to break free, taunted her to be anything but a woman who provoked him to such abandon.

Because, even through this mind-numbing arousal, there was no question that she provoked Joshua. Intensity radiates from him. The hard muscles in his back practically vibrated beneath her fingertips. His hips locked against hers as if he'd never let her off this roof.

Passion mounted a liquid fire that coursed through her veins, dragged her whole body on an upsurge of arousal. Her breasts grew heavy and tight, ached to feel his fingers in a memory that had surely been too sweet to be real. Such hot attraction to a stranger, especially this unsuitable stranger, must have magnified in her imagination during the long hours she'd spent chasing the man.

But there was no denying the way he affected her now. Her stomach melted into the aching pool of want, and her sex clenched in a plea for attention. Joshua must have known because he leaned down enough to force her legs apart. His erection branded her, a hardness catching her in exactly the right spot.

Lindy couldn't have stopped her hips from swaying if the building had collapsed and tossed them down ten stories into the street. He growled against her mouth, broke their kiss and caught her lower lip between his teeth, a hard nip that shot a bolt of want straight through her.

Tugging at her lips with those erotic bites, he tilted his hips to drill that erection against her. His sodden sweater hung heavily from her shoulders and, combined with her own wet clothes, created a friction that teased her nipples mercilessly. Yet their wet clothing was also a barrier diluting the full impact of contact, and Lindy wasn't sorry. Not when her need had grown so intense, almost overwhelming.

His hips moved. Long, sinuous strokes that convinced her he would be a man well worth blowing off the world to spend long days with in bed. He kept up that steady pressure while trailing his mouth along her jaw and down her throat, working his way to her ear to whisper, "I want to touch you."

She thrilled to the sound of his voice, barely audible beneath the pelting rain, yet somehow undeniably resolute.

Lindy wanted to touch him, too.

Burying her face in his neck, she shielded her eyes from the rain and kissed his wet skin in silent invitation. She traced the muscles around his back, her fingers gliding easily over his moist skin. He only laughed, and the sound gusted against her ear, made her tremble.

But he seemed content to let her explore, and entertained himself by nuzzling his way down her throat with open-mouth kisses and intimate strokes of his tongue, seemingly as eager to taste her, to win her reactions, to test her daring.

And test her he did. His hands were suddenly everywhere, taking the same liberties. He worked his way under the sweater, felt his way around her blouse, his fingers building the tantalizing drama with each button he popped open.

That tiny portion of her brain still clinging to reason cautioned against this abandon, warned there must be a setup coming, but instinct denied reason. The very idea of getting naked on this roof only heightened Lindy's excitement, the danger of the unknown, the possibility of capture.

When his hands finally connected with skin, Joshua's caresses grew frenzied. He dragged his hands down her ribs, along her waist, over her stomach, as if trying to memorize her. His hands warmed her, made her arch into his touch, made her mirror those touches on him.

Their breathing grew labored. The moment became urgent. The situation was spinning out of control. She sensed it deep in her gut, with an instinct she trusted enough to bet her life on. She couldn't remember the last time she'd felt this aroused, couldn't remember ever feeling so aroused.

Joshua was a means to an end, their arousal a means of

control. But she found it so hard to remember when he was lifting away her bra, clearing aside the clothes to free his path.

She wanted to press her cheek inside the curve of his neck, taste his wet skin, inhale deeply of a scent that was his alone, all male and enticing.

He broke away and she gasped, realizing just how much his body heat had warmed her. Their gazes connected in the darkness, his expression hungry. The desire she saw proved that he wanted her as much as she wanted him.

That much between them was real, at least.

So real that she couldn't deny him when he maneuvered the soaked mess up and over her head in a tangle, freed her bare skin to the elements, and his gaze. The rain sliced between them, made Lindy shiver.

His low growl of anticipation echoed off the night. She held her arms out to him, struck by how they gleamed pale and needy in the darkness. Some unfamiliar part of her was stunned by the poignancy of standing half-naked before him, the elements whipping around them, the police scouring the streets below.

She was vulnerable to this man and their situation, and she found herself excited by the sheer drama of the moment, by the biting anticipation of not knowing whether he would use her vulnerability to betray her.

He was the bad guy, after all.

But Joshua only raked a knowing gaze over her, an expression that assured her he, too, was feeling the power of the moment, the weight of uncertainty between them. He struck her with his ferocity as he dragged his own shirt over his head, mesmerizing her with the sight of rivulets streaking down the sculpted ridges of his beautiful chest, with his intensity as he moved into her embrace.

Suddenly they were skin to skin, his arms anchoring her close, arching her backward so her breasts crushed against him. She exhaled a sigh that mingled with his, sounds of pleasure carried off by the wind.

Then their hands were everywhere, fingers gliding over wet skin in an eager dance of acquaintance. Lindy wanted to feel him everywhere, drank in the strength of firm muscles, the clenching ache between her legs as he ground his crotch against her, started up that enticing rhythm again, shared his need freely, stoked the sparks of her own.

He touched places that ignited thoughts of what he would feel like between her thighs, pushing inside deep enough to ease this ache. She arched into each thrust, meeting his demand with her own, helpless to do anything but abandon herself to the promise of what they would feel like together.

He pulsed and throbbed against her in reply, his voice throaty and low against her ear, arousing. She could feel him shudder as he fought to control his need, and she savored the power of knowing she affected him so deeply.

But satisfaction was short-lived. If she'd learned nothing else about this man, Lindy knew he wouldn't let her keep the upper hand for long. He knew how to right the balance of power. And he did.

Her breath caught on a sob when he cupped her breasts in his palms, thumbing the sensitive undersides, lifting them erotically as he leaned close... He zeroed in with his mouth, sucked in a nipple.

She cried out. Another sound lost in the storm.

With his broad shoulders stretched out before her, he made love to her breasts with his mouth, exploring one nipple then the other, teasing the tight peaks with erotic flicks of his tongue. His fingers joined the game, sneaking in to tug and squeeze and drag gasps of surprised pleasure from her lips.

Lindy was glad for the wind that carried away the sounds of her pleasure, didn't want Joshua to have so much control, was helpless to resist. She melted from the inside out, felt irresistible excitement coiling within and when he slithered a hand inside her pants, she felt powerless in a way she never had before. There would be no turning back now.

And there was the real danger—she didn't want to.

Even though Lindy knew this man was all about making her climax and proving he had the control, she would be a willing participant in her surrender.

She thrilled to feel his hand curl over her sex, rose up on tiptoes to give him easier entry. Callused fingertips touched all her soft places, created a delicious friction.

This man was so bold. She gave a little, and he took whatever he wanted. Dragging his hand over her wet folds, he explored her with a skill that made her mouth go dry.

He dared her to protest, challenged her to take what he offered. He eased a finger inside her, touching places yearning to be touched. Slithering another finger back, he touched her in places she'd never considered him touching.

The pressure, the *pleasure*....

With her body clenching, her muscles gathering tightly, her legs threatened to collapse. She sank back against the roof to steady herself even though the wall dug into her spine. She didn't care. She only cared that Joshua didn't move. His hands and his mouth were right where she wanted them to be.

Locking her fingers into his hair, she held him close and gave over to his mouth's devastating attention. She rocked her hips brazenly to get the friction she needed to feed this incredible ache…her climax building, a molten heat that swelled and mounted until she rode his hand, positively wild to break the tension.

Then she came apart in his arms, just exploded in a way that stole her breath and dragged low moans from her throat. She buried her face against the top of his head, found herself strangely touched by the way he pressed tender kisses to her breasts as he rode out the clenching spasms of her orgasm with such a knowing rhythm.

He knew she was wasted, allowed her to be, assumed the control when she'd had no choice but to relinquish it. He held her, such an odd embrace that felt so entirely right with his hand caressing her most intimate places, his fingers clenched tight inside her, and his cheek pressed to her throbbing heart.

And when he whispered, "Let me make love to you," Lindy didn't deny him, not now, not with her body aching with the remnants of such pleasure.

"Yes."

He glided up her body, one hand steadying her as the other freed itself from the tangle of her thighs. She gasped as he came away, but suddenly he was there, catching the sound with a hard kiss, such a possessive kiss that she trembled, one of those full-bodied tremors that rocked her from head to toe. She felt annihilated, yet unfamiliarly thrilled to know how much one tiny word had pleased him.

There was some power in that, she supposed.

But power no longer mattered. Lindy had gone too far to turn back now. She'd admitted her attraction to this man, had intended to use it, had totally lost control.

Clinging to Joshua, she met his kisses with an almost

desperate abandon, her hands locked tight around him to hang on. But he didn't use the knowledge against her, not yet at least. He only gave her back his passion, let himself be as needy.

She didn't know what to make of his honesty, didn't have the brain cells left to figure it out. Not when he broke their kiss and left her wanting. Not with so much of her body exposed to the elements, to *him.*

Leaning against the wall, panting, she watched as he freed something from his back pocket...his wallet? In growing disbelief she watched as a familiar package appeared.

A condom?

If Lindy could have laughed, she would have.

They were on the roof in a rainstorm, harboring against security personnel and the local authorities ten stories below, and this man was thinking about protection.

She was glad, of course, particularly because she was so caught up in the moment that she hadn't thought about much but feeling him inside her—foolish, *foolish* girl.

But Mr. Gentleman Bad Guy was saving them both. How ironic was that?

"Do you always carry condoms or were you specifically hoping to score with me?" She wondered why she wanted to know, if she would even believe what he told her.

Forcing her leaden arms to reach for the packet, she took it from him, determined to prove she had some control.

Joshua unzipped his pants and maneuvered his very impressive goodies free from the fabric.

Lindy had known from the second she'd laid eyes on him that this man was dishy, so she supposed she shouldn't be surprised he was as gorgeous underneath the clothes as he was in them. Just the sight of him bare-chested and bare-crotched, pants riding low on his hips and rain sluicing over all those muscular curves and ridges, was enough to make that needy ache start with renewed force. He had a solid body honed by years of active living, a body made for touching.

Reaching out, Lindy glided her fingers along the sculpted hardness of his erection, smiled when he jumped in her hand.

"Having fun?" he asked.

"I won't answer your question unless you answer mine."

He exhaled, and she wondered why he hesitated. "Let's just say that after last night, I was hoping I might need this."

It was a good answer. Of course, he could be totally feeding her a line. There was no getting around the fact that this situation was stupid on so many levels. But Lindy had always trusted her gut—even when her instincts led her into risky places. Offering a fake-O deal to a potential informant and then doing the jiggy with him qualified as risky in the extreme.

Still, she was too in tune with her instincts to start questioning them now, no matter where they led. She didn't want to believe he was feeding her a line, either. Lindy liked knowing that Joshua wanted to make love to her, liked proof that she wasn't the only one who'd been wanting here. With a little luck—*if* she managed to focus on work ever again—getting personal might actually sway Joshua to her side.

So she rolled the condom onto his equipment, amused by how impossible it was to think of work when handling this beautiful erection.

She'd barely done the deed when he caught an arm around her and pulled her close enough to unhook the fastener at her waist. She hadn't known it when she'd dressed, but there'd been a very good reason she hadn't worn panty hose. Well, a better reason than wanting to be comfy while she traveled. Joshua dropped her casual slacks easily.

"Grab them." He hoisted her up.

Lindy laughed as she caught her slacks before they hit the wet roof. As her ensemble was trashed between the rain and the climb, the effort was pointless. She would look like a dish rag leaving here tonight no matter how careful they were now.

But the gesture was thoughtful—another surprise—and she stopped laughing quickly enough when he maneuvered her into his arms. Forced to hang on, she clung to him, which brought her breasts up against his chest. The sensitive peaks grazed his skin, sent her into a frenzy. When he clamped a hand on her bottom, she wrapped her legs around his waist until that hard erection nudged her close.

And that feeling came over her again.

Maybe it was the way he'd stilled and grown serious or how he stared into her face as if taking her measure, but she felt wildly breathless. She didn't understand why he affected her this way. But he did.

Joshua didn't dissemble—did she really think he would?—he smiled that fast smile, took aim and pressed inside.

Lindy watched, riveted by the play of emotions on his face. He was so handsome with his striking features and dark eyes.

Her body seemed to melt around him as he levered in, filling her until she could barely breathe, couldn't stop herself from squeezing her thighs tight to ride the thick feel of him.

"Ah, Lindy." He lowered his mouth to hers.

Then he began to move.

The tender sound of his voice and the stirring touch of

his kiss imprinted on Lindy's awareness. Their bodies came together effortlessly, moist folds welcoming hard heat as he pressed inside until she could feel him everywhere. Then he withdrew slowly, enough to steal her breath with the sensation.

It didn't take two slow thrusts to realize all those earlier orgasms had been foreplay to what was brewing now.

With his legs braced wide, Joshua held her anchored against him, moving smoothly, exploring the way they came together, learning the feel of her. She clung to him, using her legs as leverage to ride each stroke, grateful she wasn't the one responsible for holding them upright, otherwise they'd have collapsed into a heap long ago.

With eager fingers, she traversed the terrain of his broad shoulders, the strong cords of his neck, the silky wet hair. And they kissed. Their mouths came together then broke apart on soft sighs, the mounting tension of each thrust making it almost impossible to focus on two things at once.

Rain fell, providing the perfect cover from any eyes that might watch them on their lofty nest, allowing their bare bodies to glide together with a silken friction. The heat they created clashed with the chill water, her skin aflame and freezing all at once, driving her closer into his embrace for shelter, for pleasure.

Tension coiled inside her, stunning in intensity, as he drove her harder, forcing the breath from her lungs with each thrust. She exhaled gasping kisses against his lips, so very aware of his every tremor, the way he kissed each breath away with a growing fierceness, a possession that mirrored his hard thrusts.

Her thighs slipped around his hips and he anchored her against him with a tight grip on her bottom, lifting her in smooth moves, crushing her in his arms as he levered into her with a fury that rivaled the whipping wind and the slicing rain.

His legs began to vibrate. She didn't know how he was still standing, how he held her locked so securely against him. Lindy only knew that she didn't want to stop riding these strokes, knew that the building pleasure overwhelmed her, consumed her until she became all fierce motion.

Joshua dug his fingers into her bottom while dragging her against him harder, faster. And when their climax finally broke, their bodies exploded together, their moans breaking against each other's, their hips riding to completion together.

Then he staggered, crowding her into the wall enough to steal the little breath she had left before bracing himself with an arm above her head.

"Don't move." His voice broke in a way that made her smile.

Or *try* to.

She couldn't quite manage it, even though she wanted to savor this unspoken admission, enjoy that Mr. Gentleman Bad Guy was in danger of dropping her. But Lindy could only blink the rain from her eyes, bury her face in the crook of his neck.

He, at least, could stand.

8

PRIVATE.

Joshua frowned at his cell phone display and the illuminated word blinking insistently. Henri would be on the other end of the secure satellite signal. Was this some sort of test? Joshua had made the arrangements for the transfer of the German manuscript to happen later today at a drop point in France and hadn't expected a call until receiving confirmation of a successful pickup.

Should he answer? Only last night, he'd told Henri something personal had come up, a situation that would delay his arrival with the White Star. With this lie, he'd bought himself precious hours to figure out what that personal something would be. Only when he had a story in place would he be able to talk without evasions that might expose his lies.

Joshua needed time to devise a credible story and proof to support it. Henri was no man's fool. He would check out the story. This was business.

With each passing hour, the line Joshua treaded grew thinner. Once, he would have enjoyed the challenge of juggling Henri and Lindy, but now he could feel his future hanging in the balance, a weight that had never felt so heavy.

A sign he should consider a new line of work?

He might not have a choice. But he could choose whether or not to take this call.

Setting the cell phone down on the desk, he moved across the suite to the kitchen. He poured espresso, cocked a hip against the counter and willed the rich brew to clear his head. He had decisions to make.

Everything kept coming back to Lindy. What she wanted from him, and what she could offer—*not* some deal that would turn him into MI6's snitch. After last night, he was convinced Lindy was somehow vested in building this case against Henri, enough to ruthlessly seduce him as her point of entry.

Joshua also knew she was getting more than she bargained for with her seduction.

Unfortunately, so was he.

He'd been stringing her along with this game to swing the situation around to his favor. But that time was working against him, too. Making love to her should have been strictly a tactical move, but it had turned out to be all about satisfying desire. His. Hers.

Right down to standing in the rain to find her a taxi.

She'd resisted the effort, of course, but leaving a lady he'd just made love to standing soaking wet on a dark street corner wasn't how Joshua operated. Not that making love to a predatory intelligence agent on a rooftop was his usual MO, either.

Staring blindly into his suite, he wondered where she was now. She could be holed up inside this very hotel or one of the many within easy distance of the airport serving this city. Their game dictated tight parameters. Proximity to quick travel arrangements was one of them.

She would be tracking him down. That much was a

Play the

Lucky Hearts Game

and get...

2 FREE BOOKS
and a **FREE MYSTERY GIFT...**

YES!
YOURS to KEEP!

I have scratched off the silver card.
Please send me my *2 FREE BOOKS* and
FREE mystery GIFT. I understand that I am
under no obligation to purchase any books as
explained on the back of this card.

Scratch Here!
then look below to see
what your cards get you...
*2 Free Books & a Free
Mystery Gift!*

351 HDL EFVA   151 HDL EFZA

FIRST NAME   LAST NAME

ADDRESS

APT.#   CITY

STATE/PROV.   ZIP/POSTAL CODE   (HL-B-04/06)

Twenty-one gets you
2 FREE BOOKS
and a **FREE MYSTERY GIFT!**

Twenty gets you
2 FREE BOOKS!

Nineteen gets you
1 FREE BOOK!

TRY AGAIN!

Offer limited to one per household and not valid to current Harlequin® Blaze™ subscribers.
All orders subject to approval. Please allow 4-6 weeks for delivery.

The Harlequin Reader Service® — Here's how it works:

Accepting your 2 free books and mystery gift places you under no obligation to buy anything. You may keep the books and gift and return the shipping statement marked "cancel." If you do not cancel, about a month later we'll send you 6 additional books and bill you just $3.99 each in the U.S., or $4.47 each in Canada, plus 25¢ shipping & handling per book and applicable taxes if any.* That's the complete price and — compared to cover prices of $4.75 each in the U.S., and $5.75 each in Canada — it's quite a bargain! You may cancel at any time, but if you choose to continue, every month we'll send you 6 more books which you may either purchase at the discount price or return to us and cancel your subscription.

*Terms and prices subject to change without notice. Sales tax applicable in N.Y. Canadian residents will be charged applicable provincial taxes and GST. Credit or debit balances in a customer's account(s) may be offset by any other outstanding balance owed by or to the customer.

If offer card is missing write to: Harlequin Reader Service, 3010 Walden Ave., P.O. Box 1867, Buffalo NY 14240-1867

BUSINESS REPLY MAIL
FIRST-CLASS MAIL   PERMIT NO. 717-003   BUFFALO, NY

POSTAGE WILL BE PAID BY ADDRESSEE

HARLEQUIN READER SERVICE
3010 WALDEN AVE
PO BOX 1867
BUFFALO NY 14240-9952

NO POSTAGE
NECESSARY
IF MAILED
IN THE
UNITED STATES

given, but what Joshua wanted to know was whether or not she found herself as distracted by last night as he was.

Brutally shoving the thought aside, he gazed through the window and willed himself to stop reminiscing about rooftops and rain-soaked skin. He needed to produce some viable options for handling a difficult situation.

He needed to direct Henri one way and Lindy another, so their paths didn't cross. Joshua had things each of them wanted, but he'd committed the White Star to Henri. He owed nothing to Lindy, which made her the least pressing of the two.

That was the place to start.

So, what trail of bread crumbs could he leave for Henri to corroborate his claims of personal trouble?

Henri happened to be one of the few men alive who knew anything at all about Joshua's true identity. Not because he'd willingly shared his past, of course. His relationship with Henri was strictly business. But Henri, being the meticulous man he was, extensively researched anyone he considered inviting into his employ.

With his resources, Henri had been able to uncover the truth that Joshua had worked so hard to put behind him. Alcohol and drugs had separated his mother from her family long before Joshua had been born. By the time she'd died when he'd been a teen, he'd already learned that survival skills couldn't be learned inside a classroom. With no prospects for a bright future, he'd dropped off the grid to make his own way.

He was smart and adaptable, both qualities that powerful people employ. He'd eventually worked his way into the employ of one of the most powerful.

Henri Renouf hadn't earned his reputation without

being smart and adaptable himself. Knowledge was power, and he wanted enough to formulate an opinion about anyone he dealt with—to use as leverage in the event things didn't go his way. Not even Joshua's best efforts to bury the past had withstood the test.

In fact, those very efforts had inadvertently impressed Henri and given him a run for his money.

That had been Joshua's point of entry into Renouf's empire, the start of earning the man's respect. And as that respect—and trust—had developed, Henri had used his considerable resources to bury Joshua's true identity even deeper.

Which was why he'd been so surprised—and admittedly impressed—that Lindy had connected him to the Stuart Temple alias.

But to satisfy Henri, Joshua would need to head even further back. He could think of a scenario that would provide a plausible explanation for his delay. All he had to do was make some arrangements, falsify a travel itinerary, hire someone to carry it out and Henri would have a trail to keep him busy—one that would hold up under scrutiny.

But Joshua hated using details from his past to any purpose. His early life hadn't served much good while he'd been living it. Except to fuel his determination to create a new life. So he'd kept no connections to the past. Save one, and that wasn't one he cared to expose.

But it was one Henri was likely to believe.

Setting down the cup, Joshua shook off the restlessness that had been nagging at him ever since digging into a New York cop's past and coming up with an exploitable mistake.

Why did he keep thinking about that cop?

Their business was over and done. The cop had screwed

up, left a trail. If he hadn't, Joshua would have simply found another cop who had. So what was so special about this one?

Better yet, what was wrong with him?

He was unsettled by his contemplative mood. He was tired. Not so much physically or mentally as emotionally. Lindy's appearance had him analyzing his situation, forced him to look closely at a life he was more comfortable living than analyzing. His answers were there, waiting to be acknowledged.

This cop's intentions had been good—trying to put his kids through college.

So had Joshua's intention to make a better life.

Didn't someone once say the road to hell was paved with good intentions?

Turning his back on his thoughts, Joshua forced himself to focus on Lindy, not the rain-drenched woman from the roof but the ruthless agent who threatened his future.

She wanted to know where he was headed, which would mean discovering how he traveled from Vienna. Continental Europe opened up a variety of possibilities—train and car among them.

He counted on her wasting valuable time investigating these options. But he'd be flying out of Vienna, and not on any commercial carrier. Today, he needed to get ahead of her more than ever. Not only did he need time to put his plan into place to satisfy Henri, but he needed to arrange another peace offering to take the place of the San Gabriel. All while staying ahead of one very persistent, very desirable MI6 agent.

A beep jarred the quiet, and Joshua glanced at his cell phone that vibrated on the desk. He recognized the number. His Northumberland investigator. With his pulse upping its tempo, he cleared the display and waited for the text message to appear. When it did, Joshua smiled.

Melinda St. George.

Gotcha.

Venice, where the Adriatic Sea winds into canals and beneath picturesque bridges, paths that lure the unsuspecting into an inescapable web.

LINDY STROLLED through the Piazza of San Marco in Venice, dismayed by the crowds still milling around. By day, visitors could appreciate the famed mosaics and winged lions on the cathedral. Now, they couldn't see a thing but the silhouette of historic buildings and glare of bright lights, yet the place had transformed into a hub. A band played, drenching the clear, moonlit night with pop tunes. Fractured conversations and laughter erupted from cafés on the sides of both *Procuraties*.

Locating her quarry in this mob wasn't going to be as easy as picking him off the side of a building.

Lindy supposed she should be grateful to have made it this far. True, she was still hanging on to Joshua's money trail with both hands. He'd routed funds through several countries today. She'd been able to follow, but only because he hadn't had long enough to bury his money again. Give him a few days when he wasn't dodging her, and he'd vanish without a trace.

Since she'd trailed him through a rental car last night, she considered that he might have changed his mode of transportation. She'd wasted so much precious time running rental car companies and checking train ticket purchases.

He hadn't left Vienna by either. Nor had he left via commercial carrier. No recognizable alias had turned up, and after exhausting her list of possibilities, Lindy had been forced to reevaluate her strategy. She'd made love to this man, for heaven's sake, so how was it that she couldn't guess what his next move might be?

Sheer stubbornness prompted her to get analytical. She'd reviewed every step Joshua had made since her informant had connected him to the White Star in New York City. So far, he'd been trying to dodge her and hadn't succeeded. Knowing what she did about the man, she guessed he'd attempt a different tack.

By keeping up with him, she'd proven herself a worthy adversary, and with that idea taking root in her head, Lindy projected various ways how he might trick her.

Or *try* to.

She looked at bus departures, which would have been an unexpected mode of travel for Joshua Benedict and his five-star tastes, and had come up empty. She swung to the opposite extreme and checked private air travel. Nothing. Out of frustration, she began running every couple who'd flown out of Vienna, and had by default started with the non-commercial carriers.

That's when she'd come across her first red flag—a woman who'd charged two tickets to Venice then exceeded her credit limit with a purchase in a shop near the Rialto Bridge.

It was weak, but Lindy had been desperate.

One glimpse into the woman's credit history, though, had kick-started an idea of what Joshua might have done. He could have thrown Lindy off the scent by paying a stranger to travel with him, turning a single male traveler into a couple.

Lindy guessed he would have paid his companion cash

to charge the airfare, which would explain why she hadn't come up with anything on his money trail after several substantial withdrawals in Vienna.

So she'd followed this line of reasoning and lucked into the cell phone number of what turned out to be a college student.

Lindy had dialed, and the girl had picked up.

Yes, she'd traveled to Venice with a handsome blond man.

No, he hadn't told her why he'd wanted someone to travel with, but considering the payment he'd offered, she hadn't pushed for an answer.

Yes, they'd parted company at the airfield immediately after landing.

No, he hadn't told her where he was going.

Lindy wasn't sure what it was about her questions that triggered the girl. Something did. This twenty-year-old had obviously assumed Lindy must be a scorned lover, and "Mark"—Joshua's newest alias—had been trying to sneak out of Vienna to get away from his stalking ex, who was ballsy enough to call a perfect stranger and start grilling her for information.

The girl had sounded afraid Lindy might demand retribution, and asserted that nothing had taken place between her and "Mark" because he was way too old for her.

That had made Lindy chuckle.

Otherwise, Joshua had chosen his target well. The girl was just young and broke enough to take advantage of opportunity when it knocked. A visit to Venice fitted easily into a few days' break from classes, and a small plane with eighteen passengers including pilot and flight attendant had made providing a companion service seem safe enough to chance.

Joshua obviously hadn't cautioned the girl about talking

if she was approached, which Lindy interpreted to mean he thought he was too slick to be caught this time.

Arrogant man. But the man was also quite good, possibly the best she'd come up against.

Both in bed and out.

Not that they'd actually done *it* in a bed yet.

The thought alone was enough to sober her. With agitation fueling her strides, Lindy shook off her runaway feelings and circled the piazza again, scanning the crowds for a flash of familiar blond hair.

She had no business thinking about *beds* or *yets*. Lover or not, Joshua Benedict was a bad guy. Fundamentally opposed to all she stood for and the cause she'd devoted her life to. Justice. She'd gone into law enforcement and then ultimately the secret service because she wanted to catch the bad guys.

Lindy couldn't remember a time during her upbringing that she hadn't spiced up the routine of her quiet life with fantasies of adventure. She'd willingly sacrificed a normal existence with normal friends for a life of never-ending chases. Just because Joshua was scrumptious didn't make him any different from the umpteen other criminals....

But for some reason, Lindy couldn't stop thinking about what he'd looked like last night, not while they'd been making love—although the memory of his hungry expression made her knees go weak—but how he'd looked when her taxi had driven away. He'd stood in the rain and watched her get off safely, a noble gesture where she'd least expected one.

She would have to credit Joshua with being a study in surprises, or admit that she wouldn't have minded a little predictability right now. She was getting nowhere with these crowds, and didn't have time to question every gondolier in the city about their fares. The only tidbit the college girl had served up had been a mention of a cathedral.

Of course, looking for a cathedral in Italy was like looking for a needle in a haystack. But it reminded Lindy of Joshua's visit to St. Patrick's.

So here she was in the Piazza of San Marco, Venice's most renowned cathedral. She had no clue why Joshua might come here, just as she'd had no clue why he would have been climbing down the side of an office building last night.

She'd had Blythe run a list of all that building's occupants, though, and as soon as five free minutes presented themselves, she'd go over the list to see if anything rang a bell. She'd also had Blythe red flag the neighboring museums and art galleries to see if anything turned up missing during the time frame of Joshua's visit.

Caution never hurt with this man.

Neither would some luck, but it didn't look as if Lindy was about to catch a break anytime soon. The night slipped away and, worse still, she was gasping for some decent information.

She hadn't made it this far only to fall out of the game.

Lindy hoped.

"A magnifico," a handsome male yelled out over the music.

Inclining her head at the compliment, she continued past the open air café, cursing her lack of knowledge about Joshua. She'd gotten naked with the man, and didn't even know his real name. Of course, he didn't know hers, either.

And what was his deal with churches anyway?

Now there was a question she'd love an answer to. She tried to recall exactly what the college student had said.

We did nothing on the flight but talk. About Vienna, about our favorite cities. He said he likes cathedrals.

Lindy stared up at the silhouette of the cathedral's spire, the Gothic lines and winged lions dark and proud against the moonlit sky.

He said he likes cathedrals.

Something about that bugged her. Rubbing her temple, she inhaled deeply of the sea-tinged air, tried to clear her head and figure out exactly what didn't feel right.

An innocuous statement that didn't come as any surprise, considering she'd followed him into St. Patrick's.

Lindy sidestepped a couple who'd obviously had too much to drink, and stared into the piazza.

No, his interest in cathedrals wasn't a surprise. Nor would it be to Joshua. Not when she'd confessed to tailing him through New York City.

Lindy's instincts went live.

Joshua hadn't told his companion anything else of much value, so why would he drop a hint the size of a nuclear bomb?

She'd been operating on the assumption that he hadn't expected her to discover he'd hired a companion to travel with him… But now that Lindy thought about it, the whole situation felt too easy. Once she'd tracked down the credit card purchase, the cell phone number had followed accordingly and Joshua's young companion had readily spilled her guts.

Joshua Benedict had chosen his companion wisely then fed her exactly the information he'd wanted Lindy to have.

Damn, she'd been had.

The impulse to scream hit hard, but she'd have to make time for recriminations later. Right now she needed to make up for lost time. If she could.

He said he likes cathedrals.

Naturally, she'd have chosen the best known of Venice's churches. Joshua liked big showy places. Usually.

If he wasn't here, where would he be?

That question fueled Lindy's strides across the piazza to the café. Shouldering her way through the crowd, she queued up at the counter, deciding caffeine was in order here.

Or maybe she just needed to take action, no matter how pathetically ineffective that action might be.

One could never go wrong with caffeine.

That thought didn't offer much comfort, either. But while waiting, scowling at no one in particular and everything in general, Lindy noticed the metal rack of tourist merchandise—postcards, decorator magnets, local guidebooks.

Plucking a guidebook from a slot, she flipped through. If the dodgy man had misdirected her, where would he have gone?

He might have headed to the mainland and vanished into the Italian countryside, but Lindy didn't think so.

Where would the fun be if he didn't give her a chance to chase him? That was the whole point of the game, after all.

No, Joshua had come to Venice for a reason, as he had to New York, London and Vienna. Save for the White Star, she might not know what his business was, but instinct told her he'd come for a reason.

"Che farà lei ha?" The server jarred Lindy back to the moment.

She ordered espresso, and asked, "Is Santa Lucia the smallest church around here?"

"A tiny place compared to what we have here." The girl gestured to the café and beyond. "Not so much to see at Santa Lucia. The locals pray there because it's quiet."

"So nothing worth seeing on tomorrow's tour? What about the altarpieces? The artist is pretty well-known."

"They are altarpieces." The girl gave a shrug that effectively conveyed her opinion on the subject.

"Right. And this, too." Lindy plunked the guidebook on the counter, paid for her purchases and dropped a tip in the jar.

Moving away from the counter, she raised the cup to her lips, sipped, and grimaced as the liquid scalded her throat. She'd have preferred a cup of tea, but desperate times called for desperate measures. Her need for caffeine was great. As humiliating as it was to admit, Joshua had reduced her to the level of desperate. Lindy made her way out of the café and considered Santa Lucia.

Leaning against the café's gate, she retrieved a map from her carryall, spread it wide and pinpointed the various churches in the immediate vicinity, wishing for a place to pull out her notebook computer. But she hadn't checked into a hotel yet and didn't dare risk a table at any of these cafés.

No, she'd have to make do with the map to attempt reasoning as Joshua might.

If he'd planted his unsuspecting companion with clues, he'd expect Lindy to make for the best known of Venice's churches. That was a logical starting point, given his usual MO...the thought stopped Lindy again. She remembered his bold actions at Queen's Cross, recalled mentioning that she'd been following him based on his modus operandi. Would he expect her to head for the cathedral, while he had headed for the smallest, least-known church, which just happened to be around the corner?

Well, what did she have to lose?

Not much, unfortunately.

But taking to the dark city streets required precaution, no matter how pumped up on caffeine she was. So, stopping inside a newsstand at the corner of the piazza, Lindy bought a cheap rain poncho in the darkest color they offered. The muddy brown garment would conceal her travel clothes—blue jeans, trainers and carryall with all her high-tech gadgets—and even possessed a hood to cover her hair.

Taking a last swig of espresso, she deposited the cup in a waste receptacle and didn't don the poncho until she'd rounded the corner. Moving with a quick step over the pavement, she considered her strategy. She'd case the place the way she had the buildings around the park last night, and hope she came across something that caught her attention.

She refused to accept that Joshua might have gotten away, refused to entertain thoughts of defeat. She made her way from the busy piazza through lanes narrow and dark and twisty that carried her farther and farther from the active *Merceria* shopping district.

According to the guidebook, only the altarpieces were notable at Santa Lucia, but as Lindy caught sight of the small church, she disagreed. A survey of the perimeter revealed a semidetached building behind the church—a chancellery according to the sign.

Lindy only had to walk the block once to notice someone inside the chancellery. A shadow moved past a window, indistinct and almost unnoticeable if not for the dull glow of a streetlamp through what must have been another window across the room.

Lindy might have reasoned an overzealous administrative assistant or overworked priest burning the midnight oil, except there were no lights on inside. Whoever was there was walking around in the dark, which struck her as decidedly odd. The gate to the small yard was closed tight, and nothing about the sealed-up entrance set off any alarm bells.

But that was only before she noticed another light in the mews across the lane. A quick glimpse as she walked past, and Lindy realized she wasn't the only one casing Santa Lucia.

A cruiser sat in the alley, headlights off, only the glow of an interior light—likely a computer display—marking the *polizia*'s presence.

Keeping her pace steady, Lindy kept to her path, not wanting to draw any attention to herself. As far as the *polizia* was concerned, she was nothing more than a local heading home after a late shift at work. But as she rounded the corner to the east side of the chancellery, she wondered if whoever was inside realized they were under surveillance.

Lindy didn't think so, especially when the shadow moved again, this time passing in front of the window of a side door that the *polizia* wouldn't be able to see from this vantage.

But Lindy could see quite clearly in the dull glow of the bald lightbulb perched beside the door, and recognized a familiar silhouette.

Joshua.

DARKNESS CLUNG to the stone walls of the chancellery as if it had grown with the mold through the years. Joshua moved silently but cautiously, his infrared glasses guiding him through the obstacle course of antique furnishings.

He'd finished his work inside the office, where centuries had stuffed file cabinet drawers so full they barely closed. But he found what he'd been looking for—the most recent survey of the church grounds. While digging through those file drawers, he'd also come across a textual history of Santa Lucia's stained-glass windows. He knew someone who had collected all sorts of religious minutiae throughout a very long lifetime, and couldn't resist helping himself to that information, too.

He did resist the high-tech copy machine, though. He took photos with his digital camera inside a closet, where the closed door would contain the flash.

It wasn't until he was returning the paperwork to the office that Joshua heard a sound from the back of the chancellery. The priests charged with the church's care were tucked in across the street in their rectory, so no one should be inside until the staff arrived in the morning.

Deciding against leaving until he'd assessed the threat, Joshua moved through the hallway toward a room that had been converted into a break area, complete with the requisite microwave, coffeemaker and soda machine. He positioned himself against the wall and listened.

There was no back exit. The only doors were at the front entrance and the north side, which led directly to the church. It had presented an interesting dilemma for his break-in because both entrances were visible from bisecting streets. He'd opted for the front entrance, which was actually the less-traveled route as the chancellery sat at the rear of the church.

Crouching in the shadows, Joshua waited, his breathing stilled, his body on red alert for so long that he wondered if he'd mistaken the sound. Just when he was about to step into the break room, someone appeared from the opposite hall. The person looked shapeless in the darkness, undistinguishable as male or female while quickly moving across the break area.

Joshua stood ready for action as the person neared, closer and closer…and he pounced.

Only to find himself with an armful of familiar female.

"Lindy," he whispered.

She twisted around in his arms. Gazing up at him from under the hood of what he now realized was a poncho, she shot him a smile that dazzled the darkness. "So much for the element of surprise."

"I don't—"

"Did you know you're under surveillance?"

That stopped him cold, and when he didn't immediately reply, she said, "I'll take the scowl to mean no. *Polizia,* and they're covering both your doors."

"Then how'd you get—"

She rolled her eyes, another flash of white in the dark. "You Yanks are spoiled. Everything's always new. Didn't you see the circular window below the soffit? It overlooks the church's side entrance. Nice and quiet back there."

"You didn't come—"

"The caulking's so old the thing popped right out. Of course, the glass is leaded so it weighs a ton…I think the church needs to take up a collection for repairs."

Since she clearly wasn't going to give him a word in edgewise, Joshua didn't reply. He pulled off his infrared goggles and stowed them. She'd earned the right to her smugness tonight, especially by coming here to warn him about the police—at least he assumed she'd come to warn him.

He *hoped* she'd come to warn him, and not turn him over to the local authorities. Once again the disadvantages of his job left him vulnerable. She could explain her presence inside the church office while he could expect a trip to a local lockup.

But even that thought couldn't stop him from looking at her as if she was a lover he'd been waiting to see.

She was.

One split second of clarity, and Joshua knew he'd hoped to see her. He'd been greedy to rake his gaze over her beautiful face, curious about what move she'd next pull out of her hat.

Not a feeling he'd been consciously aware of, but one he couldn't deny. No matter what the situation between them, Lindy was also his lover, and he responded to her as such.

But he didn't get time to dwell on how big a fool he was because at that exact moment, the side door burst open in an explosion of sound.

He and Lindy reacted instantly, but hadn't cleared the break room doorway before bright lights sliced through the hallway and landed on them.

"Fermata! Le mani su!"

Even with the light partially blinding him, Joshua could see the weapons the two police held trained on them.

In that instant, before he'd followed the command and lifted his arms into the air, before Lindy made a move to do the same, Joshua knew they were facing the moment of truth.

One word and she could end this confrontation. All she had to do was call out the name of her agency, flash her badge and toss him to the wolves. The *polizia* could easily check out her claim of chasing him into Venice. She'd be off the hook. He'd be taken into custody. A few phone calls, and he'd be extradited to the United Kingdom.

Then again, with one move Joshua could also change the course of events. He still held Lindy. He could take her hostage. Or he could shove her toward the police, giving himself the precious seconds he'd need to get across the room and to the circular window in the hall. By the time she'd gotten to her feet and explained who she was and what was happening, he'd be on his way to the Rialto Bridge.

All this presupposed the police didn't shoot first and ask questions later. Since no shots had been fired yet…

Lindy had gone rigid in his arms. Joshua would have bet money she was considering the very same options.

Joshua knew what he *should* do—but somehow he couldn't force himself to move. He couldn't wrap his arm round her pretty throat or let her go, even as he waited for her to call out and end these agonizing seconds of indecision.

He gathered her against him, muscles coiling, and his heartbeat stalled in his chest as he waited for her to pull away, to call out…. In a lightning move, she tossed something down the hall, something that clunked heavily on the wooden floor and forced the police to lower their weapons and take cover. In his periphery, Joshua saw a coffee mug rolling across the floor.

He'd already started moving. So had Lindy. She streaked through the room, him on her heels, just as the police yelled out.

"Fermata! Fermata!"

Lindy barely stopped in front of the circular window opening before Joshua had her around the waist and hoisted her up. She went through the opening head first and disappeared just as he pulled himself up. He saw her hit the ground in a skilled roll as he came through. Then she was on her feet again, yanking what looked like a backpack from behind a bush and hoisting it over her shoulder as she took off. He ran after her with the cries of police behind him.

As they rounded the corner of the churchyard, she glanced in both directions, obviously undecided.

Catching her arm, he led her in the direction of the Piazza San Marco, ignoring the motorbike he'd parked several blocks away from the chancellery. They ran at full tilt, weaving through alleys and crouching low as they ran over narrow bridges to remain hidden in the shadows.

They only paused long enough for Lindy to peel off her poncho and bury it inside a trash heap. Joshua did the same with his own dark shirt, revealing the white undershirt below. When they finally burst out onto the street behind the piazza, they slowed their pace, joined hands as if they were two lovers, and melted into the crowd.

Sirens whined through the streets, but they kept an even pace while moving across the square. Joshua's only thought was to get them out of the city, whether they should attempt the road that connected Venice to the mainland or take a more anonymous route across the lagoon.

He wouldn't guess why Lindy hadn't turned him in, why she'd thrown in her lot to become a fugitive running from the *polizia*.

Just then a group of tourists burst out of a café. Americans who'd been drinking, judging by their conversation and raucous laughter. One of the girls paused to stuff money inside a large purse before slinging it over her shoulder. She stepped in front of them, unwittingly cutting them off and forcing Joshua to hang on to Lindy as he bumped into the girl.

"Scusarme," he said.

The girl frowned and kept going. Lindy tightened her grip on his arm and hissed, "You knocked into her on purpose."

"That would be rude."

"Did you rob her?"

He only stared, enjoying the sight of her lovely face in

anger. Her eyes flashed. Her mouth compressed into a line that he suspected only kisses would soften again.

"You did, didn't you?" she demanded. "Tell me, Joshua. We're in this together now."

"I might have to rethink this then. You sound awfully naggy for a woman I've only made love to once."

Her eyes widened. "Naggy?"

"Naggy." He shifted a bit to reveal the woman's identity papers, which he'd shoved into his back pocket. "Did you happen to bring along another alias?"

She scowled, which he took to mean no.

"Trust me," he said.

"Trust you? You just robbed that woman."

"Like you said, we're in this together. I'm thinking ahead."

He watched the play of emotions across her face, and resisted the urge to smile when she exhaled a heavy sigh.

"You've got a plan?" she asked.

"Always."

9

LINDY CLUNG to Joshua's waist as he maneuvered the motorcycle around a steep curve in the Italian countryside. The night wind whipped through her newly dyed hair— a lovely shade of auburn to match Joshua's dark brown. She also sported tanned skin, compliments of instant tanning lotion. The effect together worked quite nicely, she thought.

Besides the darkened hair, Joshua was sprouting a day-old stubble along his jaw, and she found the look transformed his usual polish into bad boy. It was a decidedly yummy look, and one that should—hopefully—deter them from being easily recognizable to the Italian authorities, who would circulate their descriptions.

The changes to their appearances had been her idea.

The changes to their identities had been Joshua's.

After he'd stolen the passport from the girl in the Piazza, he'd taken Lindy to a train station in Venice where he'd collected a new identity of his own from a public locker.

"Do you keep new aliases in all major cities?" she'd asked.

"Only in the ones I visit," he'd answered dryly.

Nifty trick. Lindy stashed it in her own repertoire, recalling several instances when she'd needed to make quick exits and an instant new alias would have been more efficient than contacting Blythe to do the honors.

Then they'd traveled from Venice to the mainland, visited an all-night druggist and holed up inside a petrol-stop bathroom to effect the costume changes. From there, altering their passports had been a simple matter of taking photos with Joshua's digital camera and visiting an instant photo developer. Voilà. They now traveled as Emily Stratton and Mark Chesney.

She didn't know where Joshua had gotten the motorcycle and didn't ask. While Lindy got creative in her own work, Malcolm tended to frown when she "created" too close to illegal.

A poor reflection on the Crown, he'd say and stare her down so she understood he'd enforce consequences if she kept pushing her luck.

Lindy knew what Malcolm would say about being on the run from the Italian law with their target. She'd keep this part of her little adventure a secret.

Pressing her cheek to Joshua's back, she felt the warm man beneath his T-shirt and tried to figure out why, of all the men in the world, she had to be going all soft inside over this one. What was it about him that made her forget that she had a job to do?

Who was Joshua to tempt her with glimpses of a man who wasn't anything like she'd imagined a bad-guy fixer to be?

With the motorcycle growling underneath her, the dark night whipping past as he maneuvered skillfully over the road, and his dishy bum tucked against her, Lindy closed her eyes and let herself think about the man who'd stood in the rain last night as her taxi had pulled away, watching her leave as if he'd rather have been with her.

She let herself think about what it would be like to have been two people who'd simply crossed paths and found themselves attracted to each other. No Renouf. No dodgy deals. No MI6 profile. No jobs that dictated their lives no matter what side of the law they were on.

What would she do if she had Joshua all to herself?

The question wasn't hard to answer. Not with her arms wrapped around him and her body pressed close. With every breath she inhaled his male scent. She could almost taste his rain-soaked skin in her memories of Vienna.

Lindy would make love to him in a bed.

So far their every encounter had been an irresistible ex-plosion of the senses in the most wholly unexpected places. If she could have her way, then she'd hole up with this man and get him naked for a change. She'd close the door on the world, peel away his clothes and indulge herself in this surprising pleasure they made together.

She'd explore him in long, lazy lovemaking sessions that exhausted them both so much they wouldn't get out of bed. They'd sleep wrapped around each other. They'd order room service whenever they worked up appetites.

Then Lindy realized there was no reason she couldn't.

They were on the run, so, for the moment, Joshua's game of hide-and-seek was over. By not declaring herself to the Italian authorities, she'd tossed in her lot with this man. She still needed to convince him to spill the beans on Renouf, and it wasn't as if they could stroll out of the country. They needed to lie low and avoid capture. She could *not* be apprehended.

Not only would Malcolm have something to say about having to collect her from the field, but Renouf couldn't get wind that an MI6 agent had made contact with his fixer. She wouldn't stand a chance in hell of getting close to him through Joshua. The mission would go pear-shaped and she didn't relish explaining why to Malcolm.

No, there was absolutely no reason they couldn't avail themselves of this opportunity to be alone. In fact, Lindy knew it would likely be safer that way.

When Joshua finally steered off the road and headed down a dirt path, she stared into the darkness, trying to make out where he was headed. She'd been gauging the distance they'd traveled and had a bead on their direction from the stars overhead, but at their current speed, she couldn't ask. The wind snatched away any conversation, and with only the motorcycle's headlamp to illuminate the night, Lindy could only assume he must know where he was going. All she could see were edges of fields that melted into blackness. But she hoped wherever they wound up had a hot shower and a soft bed.

A wish not fated to be granted, Lindy realized, when Joshua brought the motorcycle to a halt in front of a building that didn't look like any homey cottage she'd ever seen.

"The Piazza, hmm?"

He tipped his head back, so her whole world was filled with the sight of his handsome face. "Even safer. We can hide here for what's left of the night and head into town later, after we have an idea of how far the Venice police extended their search."

"How are we going to find out about the police inside a barn?"

He flashed a grin that dazzled the darkness and earned a swoopy feeling low in her belly.

"Trust me." He held the motorcycle steady while she slid off. "Grab the door, will you?"

She did as he asked and he moved the motorcycle inside what was indeed a big barn. But that was all Lindy noticed about their surroundings because Joshua came off the bike in a fluid burst of male grace that made her pause to watch.

And when he caught her watching… It was so stupid, but meeting his gaze made the heat rush into her cheeks.

Thank goodness for the dark that she hoped hid the worst of her reaction. As if the bloody man could read her thoughts.

"Do you keep hideouts in every country you visit?" She shot for casual.

Joshua slipped his fingers around her arm and led her inside. "I don't usually need to hide out."

"I assume you know the owner of this barn. So who is he, or she? Or am I getting too personal?"

Something about her question made Joshua frown. Lindy hadn't meant to be sarcastic, more ironic really. They'd gotten intimate yet they knew next to nothing about each other beyond the personas they wore for the public.

"I don't want MI6 bothering people who don't know anything about my life."

She wondered if that was because he didn't want her agency to glean any clues or if he didn't want said people knowing about his life. "What about a cease-fire?"

"That means we'd have to trust each other."

"That's what you keep telling me. We'll probably be more effective if we do. I don't know where your boss stands on the subject, but mine will likely leave me to rot in an Italian jail cell if I get apprehended."

"I expected you to declare yourself to the *polizia*."

"And I expected you to hang me out to dry."

Joshua appeared to consider this, that steady gaze of his

fixed on her face and forcing her to remember to breathe. "We have made a helluva team so far, haven't we?"

"I think so."

He inclined his head, decision obviously made. "Then trust it is. Within reason, of course."

"Of course. So who owns this place?"

"A crazy old man who invites me to visit whenever I'm in the country. But if I don't catch him when he's outside working, he never hears the door."

"Really?"

"He's nearly deaf. Not that he'd admit it. I've spent more than one night out here in this barn because he didn't hear me knocking."

"So you didn't date his daughter?" she asked lightly, but his joking accusation of her getting naggy suddenly echoed in her memory. Lindy really had no business asking about this man's past lovers, even less business thinking about them.

Unfortunately, she wanted to know. And not for business.

"No. He doesn't have kids. That's why he likes me to visit. Doesn't get into town much anymore."

Here was another of those tidbits that took her by surprise. Lindy was beginning to get the feeling that his profile had missed a lot of important things, such as that Joshua Benedict, fixer extraordinaire, visited old folks in his spare time so they wouldn't get lonely.

She wanted to ask how he knew the old man, knowing his answer would reveal something important about him, which might explain why he didn't offer her a chance to ask.

Switching on a pocket flashlight, Joshua illuminated the cavernous interior of the barn before steering her around a piece of heavy machinery. Shadows loomed around them, but he seemed to move more by instinct and memory than sight.

"There's a radio in here," he offered. "We can find out what's happening with the search before deciding our next move."

"Sounds like a plan."

"Not squeamish about a few hours in a barn, are you?"

"You know how to show a girl a good time."

He gave a throaty laugh then brought her to a stop by a ladder. "Stand here. I'll grab blankets. We can stay up in the loft."

Again, she thought it said something else about him that he'd hole up in a straw-filled loft smelling of cut grass and dirt rather than making for his usual five-star luxury digs.

She preceded him up the ladder while he shone the light to illuminate her way. Then she caught the blankets he tossed up. Two huge, roughly-woven blankets that would layer nicely over the straw and keep them warm—so far from the high-thread-count sheets she'd been hoping for that Lindy almost laughed.

He brought the radio when he climbed up behind her. "Here's hoping these batteries still work."

She spread the blankets in a makeshift bed while Joshua spun dials and sent crackling blasts of static through the night in his efforts to lock onto a signal. Looked like hopeless business. She'd catch snatches of an announcer's voice before he spun the dial again.

She heard him mutter, "I don't know why he bothers keeping this when he can't hear it."

"So what time does your old friend make an appearance in the morning?"

"After the sun comes up, but we won't see him."

"Don't want to introduce me?" Some cease-fire. Although Lindy understood the precaution, Joshua obviously didn't realize that as it stood right now, she wouldn't have been able to pick her way back to this farm without a trail of bread crumbs.

"He starts in the south field on Thursdays. We're safe here. We can steal some shut-eye."

But sleep was about the last thing on Lindy's mind. The glow from Joshua's flashlight only managed to make the blackness even blacker, an intimate cocoon that sheltered them from the night, the Italian authorities, the world they'd left outside.

Despite their hard-of-hearing host in a farmhouse somewhere in the dark beyond the barn, it felt as if she and Joshua were alone in the world. Shadows sliced across his features, illuminated the strong line of his stubbled jaw, the mouth that could flash such devastating grins. And kiss such arousing kisses.

He sat cross-legged on the blanket, his expression intent as he fiddled with the dials, focused on assessing their situation, revealing that meticulous attention to detail she'd become so familiar with during the past few days.

"Joshua, forget the radio for now. The morning news programs won't be on for a while. We can find out what's happening later."

He frowned at the radio then turned off the power. "Tired?"

Lindy knelt beside him and plucked the radio from his hands. "No, as a matter of fact. I'm all keyed up."

Their gazes met, and she could tell by his expression he was defining keyed up.

Lindy wouldn't keep him guessing for long.

Tossing the radio into the straw beside her open bag, she patted his thigh, gesturing him to uncross his legs.

"You do realize you've seen a lot more of me naked than I've seen of you." As he realigned his position, she scooted forward and grabbed his T-shirt. Working the hem upward, she smiled when he raised his arms to assist her without prompting.

"I'm not complaining." His voice was muffled as she pulled the shirt over his head and tossed it aside.

"But do you really think that's fair?"

His chest gleamed all bare and touchable in the soft light. Splaying her hands, she smoothed her fingers over the firm swells and ridges, examined the feel of his warm skin.

These solid muscles were a result of hard training, and she wondered what he did to stay in shape. He sailed and fished. That much had been in his profile. Did he have a gym in his villa? Work out at the country club?

"All's fair in love and war, Lindy. You've heard that."

"Quite." She pressed full-bodied against him, dragging her hands down his arms and hands to curl her fingers over his in seductive strokes. "What are we— love or war?"

"We started as war."

"Meaning you think love could factor eventually?"

"I didn't say that." He tilted his head back and caught her chin with his lips, an openmouthed kiss that made her shiver. "Do you think love could factor?"

She chuckled, running her fingers over his hands then up his wrists. He had beautiful hands, long-fingered and strong, just perfect for… With a move that would have impressed even the difficult-to-impress Malcolm Trent, Lindy had her cuffs out of her bag and around his wrists before he could topple her.

He reacted a split second too late.

Click. Click.

"I take it the cease-fire's over." He flexed his arms behind him, not the most comfortable of positions.

"Trust me." She rolled to her side and rose to her knees, biting back a smile that she'd taken him so completely off guard. "Why do you look so surprised?"

"I didn't know you carried cuffs."

"You're admitting you didn't notice them in my bag when you were planting Lady Kenwick's brooch?"

"We haven't established that I planted anything."

"What was that about all's fair in love and war again?" He eyed her with a scowl.

"Oh, Joshua. Chill. I just want equal time. You've seen me naked—"

"Almost naked."

"What?"

"*Almost* naked. I never got your bra off last night. It was still tangled under your arms."

So it had been. And the memory of standing in that rain, feeling his hard body pressed around her, in her, earned a shiver that had nothing to do with the night.

"I want equal time. If I don't take precautions, you'll start touching me and distracting me—"

"You're admitting you can't resist me when I touch you?"

He might be smiling but everything about him was earnest. This man knew very well he'd taken her apart at the seams in two countries now. To deny it would have made her a liar.

Now it was her turn.

She wanted to learn all she could about him, wanted to explore this attraction between them and understand what it was about Joshua Benedict that made him so different.

She wanted to satisfy her hunger before they resurfaced in the real world again, where they would be at odds in their goals and pitted against each other by circumstance.

Right now, the moment was out of time, a break from reality. There was no right or wrong in this place, no judgment, no ambition. They had no commitments to anything but learning as much as they could about each other through touch, sharing all the things they couldn't trust each other to share.

Lindy reached out to stroke his neck, grazing her fingers over the pulse that throbbed low in his throat. Then she leaned toward him….

Joshua's chest rose and fell on a sharp breath when she pressed her mouth to his shoulder. Dragging her parted lips along his neck, she nibbled her way up the column of his throat, sampled the salty taste of his skin.

Somewhere between escaping the chancellery and running from the law, Joshua had worked up a sweat, and Lindy found the taste of him earthy and real, a departure from the polished man she'd spent every waking hour chasing since crossing the big pond.

So many surprises. The difference between the surveillance photos to the dishy man in person had only been the first. Polished, steel-nerved Joshua Benedict with stubble on his cheeks and worn black jeans showcasing his long legs. This earthy persona suited him as easily as the man who'd worn a custom suit that cost more than her month's salary or the man dressed in burglar black rappelling down a ten-story building.

She liked the differences, thought they each revealed something about the man. She also liked the way his heartbeat quickened beneath her touch. She aroused him. His arms gathered and flexed as if he struggled not to pull her against him.

Well, she'd taken care of that little problem, hadn't she?

He still might have flipped her over—Lindy didn't entertain any illusions that he needed his hands to overpower her. Obviously he'd decided to let her explore him as he'd explored her during their breathless encounters in the dark.

Fair was only fair, after all. She was glad he respected that, liked that he didn't have to be in control all the time, could respect her enough to let her take the lead.

Lindy took it.

Skimming her hands down his ribs, she slid her fingers into his waistband, teased the smooth skin there, taunted him with the promise of where she was headed. His stomach contracted, and she laughed, her breath whispering against his skin, a warm gust that rebounded against her lips, and made him shiver.

Rocking forward enough to throw her weight, she urged him backward. With her mouth still pressed to his throat, she rode the length of his body as he sank onto their makeshift bed.

She wondered if his bound arms hurt, but when his body unfolded underneath her, compliant, tantalizing, Lindy forgot to ask.

Dragging her tongue along the curve of his neck and shoulder, she savored the sound of his hard exhalation, the contraction of muscles that assured her he was feeling more pleasure than pain.

And here she was only warming up.

Hovering over him, her mouth to his skin, breasts to his chest, hands between them, she worked the fly of his jeans, one popping button at a time, a study in teasing moves and lingering promise.

"If I'd have known you wanted me this much, I'd have let you catch me sooner." Joshua's laugh was husky and low, a sound that filtered through her in a purely physical way.

"Those are fighting words."

"Is that a promise?"

"Bold words for a man in handcuffs."

He was taunting her, she knew, but when his gaze caught hers, the candor she saw there made her chest feel tight. She forced her fingers to continue exploring onward, grazing the soft cotton of his briefs, the hard ridge of hot skin below.

Body parts that she'd only briefly made the acquaintance of the previous night were suddenly subject to her whim, and Lindy experienced a thrill of pleasure, of power, as she rose upright, intent on maneuvering his pants off.

"Hmm. Who do we have here?" She barely recognized her voice, a needy, demanding sound between them.

"You expect me to lie here while you have your way with me?"

There was irony in his voice and she reached for the flashlight, sliced its beam across his body. "Yes."

"I don't know if I can do that."

"You've got no hands."

"I've got my mouth."

That sent a shiver of pure anticipation through her. "You've got London on me."

"London?"

"I came. You didn't."

His smile dazzled the shadows beyond the light. "You think you owe me?"

"More like equal time."

"Then these handcuffs were probably a good idea."

She liked that he admitted how much he wanted her, although the truth didn't come as much of a surprise. Restraint hadn't been a big part of their interactions. She might have been the one mostly naked, but that was because he hadn't kept his hands to himself.

"Then kick back and enjoy the ride," she said. "I'll make it worth your time."

"I'm counting on it."

What was it about them that made every exchange a dare, made every glance and every touch challenge her to earn a response from this man?

Lindy didn't know. She only knew that since meeting him, she hadn't wanted to touch him more than she did right now. She tugged apart his waistband, her fingers suddenly stiff as she caught his briefs and began maneuvering the whole lot over his hips. Bit by bit all sorts of yummy terrain came into view as she coaxed his pants down, down, down….

Lindy had to unlace his hiking boots, otherwise the pants wouldn't budge, so propping the flashlight in her lap to give her light to see by, she fumbled with the laces.

"If I had free hands, I could hold that for you," he pointed out.

"Is that a promise to keep your hands to yourself?" She couldn't help but laugh. "Somehow I doubt it."

"Never know, will we?"

"Got it under control." And she did. She removed the man's hiking boots and cotton socks to reveal feet as strong and attractive as the rest of him.

She sliced the beam along his body to find out just how dishy.

Seriously dishy.

"If I'd known what you kept hidden under all those expensive clothes, I wouldn't have been the only one naked."

"*Almost* naked."

"Right."

The man was bloody to-die-for. Long, lean, sculpted, his body was a study in finely honed muscle, the solid strength of a man. And he had great legs. Long, strong with a stretch of hard thighs, not showy with bulging layers of muscle, but just perfect. The kind of legs made for admiring in cut-off shorts while he stood on the deck of a boat with a fishing pole.

Funny how Lindy kept coming back to the boat. She'd only seen one photo of his boat during her briefing, and he hadn't even been on it. But the image of him playing skipper, the wind picking up his hair and the bright sun tanning his skin to that touchable golden brown was the one sticking in her imagination.

Or maybe certain body parts were to blame; his erection stood as erect as a mainmast.

"What's turning you on the most right now?" She aimed the beam onto the target and affected a casualness she was far from feeling. "Being alone with me in the dark or being at my mercy?"

"Knowing how much you want me."

"Confident bloke, aren't you?"

He shook his head. "I see it in your face."

"Cheeky bastard."

He only laughed, a sound that made her ache to wipe the smile from his face and show him exactly who was in control.

Or maybe it was the sight of him making her ache.

Lindy flipped off the light.

Time for diversionary tactics. She intended to turn this man's knees to pudding, and his cheeky attitude along with the breathtaking sight of his naked self was a potent combination.

Kneeing her way between his outstretched legs, Lindy closed her eyes and let her hands guide her up the tight expanse of his thighs. This was a routine skill she'd learned during training—shutting down one sense to heighten the others. While she appreciated night-vision goggles as much as the next agent, she couldn't always count on having the necessary equipment.

Right now she had everything she needed.

Moving to the music of Joshua's shallow breathing, she kneaded his muscles with firm strokes, felt his skin warm to her touch, eased the tension from a body she suspected had seen as little sleep as hers had. Willing herself to absorb the tranquility, she followed the rhythm, let the methodic motion soothe away her own manic exhaustion.

He exhaled heavily into the darkness, a heartfelt sigh. She resisted the urge to open her eyes and look, instead savored the hush of their breathing combined in the dark, the tranquil sounds of the late night floating up from below.

She hadn't noticed them before, but now, with her senses so heightened, she noticed everything about the moment, the whisper of a breeze through broken boards, a croaking toad.

Sounds that reminded her of growing up in the country, of her home. A *real* home where there were people who cared for her and not just a droopy corn plant that only perked up because she'd finally watered it.

It was an odd thought, Lindy knew, especially when she was wedged between this sexy man's legs with her hands mere inches from his crotch. Maybe exhaustion made her mind wander into strange places, or maybe that was Joshua's doing. He'd been messing with her reasoning since she'd first set eyes on him, prompting her to take risks she wouldn't normally have taken.

Like staring so hard she wound up busted for loitering. She'd bypassed protocol entirely when she hadn't identified herself to the Italian authorities, and Malcolm would be fishing her out of a jurisdictional swamp if she was apprehended now.

Then there was getting naked with a bad guy.

That was the biggest risk of all, Lindy knew. Because when she grazed her fingers behind his knees, felt him shiver, she didn't think of him as a bad guy at all.

Just a man.

And a man who coaxed the most amazing reactions from her. A man who challenged her in a way she couldn't remember being challenged. A man who constantly surprised her.

A man who was proving himself a worthy match.

Yes, that was the biggest danger of all.

The thought roused her from her steamy daze, and Lindy remembered the whole point of noodling her way into his pants.

It wasn't to put him to sleep.

So she bent low over him and pressed her lips to the inside of his thigh. He trembled, and she knew the time had come to start creating new tension, to tease his body to life.

Nibbling her way along that sensitive area between his hip and his groin, she explored all his intimate places, thrilled when his erection lunged eagerly. But she never zeroed in on the target. Her sex grew liquid with wanting, with anticipation, a startlingly intense response to touching this man.

And tension built. His. Hers. Along with the tension came a question.

Did Joshua Benedict have a breaking point?

Lindy intended to find out.

10

WHEN JOSHUA opened his eyes he found Lindy nestling her cheek against his thigh, her silky hair teasing his sensitive skin. The expression of dreamy want on her face made her more beautiful than ever before.

She obviously wasn't through with him yet. Lazily she thrust her tongue out to stroke his erection, a move not meant to skyrocket him to oblivion, but to build pleasure. And she accomplished that goal big.

He lay galvanized as he clung to his restraint, fighting the languid pull of sensation as his body temperature rose and pleasure eroded his will, lured him into this fantasy.

Nothing was real about the way he felt right now.

During their previous encounters, he'd been centered on her pleasure, her undoing. Just watching her respond to his touches and hearing her sighs had tested him in a way he hadn't been tested before. Yet external circumstances had controlled the situations and shifted the balance of power to his favor—until a stormy rooftop where he'd lost his control completely.

Now he was a captive audience.

He used the dull ache in his arms to center him through this haze of pleasure. Handcuffs.

Leave it to Lindy.

A part of him felt pleased she'd needed restraints. He liked knowing he affected her control, too. He liked knowing she went to pieces in his arms, even though the knowledge wasn't proving much comfort now. Not when he couldn't reciprocate by touching her. Not when he couldn't coax those breathy sighs from her lips.

The balance of power was hers tonight. She proved it by slipping her fingers around his erection and lazily tilting him toward her lips. For a breath-stopping instant, Joshua stared at his undoing in the sight of her head lowering over him in a slow, consuming move.

Then all he could feel was her mouth.

The warm caresses of her tongue. The gentle sucking motion that pulled sensation from every part of him. The knowing fingers wrapped in a tender chokehold, and the easy rise and fall of her hand. Up and down. Up and down.

His chest constricted so tightly he grew dizzy. He tried to take in a decent breath to dispel the effect. He shifted his arms to sharpen the ache of his bound wrists, but still the urge to lift his hips off the blanket, to rise up and meet each stroke, to ride her face until he could ease this sweet torture overwhelmed him.

Which was, of course, what Lindy wanted.

Even in this white heat, he recognized exactly what she was doing—testing him.

Joshua vaguely remembered being impressed with himself for making her come apart in his arms. He'd known Lindy was using their attraction to draw him in, but he'd also known their passion had a double edge. He'd liked turning the tables, proving she'd underestimated him.

He should have known he'd invite retribution.

She guided her free hand to join the game. Suddenly her

fingers slipped below his balls and gave a firm squeeze. His hips bucked against his will, driving his erection deeper inside the recesses of her mouth.

He could feel her smile.

She gave another squeeze. Joshua groaned this time, and the sound echoed through the dark, through him, proving the hunter finally had her prey.

Another lick. Another squeeze. And he spread his thighs and sank his butt into the straw, trying to shift away enough to gain some control of the sensation.

But Lindy wasn't letting go.

She just drew him back inside her mouth with a sucking pull that made his whole body jerk unceremoniously.

"Mmm-mmm," she whispered, the vibration of sound shocking him like a Taser.

He was coming unglued fast, and Joshua tried to think enough to come up with a defense. But with Lindy buried between his thighs, paying homage with her mouth, he had to ask if he really cared who was in control. What would be so bad about taking his pleasure?

He'd recover soon enough to turn the tables.

But there was something about the thought of giving in that stopped him short of meeting her next slow stroke.

He couldn't trust this woman, couldn't allow himself to expose such vulnerability.

Lindy met him dare for dare. She bested him sometimes. She felt like his match, in every way they'd explored so far. She wielded so much power, too much as she pushed him dangerously to the edge of his restraint. Joshua wondered if she had so much power because he recognized her on so many levels.

The need to push, to test, to conquer.

When she finally pulled her hands away, he willed his head to clear, willed the tension from his body. Slowly his muscles relaxed, coming back under his control. As he shifted his position to ease the ache in his arms, he wondered what she had in store for him next.

This wasn't over by a long shot.

So he watched as Lindy rose above him, considering whether he should catch her in a wrestling move, flip her onto her back and turn the tables. She'd resist, but even off balance, he knew his strength would eventually win out.

Before he'd decided, Lindy stripped off her shirt.

Her skin gleamed pale in the darkness, a sight meant to entice, to touch. Unfastening her bra, she let her breasts spill out in an eager tumble.

"All gone," she said, arching her shoulders to slide the bra down her arms, her breasts swaying tantalizingly.

Joshua had been grateful for the handcuffs, for their distraction…until now when he wanted to reach forward and fill his hands with her, hear her moan. She was so wonderfully responsive and just the memory of his mouth on her cost hard-won control.

"I want to touch you," he said, unable to stop himself. Surely the time had come for satisfaction.

"I know." She bowed low over him, and palming her breasts, she caught his erection between them. "We're touching."

He could hear the laughter in her voice, the pleasure, and he wanted to answer, say something that would at least create the illusion of some control….

But then Lindy pressed against him, rode the length of his erection with that swell of soft skin, and the only sound to escape his lips was a groan.

She stroked again, purring against him, swirling her tongue around the head of his dick, sucking him in as far as her position would allow. A shockwave followed, and Joshua knew she finally had him.

There was no defending himself against her knowing rhythm, no denying his need. Not when her nipples hardened and her hips rocked as she caught her own pleasure.

He was a goner.

Some vaguely functioning part of his brain urged him to flip her onto her back and stop this erotic assault. Joshua only got as far as lifting his hips to meet her next thrust, to realign his thigh to catch her in a place that made her gasp against his hot skin.

Then he lost himself in her rhythm, the need building and consuming, until that stubborn reasoning assured him he should be grateful he'd hung on so long under her assault.

Joshua didn't feel grateful though, only overwhelmed when he exploded in an orgasm that dragged out a cry from him that he didn't even recognize as his own.

Then Lindy finally freed his arms, apparently satisfied.

For a moment, he blinked stupidly into the fading darkness, then took a sharp turn toward awareness as she tossed the handcuffs into the straw.

"Prove your point?" he asked.

"Quite."

The smugness in her voice provoked him enough to get over his own pain and demand some sort of compensation.

Wincing, he reached out and caught her, pulled her down. She didn't resist, but curled her long body around him, snuggling close, her curves aligned in all the right places. He savored the feel of them lying together, of holding her close, his body weak from her assault, his thoughts stunned by how good she felt in his arms.

Maybe it was exhaustion, but he could imagine spending time with this woman, long nights stretching into days where he could hold her and explore the way she felt.

Or maybe it was knowing he couldn't have her.

Not as Lindy Gardner or as Melinda St. George.

He'd learned more about the woman behind the agent since his Northumberland investigator had first text-messaged her name. The man had been peeling away the layers of Lindy's early life. Right before Joshua had headed off for the Santa Lucia chancellery, he had received his first report.

Melinda St. George was the only child of a fairly well-to-do couple from Kirks Moor. She'd excelled at school academically and athletically. She'd attended École Swiss, graduated cum laude from university before becoming a member of the local police force at twenty-three. Within two years, she'd been recruited for MI6. No surprise considering her talents.

Ironically, he'd been recruited, too.

His ability to get out of scrapes during his hardscrabble youth had brought him to the attention of some powerful people. It hadn't taken long for the money and high-flying lifestyle to overtake him. Somewhere along the way, he'd convinced himself that anything could be justified as a means to an end.

Funny, but he couldn't remember exactly when.

But without the choices he'd made or his underworld connections, he'd probably still be living that hard-knock life in a poor part of Michigan, a place where there wasn't much hope and even fewer people who cared about him.

No matter what alias he hid behind, Joshua knew this woman wasn't for him, no matter how right she felt in his arms. There was a part of him that wanted… And he despised himself for wanting to know.

"So why didn't you?" He pulled the blanket over them, tucked her closer.

"Why didn't I what?"

"Declare yourself to the *polizia*. MI6 could have pulled strings and had you back on the street in less than an hour."

She didn't reply at first, and he wondered if he'd get an answer. Then she exhaled heavily, a breath that warmed his skin.

"I would have had to give you up."

Had she only been worried about her case? It shouldn't have mattered but it did. Joshua wouldn't ask, couldn't have trusted her answer, knowing how much she wanted a link to Henri.

But there was something that wouldn't let go, some instinct that hinted he wasn't the only one conflicted, even enough to make choices that might have far-reaching consequences. He might be answering to Henri, but Lindy answered to MI6, and she'd already mentioned her boss's displeasure.

Another bond they shared.

Funny, he thought, how they could be alike in so many ways, yet so impossibly different. So right and so wrong.

San Remo, where the sparkling sea beckons in this resort city on the Italian Riviera, tempting lovers to outrun fate.

LINDY FLIPPED the lock on the loo door. She crossed the mirrored foyer and made for the sink area, which was the farthest she could get from the door. Withdrawing her notebook computer from her bag, she propped it on the counter and depressed the power button, hoping these interior walls wouldn't interfere with her uplink.

But SIS provided top-notch equipment, and while this bathroom was fairly buried within this marina in the Italian town of San Remo, the signal bounced into space where it belonged.

Pixels coagulated on the display, and Blythe appeared.

"Long time no see," she said dryly.

"Glad you missed me. No time to catch up. I'm on the time crunch today—in a public loo. I figure it'll take anyone who wants a toilet five minutes to find a manager to unlock the door. Ready?"

Blythe nodded.

"Sitrep on Vienna. Then I want you to have a look at the Santa Lucia chancellery in Venice and tell me if anything has been reported missing within the past twenty-four hours."

Lindy could hear the rapid-fire clicking of keystrokes as Blythe worked international databases, shifting her gaze between displays. "Vienna. No reported break-in at the site. No reports of any stolen artifacts from any museums, art galleries or private residences within a five-mile radius during your time frame. Building security called in a disturbance. The local police investigated. Didn't turn up anything."

While Lindy had lived that investigation firsthand, she was relieved to learn that nothing had gone missing during her watch. So what had Joshua gone to Vienna to fix? "Any obvious connections between my target and any occupants?"

"None."

"What about Henri Renouf?"

"No again."

"Download the occupant list and I'll take a look when I get a free second. Now, what's coming up on Santa Lucia?"

Blythe spun in her chair toward another display, and Lindy held her breath. She'd been debating how to handle this situation all the way from Joshua's country hideaway, located somewhere between Genoa and Cremona as best she could gauge from their journey back into civilization.

Not only did she need information about what Joshua had been doing inside that chancellery, she needed to start damage control with Malcolm. He'd have to clean up her mess if he wanted to send her back into Venice again without risking exposure. He would not be impressed that the Venetian authorities had spread the word of her escape with Joshua through all the local provinces.

She and Joshua hadn't been impressed, either. They'd deliberated long and hard on the best way to get out of Italy. Crossing the border via land wasn't even an option—the authorities would be questioning all couples traveling together.

The airport was no better. Their disguises served them while traveling through the countryside, but they didn't want to use their identity papers. Joshua's alias was in shape, but hers had required doctoring just to pass a cursory inspection. It would be sufficient for encounters within the country, but if the real owner had reported her papers stolen, the authorities might run a list of all women who tried to cross the border. Even an overworked and understaffed police department would be able to track exactly how Lindy left the country.

She made a mental note to have Blythe work up a few aliases as her first order of business after returning to London.

"Okay, here we go on Santa Lucia." Blythe squinted at the display. "Looks like more than a wee bit of trouble. Local authorities reported a break-in. The perps escaped, but the police are still searching. They've alerted all the stop points along the border."

"Really? What's missing?"

"That's the interesting part—nothing."

"Hmph." Lindy had a bad feeling. "What are they after? Seems a lot of trouble for what might have been vandalism."

"Police think they interrupted a terrorism attempt. Apparently the pastor has some pretty high-profile ties to Rome and has recently received some threats."

Damn bad luck. She wondered if Joshua had known.

"Is this your bloke?" Blythe asked. "If it is, he's working with someone."

She only nodded. No one in London needed to know who'd been in that chancellery with Joshua yet. Not until she secured his full cooperation to discuss Renouf and could justify her actions as a valid means to an end.

Blythe slanted her gaze toward the other display. "From what I've got here, your perps rummaged through the files. Looks like intel gathering."

"How important is this pastor? Santa Lucia is tiny compared to other churches around there."

"Says here there are some important artifacts."

"The altarpieces?"

Blythe nodded. "Maybe it has something to do with the Florenzia."

"I know that name."

"Two men strolled right into the national gallery and overpowered the guards in broad daylight. They shattered the display case, nabbed the most famous Italian gem and escaped by motorboat. The authorities don't have a clue where they went."

Ah, now Lindy remembered. A one-hundred-carat yellow diamond that had been part of the Grand Duke of Tuscany's treasure from his marriage to an Austrian empress. She wondered if Renouf had been behind that heist.

"Check Jean Allard's whereabouts during the time frame of the Florenzia's disappearance. I'd like to know if there's any connection to Renouf."

Blythe inclined her head but didn't shift her gaze from the display. "You might be on to something. Says here the federal government passed legislation to protect the national treasures after the Florenzia. You know those Italians—a stubborn, proud bunch. They're probably pissed your guy gave them the slip and they can't figure out what to pin on him."

Lindy would consider that. She couldn't help wondering if searching Joshua's pockets when she'd had the chance might have been smarter than searching his naked body. He'd been carrying a camera and she still didn't know what he'd done with the White Star.

"All right. Thanks, Blythe. One more thing. Be a love and tell Malcolm that I'll be off the grid for a few days."

"Trouble?"

She shook her head. "Opportunity to get close to my target. I'm all over it. Not sure when I'll be able to make contact."

Blythe narrowed her eyes. "Oh, no you don't, Gardner. Tell him yourself. He's already in a lather because you're not keeping him up to speed. You're in the field, but we have to listen to him throw a fit."

"No, Blythe, I'll just—"

Too late. The screen snapped to black before pixels converged into her boss. "Lindy."

"Hello, Malcolm."

"Are you purring yet?"

Not exactly… "I've gotten close to our target. Making contact might be hit or miss for a few days."

Malcolm's face tightened in a scowl she knew all too well—he knew that what she was saying and what she was doing didn't line up.

They'd been here before. It was never pleasant. But Lindy had never been quite this vulnerable before, either, had never walked such a tight line. She had a little leeway—there were definite perks to Malcolm's trust in her, but there were negatives, too. He knew her *too* well.

"Anything you want to share?" he asked.

"Not yet, if you don't mind."

There, she'd acknowledged something was up.

His scowl deepened. A suspended moment passed while she tried not to look inconvenienced. Joshua was making arrangements to rent a boat under his alias, and she'd excused herself to use the loo. She didn't want him to know she was checking up on him.

"Need backup?" Malcolm finally asked.

"No thanks. I've managed to get close. Don't want to frighten him off. He's good. Very good."

"I told you that."

"I've almost got him."

More silence. Then he exhaled heavily. "All right, Lindy. We'll run this your way. For now."

She nodded, unable to offer more reassurance when she was silently hoping this situation didn't blow up in her face.

"I do have something to share," Malcolm said. "Thought you'd be interested to know your old captain caught a hacker digging through their '94 through '96 personnel records."

"That's when I was there. Should I be concerned?"

He shook his head. "We erased your files when you signed on with us, but your old captain never misses an opportunity to harass me about stealing you out from under his nose, so he called as a professional courtesy."

"Did he track the hacker?"

"Unfortunately not. Whoever this person was must have had protocol to alert him to a trace because he made a clean break from the system."

"Do you have exact times of the attack?"

Malcolm nodded.

"Have Blythe transfer them to me." She wanted to see where Joshua had been then. She wouldn't put anything past the man. Glancing into the mirror, she thought the new red hair made her look cheeky. "What do you make of it?"

Malcolm's gaze pierced the distance as if they were face-to-face rather than bouncing over satellite signals. Lindy forced herself not to squirm beneath those penetrating eyes that saw too much.

"I might be able to evaluate if I had a clue what was really happening on this case."

Right.

11

Monte Carlo, where warm sea breezes, smooth white beaches and idyllic hotels offer the perfect place to hide from the world.

JOSHUA MANEUVERED the speedboat through the channel, heading toward navigable international waters. He'd plotted a course along the coast from the town of San Remo to the port of Cap d'Ail, where they could lose themselves in the busy principality of Monaco.

The conditions couldn't have been more perfect for an excursion. Warm southern breezes drifted off the Mediterranean, the sky gleamed clear overhead, and the sun sparkled off turquoise waters. Their rented vessel rode the swells smoothly. Joshua stood at the helm, hand on the wheel, feeling a sense of peace surround him, a feeling unique to being on his own boat in the pristine waters of the French Riviera.

A feeling as if he'd left the world behind.

He'd never closely analyzed the feeling, had always been content to indulge himself in a hobby that consumed him whenever work permitted. But when he thought about it, sailing had been nosing out other entertainments. He'd found himself turning down invitations that had once kept him jet-setting around the globe in favor of long weekends on his boat.

Life's challenges hadn't competed with the time he spent out on the water. Neither social, nor his work… He could barely remember the last time he'd been involved in a relationship that held his interest for more than a few dates. Joshua had thought he was bored, but maybe age really was catching up with him.

Age or guilt?

He stood with the wind whipping his hair and the bow slicing through the waves, and realized it wasn't a challenge he felt out here, but a sense of freedom.

Freedom from what?

He didn't have an answer. He'd been running from too much recently—Lindy and MI6, now the Italian authorities.

And his constantly vibrating cell phone.

Henri had first called to confirm the manuscript drop, but Joshua hadn't been able to take the call as he'd been fleeing Venice with Lindy. But he'd have to make the time soon because each time his phone vibrated, Joshua could sense his boss's growing frustration. And his own resentment grew that Henri wouldn't back off for a damn day.

Joshua couldn't help but wonder if both his reaction and so much self-analysis were prompted by the beautiful law-enforcement officer sunning herself behind him.

Leaning a hip against the chair, he turned enough to admire her stretched out on a bench seat with her long bare legs before her. They'd outfitted themselves for the trip before reaching San Remo, and she wore a bikini and floral sarong in shades of pink that accentuated her long curves and her new hair color. Stylish sunglasses covered her face as she rested her head on her backpack and tipped her face up to the sun.

His self-analysis was all about Lindy. Without question. Not only had she forced a reevaluation of his career, but she prompted him to look at his life. He wasn't sure why, except that she impacted him on so many different levels, made him feel things he shouldn't feel for a woman he needed to manage, one he couldn't trust.

But he liked watching her adapt to their circumstances and mold herself to the situation. Today, she was all sass and desirability, compared to the bold temptress who'd had him at her mercy in a deserted barn. Lindy Gardner impressed him with her abilities, but he wondered about the real woman.

Had he seen glimpses of Melinda St. George?

She must have sensed his gaze upon her because she tilted her face toward him and peered over the rim of her sunglasses. "Renting this boat was brilliant. I feel like I'm on vacation."

"And we're out of the country with a minimum of fanfare."

"What do you make of all the attention? Seems like a lot of fuss when you didn't heist any priceless altarpieces."

"You sound sure of that."

"I am."

He eyed her curiously. "You're taking my word?"

She smiled. "I'm trusting my powers of observation. You have no place to put an altarpiece. I checked out every inch of you and there wasn't an unrecognizable bump or bulge anywhere."

Joshua couldn't help but laugh, a laugh that sounded as carefree as it felt. "Was all that staring the reason why I wound up handcuffed?"

"Just keeping things fair."

"We were only two orgasms to one. I didn't mind."

Stretching her arms above her head, she let out a purring sound then swung her legs around so she could stand. "Wouldn't do not to honor my debts. I'm trying to convince you to trust me, remember?"

"So I'm all about business?"

"Those orgasms deserved a reward."

Not a straight answer but a neat sidestep from the question, which Joshua wasn't entirely sure what to make of. "Glad you thought so."

She inclined her head. "Now I have a question. How does this boat get back to San Remo?"

"Worried I'll keep her?"

"You told me you weren't a thief. Or do you only steal small things?"

"The marina will send someone to pick her up."

"Actually, I'm impressed." She crossed the deck toward him, the wind whipping her sarong around and giving him a striking view of her legs in motion. "You've been so prepared for our little side trip. Identity papers. Country hideaways. You're making me look like a rank amateur."

"For what it's worth, Lindy, I think we're evenly matched. You got cuffs on me."

"Got jammy. You were expecting sex and let me get close."

He remembered that part, but couldn't remember the last time the promise of sex had left him vulnerable. Had it ever?

"Thank goodness you're carrying enough cash to rent this boat." She came to stand behind him and slipped her arms around his waist. "Traveling on my budget, we'd still be in Venice, trying to outrun the *polizia* on a *vaporetto*."

No question that the large motorboats used for public transport over Venetian canals wouldn't have facilitated their escape. "Are you fishing again?"

"We're on a boat."

"True enough. So I take this to mean you followed my money trail to Venice."

She rested her face against his shoulder and nuzzled her cheek close. "That was how I found you in Vienna. But I assumed you already knew that. Since you didn't have enough time to reroute your money, you made three large cash withdrawals to throw me off your scent."

He only smiled.

"So tell me, Joshua. What were you doing with all your spare time when you could have been rerouting your money trail?"

"Besides trying to stay a step ahead of you?"

"You admit to *trying?*"

He glanced back over his shoulder and met her gaze. "Do I need to? You're here."

He could feel a smile twitching around her mouth before she pressed a kiss to his skin.

"How did you track me to the chancellery?"

"Got jammy again. You led me to the piazza. I fell for your misdirection, but when I got there the situation felt wrong."

"I thought you said big, busy places are my usual MO."

"For pickups and drop-offs. But you're testing me. The piazza was *too* big and *too* busy. There wasn't any easy way to leave clues for me to follow."

"You think I'm leaving you clues?"

"You're saying you aren't?"

This woman was almost scary in how she reasoned, so like him that he shouldn't be surprised that she kept showing up.

A match for him in so many ways.

"So here we are, Lindy, on the run. Have you given any thought to our next move?"

"You said you had a plan."

"I do."

"Are you taking me to your place?"

Lindy would know where he lived—that information was a matter of public record, a formality for any person of foreign nationality to live in French territory. But what surprised him was how much he wanted to take her home, to sleep wrapped around her in his own bed. Heading to Nice wasn't possible.

"I was thinking Monte Carlo. We'll disappear there."

"Worried I'll dig through your cupboards and dustbins when you aren't looking?"

"No." He didn't elaborate. Joshua never kept anything that might possibly be used as evidence against him. There was nothing in his home he couldn't leave behind if he needed to drop out of sight unexpectedly, nothing he'd have to worry about the police finding.

The precaution had always made him feel secure, but for some reason with Lindy's arms wrapped around him, it only seemed to emphasize the transience of a life that presented too many obstacles when he simply wanted to take her home.

Henri would be able to track them there, and explaining an MI6 agent in his bed would be trouble.

"So, Joshua." Her words pressed against his skin, made him tingle. "Think we should hole up for a few days before we go our separate ways again?"

"That'll be the most effective way to cover our tracks when the *polizia* notify the border countries. Standard procedure."

"What a stroke of luck this was. Now I'll have time to convince you to cooperate with me. I'm assuming we won't be staying in a barn. Do they even have barns in Monte Carlo?"

Joshua laughed. "None that I've ever seen."

"Good thing you were foresighted enough to make those withdrawals. We'll need a bundle to finance this trip."

"You think I should cover expenses when you intend to harass me?"

"Didn't I mention my budget already?" She rocked her hips suggestively. "You wouldn't believe what the Crown pays. Or *doesn't*. Besides, who said anything about harassing? I was thinking more along the lines of seduction."

Her words were enough to make his crotch throb hard in a bid for attention. "So we're back to each of us trying to convince the other to see our way."

"Feels like it." Another silky arch of her hips, and he had to fight to stay focused.

"Will dropping out of sight present any problems for you? With work? What about your family?"

Now he was fishing, but as Lindy had said, they were on a boat. He might know her true identity, but he'd yet to figure out how to put that information to work.

"Work's no problem. I'm authorized to do whatever it takes to gain your cooperation, and I don't have any family. No one but the corn plant to notice if I don't show up."

"A corn plant?"

"You know what it's like living on the run," she said.

He did, and two things struck him simultaneously. The first was that her life sounded a lot like his.

The second—she was lying. She might have a corn plant that didn't keep time, but he'd confirmed that she had parents still living in Kirks Moor, which settled in a big piece of the puzzle—she obviously cared enough to lie to protect them.

"I COULD GET USED TO the way you live," Lindy told Joshua as she dipped a strawberry into chocolate then brought the treat to her lips.

Although this hotel boasted five-star restaurants and their suite had a fully-appointed dining room, she and Joshua shared a room-service feast on the bed, where they could relax and gaze through the open balcony doors at the sun setting over the Mediterranean. They'd availed themselves of long hot showers to erase the effects of the sea, and now sat dressed comfortably in hotel robes.

A half grin played around Joshua's mouth as he handed her a linen napkin. "You were briefed that I've stayed at the Hôtel de Monaco before?"

She savored her mouthful before admitting, "I don't recall reading about any hotel by name, but this level of service seems your standard. Pricey for a working gal like me. But even if I hadn't read about the company you keep, chasing you would have been enough to convince me how you operate. You're obviously not a darts-at-the-pub kind of guy."

"I can't tell if you think that's good or bad."

"Do you care what I think?"

"Would you believe me if I said I did?"

"Would you believe me if I said I wanted to?"

Joshua laughed, a whiskey-rich laugh that rippled over her skin like an ocean breeze. "Yes."

Lindy deposited the remainder of the strawberry on her plate, unsure how to reply. Their every exchange felt like a tug-of-war, battle lines drawn between secrets and truth and deception. She'd been skirting the balance for so long now that her top-notch instincts felt sluggish and dull. Maybe she needed more sleep.

Or maybe this man and his orgasms were to blame.

"Then, Joshua, I'd be impressed by your show of faith. This situation isn't easy."

He acknowledged her with a slight nod, but she couldn't make out his expression. He hid his thoughts so skillfully behind that handsome face. The only time she knew she was getting an honest response was when one of them was naked.

"Done?" he asked.

She dabbed the napkin at her lips then set it on her plate and handed over both. Yawning widely, she stretched her arms and willed her thoughts to clear.

"Tired?" he asked.

"You've run me ragged. When I'm not outthinking you, I'm thinking about having sex with you."

"Or *having* sex with me."

"Complaining?"

"Hardly. I can't remember the last time I was so challenged, in or out of bed."

Something about his admission felt honest. Lindy wondered if she read truth into his words that wasn't there. She was positively gasping to sway him to her cause. Without a doubt.

Depositing her plate back on the room-service cart beside the bed, he asked, "Coffee?"

She nodded, and Joshua did the honors. When Lindy took a sip, she willed the caffeine to awaken her so she could think.

He helped himself then stretched out beside her again. What caffeine didn't accomplish to wake her up, the sight of him did.

He looked earthy and sensual with his stubbled jaw and dark hair. He'd belted the robe loosely around himself, and his bare legs and feet revealed just enough skin to make her imagine the rest of his naked self beneath the robe.

The moment was filled with a camaraderie that had been growing ever since they'd left Venice. Joshua was an easy man to be around, which said something, she thought, since not only were they at cross-purposes, but also they couldn't trust each other. Watching him operate up close was a bonus that should have helped her figure out how to sway him to her cause.

Instead, memories of what he'd looked like with his hands cuffed and his body being very honest made her keenly aware of how close they sat, his thigh just inches from hers.

On a real bed.

"Now that you've brought up the subject," he continued, "we need to decide what our next step will be."

"Go to London, of course."

"Ah, your deal." Arching an eyebrow, he leveled her with that inky-black gaze and won an instant reaction deep in her stomach. "I'm curious. When do you decide you're getting no place, trash my reputation and drive me underground to live as an international fugitive?"

"I hope it won't come to that."

"Still think I'll cooperate?"

"I've proven myself, haven't I?"

"Enough to trust MI6 with my future?" His gaze never wavered. "I don't trust my fate to any man."

That statement was so rich with implication that she wanted to ask why. Secret Intelligence hadn't been able to uncover his deep dark past, and she wondered what had happened in his life to hone his survival skills to such a keen edge.

"What about trusting your future to a woman?" she asked, her voice soft, the words right.

But the feeling was wrong. Her mission objective was to convince him to cooperate, and Lindy had never been squeamish about doing her job. Yet, somehow those right words laced the intimacy of the moment with a portion of something decidedly…uncomfortable.

"Trusting you won't guarantee MI6 will act in faith," Joshua pointed out. "Most government agencies will say whatever they must to get what they want. You know that. But dealing with a chain of command means unless you're running the show, you can't guarantee someone up the ladder won't change things."

The remnants of that lovely fluttery awareness vanished beneath a squirmy feeling that made her set aside the coffee, suddenly feeling the effects of how much she'd eaten. "What exactly are you worried about?"

"Besides giving up my career?"

"I think your career's moot. You can't work effectively with me on your tail."

Then she saw something flicker deep in his eyes—pleasure, she thought, or maybe amusement.

"All right, I take that back. You wouldn't have been climbing into an office building or breaking into a chancellery without a reason. I can only assume you were working."

"Are you admitting you don't know what I was doing?"

Here was the tug-of-war again. Only this time, Joshua decided to weight his efforts by running a thumb along her cheek, a warm touch that shouldn't have swayed her mood, but did. "What else besides your career then?"

"Your agency can't deliver what you've promised."

Her heart began to throb, thick slow beats that felt amplified in the sudden silence. Did Joshua know she'd lied? "You don't think Secret Intelligence can create a new identity?"

"Doesn't really matter. One of the fundamental differences between your people and my people is that my people don't play by the rules." He thumbed her lower lip, a purposeful stroke that underscored his point. "MI6 might have the resources to give me a new identity, but they can't keep me safe from someone who might feel betrayed. Not indefinitely, anyway. Not unless I pay for the privilege."

"What do you think you could do for us?"

Another stroke. "I'm not saying I can do anything. This is pure supposition."

"So you're not admitting you have any connections that my agency might be interested in?"

"Of course not."

She resisted the urge to turn away, to let him know he had so much power over her. The man had clearly analyzed the situation. She'd expected no less, but she needed to understand his concerns to offer reassurance. She didn't need to feel guilty because she was lying. What was wrong with her?

"Then let's talk hypothetically." She injected her tone with a matter-of-factness that she was far from feeling. "How do you think my agency might use this *someone's* connections?"

"Your agency would keep this *someone* around as an informant who would use his, or her, connections to dig up information whenever they might need it. A snitch on the payroll."

"Not very appealing when you put it like that, is it?"

He shook his head. "Not very healthy either. Like I said, powerful people on both sides of the law tend to dislike it when those they trust betray them."

Now there was a truth. Given what she knew about Henri Renouf, Lindy didn't see the man cutting his losses and chalking up one lost fixer to a life lesson learned.

The crime scene photos of Jean Allard came to mind, gritty images that proved how Renouf dealt with men who crossed him.

And worse still…even if Joshua decided to risk Renouf's retribution, he was wrong about Secret Intelligence. Malcolm expected her to bring in Joshua talking. No deal.

When she met his gaze, she recognized the understanding in those dark eyes. He might not know the details, but his sharp survival skills had sensed she wasn't dealing straight. Her sharp survival skills sensed it.

He didn't say another word but set aside his coffee cup. She felt relief that he seemed content to have made his point, relief that she wouldn't have to lie to him again. She should have presented a compelling argument about why he should trust her. She should be fixed on the goal, not worrying about the aftershocks on this man's life.

But when he pulled her into his arms, Lindy found herself sliding against him, letting pleasure drown out the naggy voice that kept reminding her she was luring this man to his doom.

Joshua was a bad guy. Doom was his fate to choose, and he'd chosen it—long before meeting her.

But with his strong arms around her, the scent of him filtering through her with every breath, Lindy struggled to remember that the end would justify the means. Her job wasn't to judge the value of the bad guys, but to see justice served.

Why was she finding that so hard to remember?

"Finally, we're in a bed," he whispered in between kisses.

"I'd hoped for a bed last night."

"You weren't impressed with the barn?" He nibbled her bottom lip and dragged his strong hands over her breasts, down her ribs until he made her shiver. "Was it the straw bed or the lack of electricity?"

"Actually, I was impressed."

"By what?"

"Your versatility. You segued from mixing with peers of the realm to sleeping in a barn convincingly."

"Should I believe you?"

"Do you want to?"

His only reply was a heavy sigh. Untying his robe, he shoved it off, then he stretched out against her, oh-so-breathtakingly naked.

Lindy absorbed the feel of his body, all hard muscle and hot skin. He twined his legs through hers and his arms came possessively around her. To her utter shame, she sank into his embrace, wanting nothing more than to let the newness of him override wayward thoughts, to let fantasy erase the reality of a situation that felt impossible.

Maybe Joshua sensed her struggle, perhaps even shared it. He did nothing more than hold her. His body anchored her close as if he was savoring the feel of them together, as if he wanted to capture the moment. Burying his face in her hair, he inhaled deeply, a simple gesture that stirred Lindy in places that had no business reacting to this man.

"Now it's my turn," he whispered.

Tension shot through him in a surge of gathering muscles and, suddenly, he was slithering down the length of her body.

"Joshua." She freed him from the tangle of her arms because she had no choice.

"I won't need handcuffs."

"You sound sure of that."

She made a move to twist away, but he slid his arms under her thighs and caught her, pinning her to the bed.

Just the sight of him poised between her spread thighs was enough to make her tremble, especially when he hovered above her most intimate places, dark eyes smiling a challenge. When he lowered his face, Lindy knew he had something to prove.

He dragged his tongue over her in a hot, wet glide that brought her up off the bed.

"I'm sure." He never took his gaze from hers as he dug his fingers into her bottom and held her steady.

Arrogant man. But that was her last thought before he slipped his tongue upward for another slow stroke.

Lindy gasped this time, her thighs brushing against his stubbled cheeks, and that friction alone on her skin was enough to make her insides soft.

Joshua intended to prove he had the power tonight, and some vague part of Lindy's brain registered that as she'd had a go at him last night, fair was only fair.

And when he lifted his chin, just enough so his whiskered jaw brushed all her moist folds and made her cry out, Joshua proved she didn't have much choice anyway. Not when he took aim and drew that tiny knot of nerve endings between his lips in a gentle sucking motion that made her melt. Lindy pulled away to control the sensation, but he held her steady and flicked his tongue again, proving that he had all the control.

Their power play had spiraled wildly out of control.

She'd never let her feelings get in the way of work before, couldn't possibly imagine a worse time to start than now. Lindy had damn well better bring this man in. She had to produce him with his information about Renouf to rationalize her behavior.

Because Joshua was right about one thing—powerful men didn't take kindly to being betrayed. Malcolm Trent wasn't pretty or kind when he felt he'd been manipulated or used.

With a stubborn feeling of rebellion, she abandoned herself to the moment, refusing to think about duty or consequences.

This situation was impossible, this moment so fleeting. All she could do was grasp it with both hands. She'd deal with the fallout later.

And there would be fallout.

Because Joshua was right about something else—he didn't need cuffs. Not with his face tucked between her legs. Her body dissolving beneath his skilled touches. Her thoughts spinning out of control. His touch was a weapon that coaxed sensations she shouldn't be feeling, gave him more control over her body than she had herself.

With his fingers and his tongue, he pleasured her until she buried her hands beneath the pillows and attempted to knead her orgasm into breaking. But it wasn't until her legs quivered and she exhaled his name on each breath that Joshua pushed her that final bit, and brought her to a climax that left her reaching for him.

"Make love to me." There was no more power play between them, only the need to feel him everywhere.

Then he was in her arms, covering her body and pushing inside. Her body still radiated from the strength of her climax. She could only wrap her arms around him and hang on tight, pressing kisses into his neck and lifting her hips to ride an ache that didn't want to let this man go.

Without any words between them, they explored the

pleasure they found together as the sun set beyond the balcony, bathing them in a balmy night breeze, making love to each other as if tonight would be their only night.

12

LINDY WANTED to fall asleep wrapped in Joshua's arms. Indeed, she should have fallen asleep long ago. After so many hours of delicious lovemaking, she should have been in a coma. But unlike her sleeping lover, she couldn't shut down her thoughts, all racing to make sense of what was happening.

She wanted to understand why this situation was blowing up in her face. She'd played the attraction card before to catch her thief. She'd met many men who'd found her desirable. She'd never hesitated to use them. Of course, she'd never played to this degree. But then she'd never been attracted to a target.

She'd been certain she could manipulate their chemistry to her benefit. She'd seriously underestimated Joshua.

And her reaction to him.

When he exhaled and rolled to his side, Lindy wanted to roll with him, to drape her arm across his waist and snuggle close. It would have been so easy to give in, to curl up against him and let the music of his breathing lull her.

Or she could press a kiss to that sensitive spot she'd found on his nape, sort of below his ear but not quite, the spot that made him shiver.

And if he shivered, he might wake up, would definitely

wake up if she slipped her hand around his waist and started handling the goodies…

Lindy swallowed back a sigh. She'd meant what she'd told him earlier—she'd wanted to believe he cared about what she thought. But that was the trouble with bad guys— one would be foolish to trust them.

Joshua Benedict had been charming, schmoozing his way across the globe for over a decade that she knew of. Despite his noble gestures and all the dreamy orgasms, Lindy didn't doubt for an instant he'd spotted her as a cocky fool and was playing her exactly the way she'd meant to play him.

That thought forced steel into her spine and, rolling away, she slid off the bed. She was drawn to the balcony, wanted to stand outside and let the night air soothe her restlessness.

She wasn't usually such a fool.

She made her way toward the loo instead, stopping at the room's personal safe to help herself to the small leather money belt that Joshua had carried with him since Venice.

He'd stowed it with her carryall. She didn't expect to find much of interest besides the camera. If he carried more, he would have taken care not to leave her with the key.

Not that Joshua couldn't help himself to her things if he'd chosen to. The courtesy safe wouldn't offer any challenge to a man of Joshua's talents. But it would take time to get in and out. At least she could run to the loo or take a shower without him helping himself to her equipment.

Right now she needed to do something to take charge of her runaway emotions and behave like a professional. So slipping into the bathroom, she flipped the lock on the door, passed the vanity and headed straight for the inner cubby with the toilet.

She pulled the door shut behind her and turned on the light, blinking to clear her vision when the overhead fluorescent beam nearly blinded her. Closing the toilet lid, she took a seat and spread the belt across her lap.

A wad of cash and his camera.

Like everything else about Joshua Benedict, his digital camera was first-rate, surprisingly light for such a large model. The size had struck her as odd when she'd first seen it. For a man who made his living slipping in and out of places without detection, she'd have expected something smaller. More like the imaging device he'd used inside the museum gallery. High-tech. Effective. And, fortunately for her, small enough to dispose of easily.

Depressing the power button, she scrolled through a photo list, not expecting to find tourist photos of Venice.

Sure enough, the last several shots were those she and Joshua had taken to doctor their identity papers. These were of no interest, so she kept scrolling. Then she came across a shot she didn't recognize.

Zooming in, Lindy discovered a text document of what turned out to be the history of a stained-glass window adorning the north wall of Santa Lucia's church. Squinting to focus on the text, she scanned a review of the scriptural scene depicted in the glass. She scrolled through another five photos to find more of the same—a document about every window in the place.

Why was Joshua interested in Santa Lucia's stained glass? Given the size and weight of the windows, these weren't items easily stolen. She'd gotten jammy with the window in the chancellery, but that window had only been ornamentation, a mere tenth of the size of those in the church.

Did Renouf have his eye on one of those historic altarpieces? If so, Joshua might want the details to mastermind a break-in. A thief might cut through portions of the glass to access the church. But there were much easier ways to enter.

The next photos made more sense—a recent church property survey. Joshua had shot the document from several angles then had methodically zoomed in on each portion to enlarge the detail. At a quick glance, she could pinpoint four ways to access the church without going near the windows.

She'd have Blythe red flag the church, too, to see if anything turned up missing. Although she didn't think Renouf would be bold enough to send in a thief after Joshua's run-in with the *polizia*.

But having a clear plan helped soothe her frazzled nerves. Lindy finished scanning the photos and scrolled back to the last one, and it was while powering down the system that she noticed the camera's odd shape again.

Inspecting the design, which left half the device devoid of any display in what might be a setup for an oversize battery, she tugged lightly and popped open half the camera to reveal what wasn't a battery slot at all, but a storage compartment.

The man was certainly crafty. She found herself smiling while tipping the camera to see what she might find inside—a box fell into her hand.

Bloody hell…she snapped open the box and gave a quiet laugh.

The White Star.

Even if Lindy hadn't been briefed, she would never have mistaken the value of this piece. This wasn't jewelry as Lady Kenwick's brooch had been—all showy diamonds surrounding an ungodly big ruby. This was a relic that practically radiated age and antiquity.

The auction-house photos she'd seen had accurately detailed the amulet, carved from ivory into the shape of a star, each delicate point veined with gold. But the photos hadn't conveyed the power. The White Star felt warm and heavy in her palm, as if it radiated some sort of ancient force that had acted as protection through the centuries. Lindy had never been overly fanciful, yet she found something compelling about the piece, something that felt strangely…alive.

No wonder Renouf wanted the White Star enough to murder, to be able to hold this piece…

Recalling Joshua when they'd met in the museum, Lindy remembered the gloves he'd worn. She hadn't given them much thought—gloves were a necessary precaution in his line of work. Hers, too, if she didn't want to leave a calling card. But Joshua had mentioned handling a sculpture.

Dragging a few sheets of toilet paper from the roll, she flipped the amulet into the cradle of her palm now protected from her skin. Lindy found it impossible to not touch. Was she imagining the way the ivory seemed to glow? Had Joshua felt the power of the White Star—is that why he'd carried it on him?

The risk struck her as extreme. Even if he hadn't had time to arrange safe delivery to Renouf, surely he could have concealed the amulet somewhere rather than dragging it all over Europe. Something this valuable should never be casually handled, or left exposed…

Lindy knew she'd been had again.

The spell broke. Carefully, she set the amulet inside the box and returned it to the camera's secret compartment.

For every step ahead she got with this man, she was knocked back another. For every piece of information he yielded, he took possession of two in return. A bloody never-ending tug-of-war.

Stuffing the camera and cash back inside his man purse, she flushed the toilet—not that cover really mattered at this point, but she was a professional.

After she returned Joshua's things to the safe, she indulged herself in that trip to the balcony, treating herself to a peek at the man still asleep on the bed.

Arrogant, *arrogant* bastard.

The late-night ocean breeze enveloped her like cool silk. Lindy inhaled deeply, tried to dispel the agitation that was making her thoughts race and her skin crawl. She needed to get a grip, to think rationally, to sort out the mess this situation had become so she could figure a way out. Joshua had been tiring her out with his game of hide-and-seek, scattering her wits with his delicious orgasms. He'd gotten the better of her.

The White Star was a plant. Mr. Meticulous would never casually handle such incriminating evidence. He hadn't so much as dropped a hint she might use as evidence in court since the night they'd met. Finding him in possession of the White Star would have sealed his fate, would have been the leverage she needed to force him to deal with Secret Intelligence.

Either he told her everything he knew about Renouf, or she would pick up the phone and call hotel security, who would call the local authorities. Once she identified herself, she'd start the justice process in motion. Joshua Benedict would be extradited to the United States quicker than he could have gotten his pants on.

But Lindy couldn't pick up the phone and have him taken into custody. Because Joshua had planted the

White Star for her to find as a message—one she got loud and clear.

He had something on her.

Staring into the night, at the moon glowing over the dark ocean, Lindy leaned heavily against the stone balcony and willed the moonlit darkness to calm her spiking adrenaline.

She couldn't be sure what Joshua had on her, but it would be something solid. A lot more solid than ethics. While Malcolm wouldn't be thrilled about her using seduction to coerce a target, poor behavior didn't carry the sort of weight Joshua might use as leverage to force her into erasing his SIS file or using her resources to help him vanish into oblivion.

No, the only thing Lindy's poor behavior had done was allow her to dig her own grave by giving Joshua time to come up with something solid.

Will dropping out of sight to seduce me to see your way present any problems for you? he'd asked her. *With work? What about your family?*

And then Lindy remembered what Malcolm had told her about a hacker in her old police precinct, and two plus two equaled four.

Joshua had uncovered her alias.

JOSHUA LED Lindy along the dock toward the moored motorboat. The front desk had called to notify them the San Remo Marina representatives had arrived, so they were back in their beachwear this morning.

Lindy looked lovely with the breeze lifting her hair from her face and her eyes bright from sleep. Yet she'd been quiet and contemplative. Joshua suspected she felt the tension building as much as he did.

They'd stolen a few moments, but the situation still

played out. Their game continued, influenced by external forces they had no control over and an attraction that made them vulnerable.

Even though they'd partnered up for the moment—made a helluva team, in fact—Lindy needed him to deal with MI6. He needed a way out of the impossible fix she'd placed him in.

"We have to refit." He refused to dwell on the inevitable, only wanted to make the most of the time they had together. "What do you say we hit the shops after we're done here?"

Lindy only nodded.

He wanted to smooth away the troubled crease between her eyebrows, do something to make her laugh the way she had in his bed last night, when she'd been hot and eager underneath him, as awed and satisfied by what they'd found together as he was.

Another thing he needed to defend himself from—this unexpected feeling of rightness he knew only with Lindy.

"Looks like they're already here," Lindy said.

Joshua glanced at the moored boat and the men there, one on board, the other on deck.

He didn't recognize the men from the marina. They were dressed casually for boating, and the man on deck glanced their way then turned to alert his friend.

Something about that struck Joshua as wrong. He looked closer at the men.

At first glance they appeared to be boaters readying to cast off, but he noticed that while both were dark-haired and olive-skinned—presumably Italian—neither had a tan to suggest he spent any time in the sun. The man on board joined his friend on the pier, who waved at Joshua and called out a greeting.

These men shouldn't be able to identify him—only the name, not the face.

Joshua glanced down at Lindy, somber expression still in place. Had she set him up?

Stalling, he dropped the folder holding the boat keys and rental papers then knelt to retrieve the items, pulling Lindy down beside him. She looked surprised.

"Are they yours?" He watched her closely.

She glanced out from under the fringe of her lashes at the approaching men, and her frown deepened....

"Bloody hell," she hissed on a breath. "They're not—"

Joshua shoved her off the pier just as the first shot rang out. He went over on top of her, hitting the surface hard and plunging them into the water between two power-boats at anchor.

Not MI6, unless Lindy's people had decided to take her out of the situation, too. Joshua didn't think so. Her people didn't operate this way.

His people did.

Two more bullets sliced through the water near them, one so close Joshua could feel the heat streak the bare skin of his thigh, the sound eerily muffled by the depths.

Lindy clutched at his arm, fighting to continue their descent and not resurface, motioning in a direction that would take them under the pier. Her hair wisped out on the water, her cheeks filled with breath, her face pale and purposeful.

Catching her tight against him, he lent his strength to their descent, and they swam into the murky depths, the only place to hide in this pristine water, using his free hand to maneuver through the snare of anchor lines that created an underwater web.

They couldn't stay down for long—a fact all too obvious. The hit men would be searching, waiting for them to surface. With any luck, someone would hear the shots. Any commotion might force these assailants to flee, even if the last thing he and Lindy needed was an interview with the cops.

Clutching Lindy's hand, he led her up toward the pier above, his heart throbbing in his chest, his breath burning like white heat in his lungs.

They broke the surface with barely a sound, dragging air into their lungs, trying to tread water without splashing.

A shout then footsteps hammering above forced them into action again. Sucking in another hard breath, he dove back in. This time Lindy beckoned him to follow, and he swam after her, trailing after her long pale legs that sliced in clean strokes as she led him under a hull's draft.

They cleared the channel between the piers, deep enough not to draw fire, and headed below the next pier before resurfacing in the shadows for air.

"You thinking we should make our way toward the far end?" he whispered in between breaths.

She nodded, not risking a sound, but from above they only heard raised voices, no more gunfire.

Then they dove again. Joshua knew she was thinking— exactly what he was thinking.

Make their way to the end of the marina and surface with the maintenance vehicles that fueled the moored vessels.

Had shots not been fired and had he not had a sick feeling in his gut that Henri was responsible for this hit, Joshua might have appreciated another reminder of how this woman complemented him in so many ways.

But right now he was just relieved that she was skilled

enough to carry her own weight because the very idea of getting Lindy killed felt a lot bigger than he was.

Marseille, where ships from all over the world clear this seaport, filling the streets with mobs that provide the perfect cover to vanish.

JOSHUA WATCHED Lindy disappear into the bathroom and pull the door shut behind her. After a long day of travel, she wanted to shower and he hadn't been invited. He cautioned himself not to take it personally. Lindy wanted privacy right now, and he'd done nothing to earn the right to infringe upon it.

He wondered if she'd barricaded the door, wouldn't blame her if she had.

They'd been on the run all day. After escaping the marina, they'd had no choice but to risk a return trip inside Hôtel de Monaco to retrieve their things and had managed the trip without detection. From there it had been a matter of a television remote to learn the Italian authorities had decided to use the paparazzi to aid in their search.

The Santa Lucia break-in wasn't big news by any stretch, but it had caught the Italian authorities at a bad time. Timing could be a roll of the dice in Joshua's work. His timing couldn't have been worse. Under normal circumstances, he would have researched carefully. Most likely he'd have opted out of Venice while the country was still stinging from recent terror threats and a religious artifact theft that hadn't been one of Henri's acquisitions.

These weren't normal circumstances. He'd been working too hard to dodge Lindy, to set up a fake trail for Henri and to add to his cache for leverage.

As it was, the Italian authorities had sent his and Lindy's

descriptions to the press, along with police artists' render-ings that were all too accurate.

Piecing together the course of events from there had been easy. Joshua's cell phone had stopped ringing with calls from Henri about twelve hours ago—shortly after the authorities had released their descriptions.

If Henri had connected Joshua with a woman, he'd have used his resources to discover who the woman was. No doubt he'd placed Lindy as a British agent and would natu-rally assume Joshua had double-crossed him with the amulet.

Hence the hit.

Exactly what Henri had done in New York when Jean Allard had upped his price for the White Star.

Since Henri obviously knew how they'd left Italy, leaving the principality of Monaco by sea had no longer been an option. So Joshua and Lindy had stolen a motorcycle to leave a trail to the train station, bought two tickets for the TGV, the high-speed train that linked Nice and Paris, then hopped a taxi for the Nice-Côte d'Azur International Airport.

They'd hired a private helicopter to cross the Franco-Monégasque border without having to produce their papers and had flown to a shuttle stop in Nice. That flight had taken them over what were, in Joshua's opinion, the most beautiful shores along the Côte d'Azur. Ironically, they'd flown close to his place.

He hadn't bothered pointing it out to Lindy.

After leaving the shuttle stop, they'd taken a bus trip to Marseille, where they were currently holing up in a waterfront pension he'd stayed in before when keeping a low profile.

He gazed around the tidy room. Functional, clean and even well-decorated with a Battenberg lace comforter on the four-poster and matching curtains on the window. Nothing that would impress the woman currently shower- ing behind closed doors. Except perhaps for its anonymity, which was requisite right now.

Henri had driven them underground until Joshua could tap back into his resources without detection. Holing up to regroup had made the most sense. He wondered whether Lindy still thought they were in this situation together.

When his cell phone vibrated, Joshua pulled it from his pocket, resigned at what he'd find on the display.

An incoming text message from his Northumberland investigator.

Target acquired.
Randall and Hope St. George
Newcaster Road
Kirks Moor, YA6 3HN
England
United Kingdom
+44 (024251) 41925
   Randall St. George is a barrister. Hope runs his office. Elders in the Anglican Church. Only child: Melinda. Listed as a private financial consultant based out of London. Awaiting instructions.

Joshua confirmed then disconnected and stored the message. He had information on Lindy's parents and could make his move.

But what would that move be?

In New York, Lindy had threatened to expose his alias. Now he could threaten to expose hers. He'd acquired her parents' information as verification. Collateral, if necessary. That would depend on whether she helped him by erasing his MI6 file.

It was a simple maneuver, one he'd used before. Just days ago, in fact. But the NYPD officer had made a mistake that Joshua had used as a bargaining chip. Lindy's only mistake had been doing her job too well. She'd simply been unlucky to have been assigned to him.

Would he force Lindy to risk her career to bail him out of the mess he'd made of his own?

He was beginning to see just what a mess he'd made.

Joshua knew his best chance to stay alive was to blackmail Lindy into erasing his file. Then he would disappear. He'd always had a failsafe. A man in his line of work could never be too cautious. But if Lindy could contain the threat of the international authorities by eliminating his file, his disappearance would be that much easier.

Henri would never let him go, of course, not with Joshua knowing so many secrets. But if he sent along the White Star as a show of faith and could avoid a hit, perhaps in time, Lindy would actually build a case against Henri that would stick.

If she didn't wind up dead.

Clearing his cell phone display, Joshua stepped outside onto the small balcony that overlooked the busy wharves. The familiar feel of the warm ocean breeze under the setting sun should have chased away his chill. Tonight, that familiar feel only melted the numbness that had shielded him from looking at his actions too closely for too long.

When had he sunk so low?

He'd been running from the answer lately, before Lindy. He hadn't realized what the problem was. Now he knew his conscience had been nagging for a while. He hadn't been able to outrun the truth, not even on a boat cutting through that crystal water.

The truth had been inside him, dogging his heels wherever he went.

He'd blackmailed a police officer, had forced the man to risk career and family to deliver the White Star, had forced him to sacrifice his self-respect to cover up a past mistake.

And even worse than corrupting the man was the ease with which Joshua had managed it.

As easily as he'd dug up something about Lindy and considered using it against her.

He'd finally met a woman who was his equal in so many ways, a woman he admired and respected, and he was poison to her.

Leaning heavily on the stone railing, Joshua felt the exhaustion of the past few days suck at his strength. Or maybe that was the weight of his actions and finally facing the truth.

He deserved this turnabout. He hadn't given a second thought to right or wrong when vowing to put the past behind him. When he was growing up he'd hated dropping by friends' houses for meals because his mother hadn't come home. As much as he'd appreciated the handouts, he'd thought pity was too high a price to pay.

As well-meaning as the concern had always been, his pride had taken hits year after year because everyone in the neighborhood had known about his sorry situation.

And Joshua had accomplished what he'd set out to do— to get far away from the poor, lonely kid he'd once been.

But at what cost? Had he ever considered the cost?

A cop's self-respect.

Lindy's career.

His soul.

He laughed, a brittle sound that melted on the buzz of the busy wharves. All it had taken was an MI6 agent with sparkling eyes and a sexy smile to make him see the truth. He hadn't wanted to become a slave to her agency, had been trying to outmaneuver her, willing to sacrifice her to escape fate.

But he was already a slave—not to Henri, but to himself. The past had dictated his life. He'd sold his soul to live a lifestyle that had turned him into a ruthless bastard who would use anyone or anything to get ahead.

And now… The weight of his choices sat heavily, and one locked door between him and a beautiful woman felt like an obstacle he could never overcome.

But at least now he knew what he wanted to do.

Good, bad or otherwise. He'd had enough.

13

BY THE TIME Lindy was ready to face Joshua again, she'd showered, dried her hair and gotten fully dressed. She'd had enough time to sort through her thoughts, to clear away the emotional debris so she could assess the problem rationally. Unfortunately, she still didn't feel rational, which probably had to do with the fact that she didn't see any solution with consequences she cared to live with.

She'd made a bloody mess of this whole situation.

Malcolm would not be happy when he saw her face go public as an accessory to a break-in, and the only way to rationalize the choices she'd made was to bring Joshua in.

Joshua didn't want to go, and knowing what SIS had in store for him had dulled the edge on Lindy's determination.

The only thing she could do was force his hand and try to deal. She couldn't do anything with the Santa Lucia photos, but he was in possession of the White Star.

A new deal. A *real* deal.

He knew her true identity. If she took a leap of faith and trusted that noble streak she'd glimpsed, perhaps she might convince him to walk away, if she promised to walk away.

They'd be square.

She'd tell Malcolm he'd given her the slip. What did it

matter if her reputation took a dive? She was the target of Renouf's hit man, which had changed everything.

Working in covert operations meant living life away from the general public, a sacrifice she'd always considered worth the end result. Sure, she didn't date often or have normal friends, but she still had a circle of nearest and dearest. She wasn't totally isolated.

Now that she'd been compromised, those closest to her would also be at risk, which meant a serious alias overhaul and another layer of protection around family and friends.

No problem for SIS, but a problem for her career goal.

Renouf's hit had put an end to any hope of running her own ops. She had to wonder if her chances had ever been that good anyway. If she'd had to go to such extreme lengths to force Malcolm's hand, had she ever been a contender?

She didn't like the answer.

So, hiking her carryall onto her shoulder, she steeled herself for the battle ahead, pulled the door wide and left the loo.

"Joshua, we need to—"

She came to an abrupt stop in the doorway when she found the room empty. Crossing to the small balcony, she pushed the door open. "Joshua?"

The man had gone.

They'd checked into this room with nothing but the new clothes on their backs and their respective bags. His leather money belt with the White Star was nowhere to be seen.

Then she saw a note on the pillow… A sheet of plain stationary with the pension's name and address stamped on the bottom in blurry ink. On it, brisk cursive strokes read:

No deal, Melinda. Go home and change your alias.

Underneath was a wad of cash—more than half of what he'd had, enough euros to pay the room bill and make her way back to London in whatever fashion she felt safe.

Lindy stood there, staring at the cash, the letter clutched in her hand, but it took time for full comprehension of what he'd done to sink in. Or what he hadn't done, more precisely.

He *hadn't* blackmailed her.

If he knew her real identity, it was a safe bet he knew about her parents. Yet he hadn't threatened to expose her, or harm her family. He might have tried to maneuver her into eliminating his file, so he could drop off the grid.

He hadn't. Instead, he'd left her in a dockside room in Marseille. The bloody man had *left* her!

Lindy took off down the three flights of stairs to the lobby, where she hurried through the house, looking for the woman who'd registered them not so long ago.

She found the old woman wielding a dust cloth with a vengeance over the antique buffet. Lindy strolled into the dining room, nearly gagging on the lemon scent of wood polish.

"Excusez-moi," she said.

The woman kept on scrubbing the surface as if she wanted to see her reflection.

"Excusez-moi," she repeated, more loudly this time.

When the woman finally glanced up, she peered at Lindy from beneath a head full of steely gray curls and smiled. "You like the room?"

"The room's fine. The man I checked in with. Did you see him leave?"

"Non, non." Her gaze brightened with interest. "You fight?"

Lindy shook her head. "He was running out to grab something for us to eat. I wanted to tell him to bring me tea."

The lie tumbled easily off her lips. Lindy knew the old lady wasn't buying because she tucked her dust cloth inside her frilly apron and motioned toward a door at the back of the room.

"Come into the kitchen. I will make you a cup. We can chat until your young man returns."

Young man? Lindy almost smiled. Hadn't a college student recently accused Joshua of being exactly the opposite? It was all in the perspective, she supposed.

"Come, come," the old lady prompted.

Lindy eyed her for a moment in indecision, torn by the need to head out to look for clues to Joshua's whereabouts. But if he meant to vanish, he'd be long gone by now. A few minutes wouldn't make any difference tracking him down. She knew that firsthand. And there was an urgency about this woman that made declining the invitation feel rude.

The old lady's face was angular and gaunt, a face that had seen a lot of years and too many of them hard, but her bright blue eyes were kind.

Lindy smiled. *"Merci."*

The woman led her through the dining room into a kitchen that was as immaculate as the rest of the house. She told Lindy to sit while putting a kettle on the stove and fishing out tea bags from a porcelain canister.

Lindy did as instructed, surprised to find her agitation fading. Maybe she just felt better not being alone.

The woman's name was Nanon, and she'd owned this pension since before the war when her husband had gone off to fight for the Resistance and wanted to leave her some source of income in the event he didn't return.

But he had come home and lived to a ripe old age before closing his eyes in his favorite chair and not opening them again. As that night didn't sound as if it had happened too long ago, Lindy thought loneliness might explain Nanon's predilection for inviting strangers to tea.

"What did you fight about?" Nanon brought the cups to the table and set one in front of Lindy.

The old dear had obviously forgotten Lindy's earlier denial, or maybe she just assumed that dealing with a man meant a fight. After so many years of marriage, she was likely the authority. Either way, she looked so hopeful that Lindy decided to go with it.

"We're at cross-purposes," she said. "He made choices about some things, and I made choices. I don't see a resolution."

"Ah, those men always think they know best when they should know to listen to their women."

No argument there. They were the target of a hit, and instead of discussing the situation rationally, Joshua had run off and left her to fend for herself.

Not that she minded fending for herself, of course, but she minded that he hadn't even consulted her, had assumed he knew best. The man had practically patted her head and told her to run along home.

"He was very high-handed, really," Lindy admitted. "Never even asked what I wanted, just took charge of the situation and barreled off to do things his way."

The kettle whistled, and Nanon lifted it from the burner and carried it to the table. "High-handed, *oui*. Probably never occurred to him that you might know better. Women usually do."

Lindy laughed. "Agreed."

Dunking the tea bag in the steaming water, she considered where Joshua might go and how he would get there. To Renouf's stronghold in Spain to buy his way out of a hit?

It was hard to say, since Joshua had all the information on Renouf. Would it have killed him to share some, just enough to make sure she steered clear of the man on the way back home?

Nanon returned the kettle to the stove then sat across from Lindy. She settled the tea bag in her cup with a hand made unsteady by age. "Your young man is very handsome."

"Yes, he is."

"Have you been together long?"

"No."

Nanon seemed to consider that, unsure what sage advice to offer. She finally raised her cup in salute. "The handsome ones are always trouble. Remember that. They strut like roosters, thinking they can have any hen in the house."

Lindy only nodded. If she were a hen to Joshua's rooster, then there was no denying that he'd strutted into her life and helped himself.

They sipped their tea in silence for a few minutes, only the street noise filtering in through the open window.

"Does your young man love you as much as you love him?" Nanon asked.

Lindy winced. She lusted after Joshua. Figuratively and literally. Enough to make some seriously ill-advised choices to get him to confess what he knew about Renouf.

To get her hands all over his dishy self.

"Love, Nanon? What makes you think I *love* him?"

That bright gaze twinkled. "It's all over you."

Lindy gulped more tea to avoid correcting her hostess.

Obviously the old dear needed something more interesting to do than polish her furniture.

But love?

Lindy didn't love Joshua any more than he loved her. They were attracted to each other. And challenged. And well-matched, aside from a few obvious differences.

Their views about the law for starters.

But *love?*

The man had seduced her with yummy orgasms then abandoned her without a backward glance.

But he hadn't sacrificed her to the Italian authorities in Venice, an unbidden voice inside her head reminded.

And he hadn't let her get shot on a pier in Monte Carlo.

He hadn't blackmailed her, either. Instead, he'd admitted to knowing her real identity.

Why would he admit to knowing her real identity?

Lindy stared into her teacup, recalling the man who'd stood on a street corner in Vienna, watching her drive away in a taxi.

Why would that man leave her on the docks in Marseille to make her way back to London alone?

Unless he didn't think she needed protection.

That thought came at Lindy sideways.

After dodging bullets together in Monte Carlo, why wouldn't he think she needed protection?

"Exactly what does love look like?" Lindy tried not to sound cynical, didn't think she'd managed it.

"Ah, *l'amour.*" Nanon heaved a dramatic sigh. "It makes you rush around looking frantic and asking strangers if they have seen your man."

"Hmph." The old lady didn't have a clue, Lindy thought

mutinously. She was an agent of the British Crown, and Joshua a target who had given her the slip.

But why had he given her the slip? Had he thought she'd be safer without him?

Lindy remembered the man who'd stood on a rainy rooftop, fishing a condom out of his wallet to save them both.

"Nanon, can you fall in love with a man and not know you're in love?"

"Can you jump off a cliff and not know you're falling? Only if you're a fool. Are you a fool?"

Lindy remembered a night in a barn and the urgency she'd felt to rattle Joshua's self control, to prove she wasn't the only one who couldn't resist temptation.

While she might be a lot of things, reckless and ruthless among them, Lindy had never been a fool.

"How can I fall in love with a man who's all wrong for me?"

Nanon's laughter filled the kitchen, a sound that made the place feel alive for the first time, a sound that hinted at the many years of life that must have happened here, years filled with love and laughter.

"The French know about true love. You are not French, so I will tell you." She set her cup down on the saucer with a rattle. "True love doesn't know right or wrong. True love only knows the heart. One heart recognizes another. It doesn't matter if two people are friends or enemies. It doesn't matter if two people can be together or not."

The wistful expression on Nanon's face made Lindy think she might be remembering the years she'd spent apart from her husband, separated by the war, by death.

"True love is never, ever easy. How can it be when you're in love with a man?"

"How do you know, Nanon? I mean *really* know."

She sighed and clasped her withered hands over her heart. "True love makes you mad with passion. True love makes you throw caution to the wind. True love makes you risk yourself and sacrifice everything to protect your lover."

Bloody hell.

Lindy suddenly *knew*. And, no, it wasn't easy. Not even when she realized that she wasn't the only one to throw caution to the wind.

"DON'T EVEN TALK to me, Gardner," Blythe told Lindy. "You're persona non gratis around here."

The display went blank before Malcolm's scowl appeared.

"Lindy, nice of you to drop in." His tone cut across the distance between London and Marseille like a slap. "I've heard you're not meowing anymore. Care to elaborate?"

Not really. Staring at the display, she mentally steeled herself to throw caution to the wind, to hand her career to Malcolm on the proverbial platter. "I've gone balls-up."

"Define that."

"I gambled and lost."

She explained how Joshua had uncovered her alias and how Renouf had drawn her connection to SIS and sent a hit man. She left huge blank spots where anything about mad passion and true love might fit in. She simply couldn't admit aloud that she'd fallen for her target. Malcolm's darkening expression assured her she didn't need to—he was filling in the blanks quite nicely without help.

"I think Joshua offered Renouf the White Star in exchange for calling off the hit on me."

"Let me get this straight." Malcolm sounded strained,

as if she'd unwillingly dragged him inside a telly serial. "You think your target is going to Renouf to use the White Star as leverage to protect the agent who's trying to bring him in? Did I get that right?"

Lindy let her eyes flutter shut, a moment's respite from that accusing, incredulous stare. Her gut reassured her that she wasn't the only one who'd fallen in love. "Yes, that's right."

"Do you think Renouf will go for that trade?"

"He wants the White Star. I think he'll agree to the trade then eliminate Joshua once he gets it."

"Which still leaves a hit on you." Not a question. "I'm bringing you in."

"No." She delivered the word simply, but there was nothing simple about arguing with a direct order, as Malcolm's thunderous expression proved. "Please listen to me. I need to track down Joshua. I'm sure he's going to meet with Renouf."

"What makes you think Renouf will meet with him? What makes you think Renouf will leave his stronghold in Spain when he could send someone to make the pickup instead?"

"When I made contact with Joshua in New York City, I compromised his position. Renouf wants the White Star, and Joshua knew he might need leverage. That's why he kept it all this time and didn't make the delivery."

"He told you that?"

"No, but I know that's why. Trust me. I've been studying this bloke up close." *Seriously* close. "I'm right."

"So you think Joshua will force Renouf into the open because it's his only chance to make the trade and get away?"

Lindy shook her head. "Joshua won't be able to get

away. He knows that. Renouf will eliminate him the instant he has the White Star."

"Then why force him into the open?"

"To give us a chance to catch him. If we've got Renouf in custody, there will be no one to fund the hit. I'll be safe."

Lindy forced herself to hold Malcolm's gaze as a silence fell between them so heavy it almost hurt. All the implications of her words passed between them, carrying even more weight because they remained unspoken.

Malcolm had trained her. He'd commanded her. He'd indulged her. He'd trusted her. He'd kept her in the field knowing she'd wanted to run her own ops. She'd had a love-hate relationship with him for over a decade. Above all, Malcolm *knew* her. He knew everything she wasn't saying.

And he didn't make her say it.

In that moment, no matter how many times he'd sidestepped her request to run her own ops with lateral job moves, no matter how many times he'd questioned her judgment, Lindy only felt grateful that he didn't make her admit she'd been so unprofessional as to let her heart get mixed up with a target.

He knew, of course, but he didn't make her admit it aloud. That was a show of respect.

"I suppose you want to interfere?"

Lindy heard the sigh in his voice and nodded, not trusting herself to speak.

Malcolm's dark gaze caught hers, searched inside places only he knew to look. His gaze promised her hell to pay, *after* they'd finished the job.

That was Malcolm Trent, ever professional.

"You're not working alone on this," he said. "I'm sending in backup."

This time Lindy didn't argue.

Paris, where priceless objets d'art and centuries of legend fill the elegant George V, a palace hotel that inspires lovers to throw caution to the wind.

THE CITY OF LIGHTS had always been one of Joshua's favorites. Whenever visiting Paris he stayed in this legendary palace hotel that Henri had introduced him to over a decade ago.

In the superb Parisian fashion of lavish opulence, Henri's favored suite was not only the best in the house, but quite possibly the most elegant in all the chic Eighth Arrondissement.

The two-level suite took up the top floors of the hotel. A generous front entrance foyer and a spacious salon made this an impressive and comfortable place to conduct business on Henri's rare trips out of his stronghold in Spain. From several private terraces, he enjoyed an incredible view of the city skyline, including Saint Louis des Invalides, the Panthéon, Charles Garnier's Opera House and the Grand Palais.

Until this visit, Joshua would have exited the elevator and walked up to the bodyguards flanking the door, exchanged greetings then headed inside to visit the guest within. But today those bodyguards—Henri's private stock—took one look at him and went on red alert. One casually lifted his jacket enough to reveal a sidearm.

Joshua submitted to a weapons search without conversation.

"You're clear." The guard opened the door while the

other stepped inside to announce him, these formalities driving home how far from grace Joshua had fallen.

He moved inside the suite, through the impeccably appointed foyer where a gilt antique mirror reflected the room beyond and made him a visual target of the man who reigned over the lavish surroundings as a king might sit upon a throne.

Or a spider in his web.

A short man in his sixties, Henri was dark, well-groomed whether socializing or at leisure. The wingback chair he sat in had been positioned to maximum effect between the sweeping windows while mastering the view of the suite.

With a flair for drama that was as much responsible for his fearsome reputation as any ruthless business he'd conducted, Henri sat in his custom-tailored suit, watching his guest's arrival with an implacable, proud manner that commanded the power both to intimidate and to impress.

As Joshua had never been easily intimidated...

Their gazes met across the distance, Henri's gaze cool, almost remote. Joshua met that stare evenly as he moved inside. He'd never dissembled with the man and wouldn't start now.

"Henri, you look well."

"You disappoint me," Henri said.

Joshua hadn't expected to feel anything, but supposed he should have. Henri had been a mentor of sorts, one in a long line over a career that had raised him from a forgettable life to one of indulgence.

In business, Henri possessed many qualities to emulate. He'd hewn a vast empire of holdings over decades, but his initial rapid-fire rise to the top made him seem to emerge in the international business arena before people had even realized he was a man to watch.

His own origins were veiled in secrecy, lending to the mystery surrounding him. Joshua had long held the opinion that Henri's rise in power wasn't unlike his own—Henri had started far from where he'd wound up. A phoenix rising from the ashes. Whatever those origins, Henri's ruthless reputation fueled a success that made his a name to fear worldwide.

Once, Joshua had been proud to have earned this man's trust and respect.

Definitely impressionable.

"I'm sorry you feel that way, Henri. Especially since you don't understand the situation."

"Excuses? That's not like you."

"No excuses. Just fact."

Until this visit, Joshua would have been offered a glass of Henri's preferred cognac and an imported cigar. They would have exchanged pleasantries and slowly settled in to discuss business.

"Fact," Henri finally said. "The only fact I have is that what you told me is a lie. We've worked together for years. I respected you and believed I held your respect in return. So tell me why you would betray me now. Surely I deserve some explanation."

"It's called life. Sometimes unexpected things come up. I couldn't deliver the White Star safely. I asked you to trust me for a few days while I took care of the situation. I even passed along *Mit Vergnügen!* as a show of faith and this…"

Withdrawing a jewel case from inside his jacket pocket that contained a CD on to which he'd burned the Santa Lucia survey photos, Joshua set it on the coffee table between them.

"We discussed acquiring this church survey some time ago, Henri. I took the liberty of acquiring it when I was in Venice."

He had Henri's complete attention, and paused for effect before saying, "For the record, I'd hold off on trying to acquire the San Gabriel from London. I have it on good authority British Intelligence has the residence under surveillance."

"Very good authority." Henri almost smiled. Almost. "You have been busy."

Joshua inclined his head.

"The White Star?"

"I have it."

The silence grew between them, Henri reevaluating and Joshua gladly giving him time to draw his own conclusions.

Finally, Henri spread his hands in entreaty. "You were keeping company with a woman I discovered to be an MI6 agent, Joshua. What was I supposed to think?"

"Here's where our trouble starts. No trust. I couldn't tell you I'd been targeted by a British agent—"

"You *should* have told me. I have far greater resources than you do. I could have handled the situation."

Joshua couldn't keep from smiling. "You would have considered me compromised and sent a hit man after me and the agent so I wouldn't compromise you."

Henri had the grace not to deny the charge, which was another of those qualities Joshua had once admired—honesty. Henri waved a dismissive hand. "So you think I should have given you the benefit of the doubt? Even knowing you weren't being honest? Not to mention that the trouble I sent you to fix was with a man who tried to keep me from the White Star?"

"In America we call it being between a rock and a hard

place. I didn't have many choices. I went for damage control. I reassured you, then hoped for the best."

That earned a smile. "Where is it?"

He produced the box from his pocket and slid the amulet into his palm.

Joshua remembered the first time he'd handled the piece, the odd pulsing he'd attributed to adrenaline. The feeling was curiously absent now. He couldn't help but wonder about the curse, whether there might be something to it after all. He'd touched this amulet and Lindy had appeared.

Obviously, he wasn't pure of heart, which meant the amulet's curse made him glimpse a future that might have been his if he'd kept his heart pure instead of selling his soul.

Joshua handed over the piece.

There was a certain cringe factor to watching Henri handle the amulet, his expression growing glazed, obsessed. Here was a man who didn't let emotion leak through—because he didn't have much to leak, Joshua had always thought—but Henri touched the White Star reverently, as if the ivory radiated with energy.

Then he laughed. Joshua felt a shiver trail down his spine as the sound reverberated between them, wildly out of balance with the moment, a sound of the most perverse pleasure that Joshua thought of the curse again and considered that this amulet might have some sort of otherworldly hold on Henri.

Slipping the amulet back inside the box, Henri pocketed it. "Unfortunately, sometimes I make mistakes."

Joshua supposed he should feel some consolation that Henri sounded genuinely regretful, but when he found himself the target of a nine-millimeter, he couldn't rally anything but a vague feeling of inevitability.

"Doing your own dirty work, Henri? This isn't like you."

"This is personal."

Yes, it was. Joshua also thought it ironic that he'd spent his life fixing situations for men like this one only to be unable to fix his own, to atone for past mistakes and make different choices. "I'll take that as a compliment."

"It is. You lent a great deal to my organization, and I genuinely enjoyed your company." Henri's gaze held Joshua's above the gun barrel. "But I will admit to being surprised that you're not trying to outmaneuver me."

"Back to choices again. I chose to honor my commitment and hope for the best. You and I both know you've got men all over this hotel. I'm going nowhere without your consent."

"Which I'm afraid I can't give. You're a liability now. Quick and clean is the best I can offer you."

Joshua had taunted death often, had always believed he'd win the contest. Now, he didn't feel challenged, or even frightened. Just tired and moved to realize the things he'd always considered important weren't.

A realization coming too little too late.

The barrel steadied at his heart. The chamber clicked. The shot rang out, barely a muffled hiss from the silencer.

Joshua waited for the impact, held his breath expecting to feel the slam of cold steel pound through his chest.

But he didn't reel with the blow…Henri's arm jerked at an awkward angle. He cried out. The gun spun out of his hand and thumped onto the thick oriental carpet.

Then everything happened at once. Joshua was on the gun, kicking it out of reach as Henri exploded from the chair. When Joshua spun around to see who'd fired the shot, he found Lindy, arms outstretched and gun in hand.

"Lindy!" He took aim as a guard emerged from the stairs behind her.

Joshua never got to squeeze off the shot because Henri barreled into him in a bid for the door.

Catching himself on the coffee table, he didn't glance back at Henri, but launched himself over the sofa to join Lindy, who was subduing the guard hand-to-hand. He got to use Henri's gun, cold-cocking the man so he collapsed in a heap.

Lindy sank to her knees and cuffed the dazed guard before Joshua thrust open the foyer door looking for the others, and he couldn't help but smile. She had a knack with those restraints.

"I'm impressed," he told her. "Another old window?"

"Climbed to the terrace and hid in the shrubs." She stood and shot him a fast grin. "Can't you see the twigs in my hair?"

Raking his gaze over her, he drank her in, captured every detail in memory. "You did realize the point was to catch Henri in possession."

"When it came right down to it, I'd rather have you alive. Imagine."

Her matter-of-fact admission hit him in so many places that he hadn't let himself feel in so long…. The relief in her beautiful face humbled him.

And in that instant Joshua knew that no matter where he went from here—prison most likely—he would take away the knowledge that he'd earned this woman's respect.

An accomplishment that felt like so much more than anything he'd pulled off in his life.

"Something's not right. My people should have

Renouf." She cocked her head to the side and said, "Talk to me, Blythe. What's happening out there?"

Joshua watched Lindy's expression harden as she received information over an audio device wedged in her ear.

"Damn it," she said, heading for the door. "What about Sanders and Hargrove in the lobby?"

Joshua didn't have to wait for an explanation to know what had happened. Renouf's army was taking out Lindy's backup.

Henri didn't enjoy his reputation without good reason. That meticulous attention for detail that had so impressed Joshua long ago still served Henri well. He never left the safety of his stronghold without layers of protection in place.

Without a word, they flanked the door. Lindy took point and swung it wide. Two men sat in a heap on the floor, apparently unconscious. Renouf's bodyguards were nowhere to be seen, but a metallic hiss sounded down the hallway....

The service elevator.

"The stairs," Lindy said.

"Henri will have people waiting outside for him," Joshua told her. His first official act as a snitch, and he wasn't even on the payroll. But one good deed might count for something. A chance he wouldn't pass up. "He'll have all the exits covered."

Lindy relayed the information to her audio contact as she took the stairs two at a time. "Pull in the outer perimeter. Tell them I injured Renouf's right arm."

Circling the last of the stairs, they headed toward the door that led to the lobby. Lindy took point again, only this time she tucked her hand inside her jacket to conceal her gun.

They burst out, heading away from the main lobby where

the sudden noise of activity alerted them to a problem. A quick glance over his shoulder and Joshua groaned.

Hotel security.

"I can't catch a break," Lindy exclaimed when she caught sight of the three goons in dark suits barreling toward them.

"Mademoiselle!"

She didn't slow down, but flashed her badge over her shoulder and continued to the service elevator. Each second dragged by, security on their heels…they made it to the elevator as it thumped to a halt behind closed doors and a buzz signaled its arrival.

"Mademoiselle—"

"In pursuit of a suspect," she fired off in French, stalling for time by handing the man, whose nameplate labeled him the security chief, her badge.

Then the elevator doors shot open.

A uniformed maid glanced up, surprise frozen on her face, white knuckles clutching the service cart she'd been about to steer through the doors.

"Was there a man in here?" Lindy demanded. "A guest?"

The maid fixed them with a startled look then nodded. *"Le plancher au-dessus."*

Second floor.

Joshua exhaled a sharp breath.

The second floor would leave Henri his choice of elevators to obtain the main lobby or any of the guest rooms to hole up in. Joshua was betting on the elevators. Knowing Henri, he'd stroll right out the front door the way he'd arrived. By the time Lindy convinced security to let her conduct a search—if they let her conduct one, which looked doubtful—Henri would be long gone.

His injury might have made his arm a bloody mess but he still had two working legs.

"I'm in pursuit—"

"Non, mademoiselle. Not inside this hotel. You have no jurisdiction over my guests," the security chief insisted. "You will come to the monitoring station and we will discuss—"

"Not until I have my suspect." Lindy sidestepped him, but the man grabbed her arm to halt her passage.

Joshua stepped in as Lindy exploded away from the chief.

"Tell them to pursue," she hissed into her audio device, startling the security goons who crowded around her.

The security chief growled. "If you were in pursuit of a suspect inside this hotel, you were obliged to inform us. We cater to our guests, Mademoiselle Gardner, not apprehend them."

Parisian hospitality was just that zealous. And Henri was getting farther away with each precious second wasted.

Static crackled, ending the power play. The security chief reached for his radio.

"Report," he spoke into the receiver.

"Captain, we've apprehended three more suspects outside the service entrance," a voice shot back.

Lindy cocked her head, clearly receiving a report of her own over the audio device. Her expression grew thunderous. "Those were my men. You're interfering to give my suspect time to escape."

The security chief obviously didn't like accusations hurled by a sexy British agent. With a scowl, he grabbed Lindy by her upper arm. "To my office, mademoiselle. Our manager will meet us. We will straighten the situation out, away from our guests."

Joshua stepped in close enough to Lindy to crowd out the security chief, forcing the man to release his grip on her.

"Monsieur—" another security goon said.

Joshua motioned him off with a scowl. "If you want to move the party out of range of your front desk then keep your hands to yourself."

Lindy stepped out of the security chief's reach and said, "All right. Let's go."

Joshua knew by her expression that all was not going well with whoever was on the other end of her audio device.

"Let me guess," he whispered as they were escorted to the monitoring station. "Cars posted at all exits?"

She nodded.

Bait and switch.

Maybe MI6 would luck out and track Henri, who would have several avenues of escape available. Joshua wasn't optimistic. Unless Lindy had a small army of agents in pursuit…

So, once inside the monitoring station, he stood to the side while Lindy secured medical help for her injured agents and explained the situation. He was treated to a firsthand glimpse of international jurisdiction at work.

If his future hadn't been caught in the balance, Joshua might have enjoyed the ensuing pissing contest.

Security withheld their assistance as they claimed their British neighbors should have had the courtesy to contact the French police before conducting a sting within city limits. Inside the George V.

The hotel's general manager knew who buttered his bread, too, and pompously spouted rhetoric about how his job was to ensure his guest's safety while within these hallowed walls, and no one would be apprehended inside his hotel, especially such a special guest as Henri Renouf.

Lindy's only recourse was to contact the French police, but Joshua guessed she hadn't contacted them initially because MI6 hadn't wanted this investigation to go public. Lindy wasn't likely to find many allies there, either. The French police wouldn't like MI6 operating on their turf without greasing the requisite palms and weren't likely to cooperate. At least until Henri, who also held French citizenship, was long gone.

By the time Lindy had wrapped things up and security escorted them to the back entrance, she looked livid.

"Bloody arseholes." She didn't seem to care if her voice carried to the security goons a few steps behind them. "At least you didn't take off. I suppose that's something."

"Would your people have let me?"

"My people are all over Paris right now chasing a shadow." She cast another meaningful glance back at their armed escort. "We need to talk. But I can't right now."

"I'm not going anywhere."

She finally lifted her gaze to him, and he recognized the worry he saw in those beautiful gold-flecked depths, was amazed at how much he wanted to smooth away the crease between her eyebrows, to reassure her.

"Henri might know you're on to him, but he's out in the open. If you move fast, you might still catch him."

She exhaled in exasperation and moved in close to whisper, "That's not it. I'm balls-up now. I don't know what's going to happen. To either of us. You know how the chain of command works, and I'm going to be in a bit of hot water myself."

Joshua recognized the understatement. A team they were, in so many ways. He nodded to the hall leading to the service entrance. "Are you telling me to slip out the back?"

"I lied about the deal, Joshua. There never was—"

"You thought I believed you?" He laughed and side-stepped a security goon to push open the door. "Should I be insulted?"

Lindy paused. "You didn't believe me?"

"I already told you, I know how governments work." He reached out to thumb the frown from her mouth, wished he could kiss her. "It would have been rude to call you a liar. Why don't we leave it at this—I knew that if there was a deal, the best you could possibly offer me was to become a snitch."

"Then why are you still here?"

Dragging his thumb across her lower lip, a slow, suggestive stroke, he willed her to understand everything he had no time to explain, to feel what he felt in one touch. "Because it's the right thing to do."

Then one of her agents called out and the moment was broken. Glancing at the street where a limo awaited, Lindy stepped through the open door, and when she did, Joshua thought he heard her sigh.

The chauffeur opened the door, and he followed Lindy inside the vehicle to find a dark-haired man waiting.

"Malcolm," she said dryly. "I suppose I shouldn't be surprised you came out to play."

"I don't suppose you should. Not only do I have to clean up your mess with the French and Italian authorities, but I wanted to personally meet the man who made me come into the field to collect my best agent." Extending his hand, he summed Joshua up in a glance. "Malcolm Trent, director of Secret Intelligence."

Joshua shook. He wasn't in cuffs yet and considered that a decent first step.

He sank into the plush seat beside Lindy, who'd already begun grilling her boss for details of the pursuit.

Malcolm folded his arms across his chest and shifted a narrowed gaze between them. "Renouf's somewhere in France but out of our reach. We tracked him to a private airfield where he escaped via helicopter."

"Damn." Lindy rubbed her temples as if trying to soothe an ache.

"Quite. You brought me this man when I might have had Renouf in possession."

"I didn't have a choice."

"Oh, you had a choice. I'm just surprised by the one you made." The director's dark gaze shot to Joshua.

Lindy winced, and Joshua understood that when she'd made the call to place his safety above apprehending Henri, she'd knowingly opened herself up to the consequences.

He still couldn't believe she'd made that choice.

He also wanted to know how she'd tracked him down, but all he could do was curb his impatience. The future loomed dead ahead. He wasn't in any hurry to rush it.

Not when he could sit here and admire Lindy as she handled her boss, gorgeous and brilliant as she smoothed the man's ruffled feathers with fast smiles and calm-voiced logic.

Not when she caught Joshua's gaze, her own bright eyes mirroring what he felt—resignation, uncertainty, relief.

It was enough.

14

London, where a maze of secure surveillance sectors form the Secret Intelligence Service, where reversals can and do spin situations off in unexpected new directions.

LINDY HADN'T GOTTEN a chance to speak to Joshua alone before being whisked away for a week-long debriefing by SIS brass. She had no clue what was happening with him since she hadn't been allowed to speak with Malcolm since her return.

She had, however, gotten to share every gory detail of this mission from hell, from being busted on the New York City pavement to declining to identify herself to the Italian authorities. If this hadn't been agonizing enough, she'd also learned the reason she'd been treated to lateral move after lateral move rather than running her own ops.

Be careful what you wish for...

Words to live by.

She was admittedly the best damn field agent Secret Intelligence had—the field director's words. She was also a great trainer and team player, when she chose to play on the team—the training coordinator's words. But she liked challenges a bit too much for her superiors' comfort. She could be reckless, evasive in her reports and so devoted to her work that she didn't draw a proper balance with her personal life.

Of course, defending herself against this list of faults was impossible after having confessed to being reckless and evasive in her reports about Joshua Benedict. She did not, however, admit to a lack of a proper personal life.

And she argued that challenges weren't a bad thing. Complacency was the kiss of death to a field agent. How else was she supposed to keep her skills sharp?

The brass hadn't wanted to hear it, which left her wondering why she'd ever wanted to run her own ops in the first place. At least in the field, she was far from headquarters.

When the brass finally cut her loose, she wound her way around the corridors of Headquarters, slicing her access card through security devices, ignoring agents who X-rayed her. She actually growled at a young retinal-scan technician who tried to get chatty.

As long as she had clearance to be inside Headquarters, she was going to Malcolm for answers. Two answers in particular.

One…did she still have a job?

And two…what had he done with Joshua?

By the time she made it to Communications, Lindy knew without question that she should have first detoured for home and a decent night's sleep to replenish her supply of self-control. But making that decision would have required some. Self-control seemed to be in very short supply today.

Stalking inside, she looked for Malcolm, but didn't see him anywhere among the agents who buzzed around the various comm centers. Zeroing in on Blythe, Lindy asked, "Where is he?"

"Sounds like someone's in a strop." She spun around in her chair. "Looks like it, too. Why don't you scurry back to whatever rock you've been hiding under and not come out until you've had a rest. A shower, too. You look like hell."

"Be careful, I bite. Now where is he?"

Blythe turned back to her display. "You didn't say please."

Scowling, Lindy headed to the nearest station and grabbed a headset. Suddenly her voice rang out over the intercom. "Two Man U tickets for a location on Malcolm."

"Bloody hell," Blythe cursed as several voices called out his location in the sublevels.

"They're yours, Deckard," Lindy said. "Have fun."

The agent gave her a thumbs-up before disappearing behind his station again, and Lindy shot Blythe a smug smile. But her smile faded fast when she heard laughter coming from behind her, *familiar* laughter. Spinning around, Lindy's mouth went dry.

There he was. Just as dishy as he'd been the first time she'd laid eyes on him. Just as blond. His smile just as dashing.

His dark gaze swept over her, almost a physical caress, a look that reminded her of the intimacies they'd shared, a look of mingled pleasure and relief.

Her temperature spiked hot and cold all at once, and a crazy sense of relief collided with questions about what he was doing here. If Joshua was spilling his guts about Renouf, he would be in Containment, not sitting here like a bloody guest.

Lindy never got a chance to ask because he chose that moment to cover the distance between them. In a few long strides, he was suddenly there, pulling her into his arms.

He didn't seem to mind that they were standing in full view of her coworkers.

Funny thing…neither did Lindy.

She was glad to feel his arms around her, feel his hard self crowding up against her and doing all sorts of screwy things to her insides.

Then his mouth came down on hers, and Lindy knew in that moment, as their breaths collided and their tongues tangled in a rush of awareness that made her knees weak, no matter what the outcome of this fiasco, no matter what the consequences, she wouldn't have missed this ride with Joshua.

Not for anything.

"Get a room!" Blythe's voice startled the moment.

Lindy and Joshua broke apart to the sounds of whooping and applause and not a few raw comments.

Joshua didn't let her go. He anchored an arm around her waist, laughing good-naturedly.

"Best idea you've had all month," Lindy shot back, all bravado, when she could feel the heat searing her cheeks. "We need some privacy," she whispered to Joshua.

The best she could come up with was an empty briefing room, and the instant the door closed behind them, Lindy found herself in Joshua's arms again.

"Hello." One simple word, spoken in that bedroom voice, and her stomach lunged.

"Hullo."

The moment swelled between them. They were together. Alone. Joshua's dark gaze caressed her as if he were ever so pleased to see her. She wanted to kiss him again, but forced herself to ask, "What's been going on with Malcolm?"

Leaning against the conference table, Joshua spread his legs and pulled her between them. Looping her arms around his neck, Lindy caressed the hair there, enjoying the luxury of touch that had never been properly theirs.

"So?" Lindy prompted.

"Your boss and I have been negotiating. I have something he wants. He has something I want."

"I already know what Malcolm wants from you. What do you want from him?"

"A future."

Lindy stared into his face, at the amusement she saw there. She wanted to believe she'd impacted this man as much as he'd impacted her, that more was happening between them than a few hot nights and a tug-of-war. Lindy knew how she felt, but that was the problem with gentlemen bad guys—she couldn't be entirely sure what they felt.

"What sort of future?" she asked. "Last I heard you weren't interested in being a snitch for MI6."

"I pitched your deal idea."

"Oh, and what did he say?"

"He's been...accommodating."

"I see." Lindy steadied her voice, refused to let Joshua see how his admission affected her. "So you dish out what you have on Renouf and Malcolm erases your file. Is that it?"

"Not quite."

"Joshua, stop toying with me. I've just spent my week sequestered, debriefed and interrogated. I am not in the mood for games. What did Malcolm say?"

He idly thumbed her cheek, that almost-smile still playing around his mouth. "He told me how you tracked me to Paris."

"What does that have to do with anything?"

"Everything." His thumb trailed along her jaw, as if memorizing her features. "Malcolm told me how you tracked the fake travel plans I made to lead Henri back to the States while I led you to Venice. He told me how you tracked your way to a nursing home in Michigan—"

"I already know how I tracked you down. What difference does it make?"

"You're so clever."

"You already knew that."

He smiled.

She scowled, growing more impatient.

"What difference, Lindy? It made *all* the difference. Not only did Malcolm get a chance to see how clever I am, but he got to see how well we complement each other."

"So, and—"

"And it means you uncovered my real identity."

"Not rocket science, Joshua. Once I discovered your planted trail, I knew you were trying to divert Renouf. He backstopped your cover by making phone calls to a nursing home. I thought that was odd, so I called the place and talked to a nurse. Turns out that a very elderly man lives there who has no family except for a grandson named Tom Davis who funds his care. Even though this grandson doesn't often visit, he sends his grandfather religious minutiae from all over the world and keeps a candle lit for him every week."

"So you assumed I was Tom Davis."

"I did follow you into a New York cathedral and watch you light a candle." Lindy rolled her eyes. "Okay, and I admit to pilfering your camera in Monte Carlo while you were asleep. I saw the photos you took at the chancellery. I guessed what you wanted the property survey for, but I couldn't figure out why you'd care about all those stained-glass windows."

"So two plus two equaled four." He brushed the hair from her temple, light strokes that made her shiver. "You uncovered my real identity. You know all about where I came from and what I've done to get where I am today."

"Mmm-hmm."

"Yet you're still standing in my arms, demanding answers, getting impatient with me because all you really want to do is kiss me."

"Oh, you think so?"

He nodded.

Then Lindy understood. She hadn't thought much about Joshua's early life except that his tough origins could have explained some of the choices he'd made to land him on the wrong side of the law. But there was so much in his expression....

Apparently Joshua had given it a lot of thought. He was such a proud man. Did he think his past and his choices would influence the way she felt about him?

Lindy wasn't sure what to say, so she rested her head on his shoulder. "Tell me about your grandfather."

He exhaled deeply and stroked her hair. She sensed it was difficult for him to talk about himself—his real self— so she burrowed her face against his shoulder and waited, savoring the feeling of his arms around her, a simple, *right* feeling that proved a welcome respite from the turmoil her life had become.

"Not much to tell," he finally said. "My grandfather is a religious man who didn't approve of the way my mother chose to live. She wanted no part of him. But whenever she was down and out, she ran to him for help. He always came through. I only saw him a few times while I was growing up. He took me fishing on Mackinac Island once."

So Joshua cared for his grandfather now, took the time to send him things he'd enjoy from around the world.

She remembered something else Joshua had said, in a barn in the Italian countryside. "Your grandfather doesn't know about the work you do, does he?"

Joshua shook his head.

"So who owns the farm in Italy?"

"A friend of his. They met during the Second World War. Opposing sides, of course, but they've stayed in touch."

Friendship where one least expected it, Lindy thought. Not so different from her and Joshua.

"You still haven't told me what happens next," she said. "Is Malcolm going to erase your file in exchange for your cooperation about Renouf?"

"Yes."

Closing her eyes, she told herself to be glad. She didn't want to see Joshua driven underground. Yes, he'd made hard choices, done things he obviously wasn't proud of, but did that mean he couldn't fix things?

That was, after all, what this man excelled at. And wasn't that the argument she planned to use on Malcolm about herself?

When it came right down to it, she wasn't so different from Joshua. She'd been driven and ruthless and had bent the rules. She hadn't cared about anything but achieving mission objective, and this time she couldn't even claim the noble purpose of justice because she'd been more concerned with leverage.

She'd been no less driven than Joshua. Their circumstances had simply been different.

"Is Malcolm going to create a new identity for you?" She knew there'd be no other way.

"Yes."

"After we apprehend Renouf?"

"No."

Tipping her head back, she stared into his face. "Stop making me drag out every detail. Tell me what's going on."

Joshua pressed a kiss to her brow, such a tender gesture that Lindy sighed despite her irritation.

"As it turns out, your boss wants more than the information I have on Henri. If I help your people keep Henri under surveillance until they apprehend him, your boss has a job in mind for me."

"A snitch on the payroll?"

Joshua snorted. "Not interested. Malcolm wants me to become part of a team. A task force."

"What sort of task force?"

"A team with very specialized skills for deep-cover ops."

"What sort of ops?"

"Retrieval. Black ops stuff that Malcolm doesn't want readily connected to the agency. He said there were fugitives that need to be hunted down, not to mention all the stolen British artifacts that need to be recovered. Thought with my particular skill set this might be up my alley."

"Is it?"

Joshua nodded.

She eyed him narrowly. "You said he wants you to be part of a team. Who's going to be on this team with you?"

"He didn't authorize me to say."

"A bloody little agent you are, hmm?"

Joshua shrugged. "Maybe you should ask your boss. I don't want to run afoul of the man just yet."

Scowling, Lindy disentangled herself from his arms and headed for the comm unit on the wall. Depressing a button, she said, "Blythe, I want Malcolm."

"Do I get Man U tickets like Deckard?" Blythe shot back.

"One-time offer. You missed it."

"What makes you think I'll help you?"

"Because you know I'm in a foul mood and not above running to Malcolm with sordid tales of the last time we hit the underground clubs—"

"Bitch." The connection crackled and suddenly Malcolm said, "So you're out on good behavior."

"Is that what's happening? You'll have to tell me because no one else is talking around here. Oh, except for someone I thought was a target, but who's suddenly strolling around like he owns the place."

"Didn't he tell you about the deal we worked out? I think it's a damn clever use of his talents."

"Bloody brilliant. I'm happy for him. Really I am. But what about me? Do I still have a job?"

"You can take point on this new task force if you want. Action. Adventure. Sounds like your thing. You'll get to run your own ops and train our new employee however you want."

Lindy stared at Joshua, who met her gaze evenly. "Why are you doing this? What's in it for you?"

"Aside from not losing my best field agent? You were willing to sacrifice your career for this man, Lindy. What should I make of that? If you saw something of value, I thought I should at least take a look."

"You're going to make me cry."

"Before you break down in floods, tell me whether or not you want the job. Or do you need time to think about it?"

Lindy's finger froze over the comm button. Her eyes fluttered shut as she managed a crazy feeling of…*something*. Relief. *Profound* relief. But along with it came the first niggling grains of excitement.

It wasn't a promotion in the conventional sense, rather another lateral move suited to her skills. But how could she complain? She'd be running her own ops, enjoying the challenges she so adored in the field. And working with Joshua would mean plenty of time and opportunity to pay attention to him.

When she opened her eyes again, she found Joshua watching her with a tight expression on his handsome face.

Did he really think she wouldn't jump all over this?

Depressing the comm button, she fought a smile that suddenly felt all over her face. "Training a partner *and* running my own ops? I'll want a raise."

Malcolm gave a short laugh. "Go home and sleep. Come back in a few days and we'll hammer out the details. Okay?"

"You got it, boss." She held Joshua's gaze steadily, feeling that crazy swooping feeling inside as his dark eyes caressed her, that same insane feeling she always got around him. "And, Malcolm? Thanks."

With a static crack, the connection severed, but Lindy could practically feel Malcolm's smile. Before she got a chance to mull over this unexpected turn of events, to register that her future was about to change, her new partner was suddenly on her. He caught her in his arms and pulled her close.

Threading his fingers into her hair, he tipped her head back, stared into her face with a possessive gaze. "You won't be sorry, Lindy."

"I know."

And that seemed to be exactly what he needed to hear because suddenly he rested his brow against hers and exhaled heavily, as if shrugging off the weight of the world.

"What do you think about going legitimate?"

"It's time." He stroked her cheek, a gentle touch, a promise. "We'll need new aliases."

Twining her fingers through his silky hair, Lindy savored the knowledge that she could touch him now freely, and without reservation or shame. "No problem. I don't know if I could get used to calling you Tom, and I was a bit knackered of Lindy."

"How about something sexy like Angel or Mona?"

"Those are horrible."

He just laughed softly, and everything about him sounded pleased.

"So you're officially on the payroll, Joshua. Does this mean you're admitting you love me?"

"Will you believe me if I tell you I do?"

With her fingers in his hair, Lindy dragged him close, breathing a word against his mouth, the one word that mattered.

"Yes."

Silhouette® BOMBSHELL™

The Marian priestesses were destroyed long ago, but their daughters live on. The time has come for the heiresses to learn of their legacy, to unite the pieces of a powerful mosaic and bring light to a secret their ancestors died to protect.

The Madonna Key

Follow their quests each month.

Lost Calling by Evelyn Vaughn,
July 2006

Haunted Echoes by Cindy Dees,
August 2006

Dark Revelations by Lorna Tedder,
September 2006

Shadow Lines by Carol Stephenson,
October 2006

Hidden Sanctuary by Sharron McClellan,
November 2006

Veiled Legacy by Jenna Mills,
December 2006

Seventh Key by Evelyn Vaughn,
January 2007

UNCUT

Even more passion for your reading pleasure!

You'll find the drama, the emotion, the international settings and the happy endings that you love in Harlequin Presents. But we've turned up the thermostat a little, so that the relationships really sizzle…. Careful, they're almost too hot to handle!

Are you ready?

"Captive in His Bed weaves together romance, passion, action adventure and espionage into one thrilling story that will keep you turning the pages…Sandra Marton does not disappoint."
—Shannon Short, *Romantic Times BOOKclub*

CAPTIVE IN HIS BED
by Sandra Marton

on sale May 2006

*Look out for the next thrilling
Knight brothers story, coming in July!*

www.eHarlequin.com

What are *your* forbidden fantasies?

Samantha Sawyer is a photographer who's
dying to live out her sexual fantasies....
The tricky part is her new assistant
has morphed into her dream man.
And once he's tempted,
there's no going back....

DON'T TEMPT ME
by **Dawn Atkins**
On sale May 2006

Look for **Sue Johanson's Hot Tips**
in the back pages of every *Forbidden Fantasies* book.

*Sue Johanson is a registered nurse, sex educator, author and host of
The Oxygen Network's* Talk Sex with Sue Johanson.

If you enjoyed what you just read,
then we've got an offer you can't resist!

Take 2 bestselling love stories FREE!

Plus get a FREE surprise gift!

Clip this page and mail it to Harlequin Reader Service®

IN U.S.A.	IN CANADA
3010 Walden Ave.	P.O. Box 609
P.O. Box 1867	Fort Erie, Ontario
Buffalo, N.Y. 14240-1867	L2A 5X3

YES! Please send me 2 free Harlequin® Blaze™ novels and my free surprise gift. After receiving them, if I don't wish to receive anymore, I can return the shipping statement marked cancel. If I don't cancel, I will receive 6 brand-new novels each month, before they're available in stores! In the U.S.A., bill me at the bargain price of $3.99 plus 25¢ shipping and handling per book and applicable sales tax, if any*. In Canada, bill me at the bargain price of $4.47 plus 25¢ shipping and handling per book and applicable taxes**. That's the complete price and a savings of at least 10% off the cover prices—what a great deal! I understand that accepting the 2 free books and gift places me under no obligation ever to buy any books. I can always return a shipment and cancel at any time. Even if I never buy another book from Harlequin, the 2 free books and gift are mine to keep forever.

151 HDN D7ZZ
351 HDN D72D

Name _____ (PLEASE PRINT)

Address _____ Apt.#

City _____ State/Prov. _____ Zip/Postal Code

Not valid to current Harlequin® Blaze™ subscribers.

Want to try two free books from another series?
Call 1-800-873-8635 or visit www.morefreebooks.com.

* Terms and prices subject to change without notice. Sales tax applicable in N.Y.
** Canadian residents will be charged applicable provincial taxes and GST.
   All orders subject to approval. Offer limited to one per household.
  ® and ™ are registered trademarks owned and used by the trademark owner and/or its licensee.

BLZ05 ©2005 Harlequin Enterprises Limited.

With these women, being single never means being alone

Lauren, a divorced empty nester, has tricked her editor into thinking she is a twentysomething girl living the single life. As research for her successful column, she hits the bars, bistros, concerts and lingerie shops with her close friends. When her job requires her to make a live television appearance, can she keep her true identity a secret?

The Single Life
by Liz Wood

HARLEQUIN®
Blaze™

COMING NEXT MONTH

#255 THE PLAYER Rhonda Nelson
Men Out of Uniform, Bk. 1

There's nothing like a man in uniform…or out of it! Especially when he's as hot as former Ranger Jamie Flanagan. No longer in the military, tall, dark and sexy Jamie is now a top security specialist. Only, when he's hired to protect Audrey Kincaid, he never dreams he'll take such a personal interest in guarding her body….

#256 HIDDEN OBSESSION Joanne Rock
Perfect Timing, Bk. 1

One minute Detective Graham Lawson is looking at a painting of a medieval woman disrobing, the next he's watching the live version. And while he might not buy that he's somewhere in history, he can't deny the effect sexy Linnet Welborne has on his libido.

#257 LETTING GO! Mara Fox
The Wrong Bed

Shy Emma Daniels needs a life—a sex life. So when she meets a sexy stranger on a Caribbean cruise, she decides to go for it. After all, Andres is tall, dark and temporary—the perfect man for a vacation fling. Only, little does she guess that Andres is on vacation, too….

#258 MIDNIGHT TOUCH Karen Kendall
After Hours, Bk. 3

There are a lot of things blue-blood Spinneys won't do. And Kate has missed out on good times as a result. Especially once she meets the hot-blooded Alejandro Torres. He's so wickedly tempting she discovers there are many—sensual—things *this* Spinney will do.

#259 TWO HOT! Cara Summers
Forbidden Fantasies

Torn between two lovers? That's Ph.D. student Zoe McNamara's latest dilemma. Heck, she hasn't had even one man in her life for a while, let alone two. So how is she going to handle the electrifying chemistry she has with sexy Jed Calhoun—*and* with mysterious Ethan Blair? And what is she going to do when she realizes they're one and the same…?

#260 DESTINY'S HAND Lori Wilde
The White Star Continuity, Bk. 6

The legend concludes…. When Morgan and Adam Shaw jet off on a special vacation to rekindle their once-blazing passion, little do they realize it'll turn into the adventure of a lifetime. They find not only their second chance, but the chance to save the charmed amulet, The White Star…and themselves!

www.eHarlequin.com

HBCNM0506